THE WIZARD OF 4TH STREET

SIMON HAWKE

D0003904

POPULAR LIBRARY

An Imprint of Warner Books, Inc.

A Warner Communications Company

POPULAR LIBRARY EDITION

Copyright © 1987 by Simon Hawke
All rights reserved.

Popular Library®, the fanciful P design, and Questar® are registered
trademarks of Warner Books, Inc.

Cover illustration by Dave Mattingly

Popular Library books are published by
Warner Books, Inc.
666 Fifth Avenue
New York, N.Y. 10103

W A Warner Communications Company

Printed in the United States of America

First Printing: October, 1987

10 9 8 7 6 5 4 3 2 1

"If you want to come out of this alive, you'll do exactly as I say...

We're going to walk down the hallway to your room."

Wyrdrune swallowed hard and nodded.

They went out of the stairwell and down the hall together, the man holding onto Wyrdrune's arm, keeping the knife pressed against his side. They stopped at the door to Wyrdrune's room.

The corridor was empty. The blond man had disappeared.

As Wyrdrune glanced wildly about him there were three soft coughing sounds, coming in rapid succession from inside the room. Splinters flew from the door and three holes appeared in the corridor wall. Then the door opened and the blond man said, "Inside quickly."

He pulled Wyrdrune into the room and closed the door. A man's body lay sprawled facedown on the floor, staining the carpet with blood.

"My God, you've killed him."

"I should hope so," the blond man said.

"But how—how did you . . ." and then he realized there was only one way the man could have disappeared and reappeared so quickly. . . .

THE WIZARD OF 4th STREET

For John "Bud" Sjoden,
of Leadville, Colorado, for being a gracious host, for supplying good beer and better conversation, and for putting up with the bumming of endless cigarettes; for the quiet nights spent listening to old '78s and for the sanity-inducing days on the riverbanks and high trails and old mining roads of the Colorado Rockies; and for all the smart-assed cracks about my Stetson.

CHAPTER
One

The cabdriver was a rookie; Wyrdrune could always tell. The photo on the license fastened to the dashboard showed a dark young Puerto Rican with perfect teeth and pockmarked skin, wearing his brand-new yellow turban and smiling into the camera lens. It identified the driver as Jesus Dominguez, Certified Adept, Class 4 Public Transport, New York City Taxi and Limousine Commission. The lack of conversation was a dead giveaway. Wyrdrune glanced up at the driver's face, reflected in the rearview mirror. Sure enough, his lips were moving, repeating the simple impulsion spells over and over to himself. A veteran cabbie could easily maintain the relatively undemanding levitation and impulsion spells while carrying on a nonstop conversation, but the rookies who had just passed their first-level adept exams were always a little nervous at the start. Wyrdrune closed his eyes and thought, *Please, let's not have an accident, okay? Not today. Let's just get there on time and in one piece. There's too much riding on this.*

He glanced out the window as the vaguely turtle-shaped cab skimmed silently along about two feet above the surface of the disintegrating street. Traffic on Fifth Avenue was light. It was the time between the morning rush hour and the noon break, when the streets became almost completely gridlocked and the sidewalks were choked with pedestrians, making it next to impossible to go crosstown. The cab floated past expensive boutiques and bookstores. They went by Fiorello's, the fashionable and overpriced alchemist's that catered to the herbal and thaumaturgic needs of the chic set; Bloom's department store, with its display windows full of mannequins wearing the lastest haute couture fashions, short hooded cloaks in multicolored pastels, loose trousers bloused at the ankle over short boots, and embroidered tunics with fake chain-mail shoulder pads. They passed an elephant-shaped bus bearing a placard on its side advertising "A Chorus Line—the longest running show on Broadway!" It was the latest in a series of pre-Collapse revivals, and it was packing them in.

Wyrdrune couldn't understand the pre-Collapse nostalgia craze. While preparing a thesis he had once spent several weeks in the Broadcasting Museum, viewing old pre-Collapse tapes. Unlike most people, he had concentrated on news and documentaries rather than entertainment programming, and he didn't see what was so good about "the good old days." He couldn't imagine how people could have lived like that, breathing air that turned their lungs black and going deaf from all the noise. It had been a poisoned world, riddled with the cancer of technology. The Collapse had almost finished it once and for all.

It had happened at the close of the twenty-second century, an urban dark age brought about by international conflict and abuse of the ecosystem. Solar energy, fusion, and other alternative energy programs were unable to compensate for the dwindling natural resources due to persistent political and economic problems that curtailed their full development. The pre-Collapse civilization had poisoned itself for profit and finally ran out of time. Cities burned. The world was plunged into total anarchy, people killing each other for food, eating rats, freezing to death. Back then, the sky over Manhattan had been a putrid brown-gray, at night turning an irradiated purple. The water in the Hudson River had been so polluted, you could practically walk across it, and New York Harbor was a sea of sludge. The streets had been oil-slicked, the pavements cracked and filled with potholes. Now, a century later, they were turning green with flowering meadow grass and planted with gardens that had a chance to thrive in the clean air. There was an atmosphere of great age about the city, but rebirth was taking place amid decay. Rain, no longer laced with acid, was gradually washing the ancient buildings clean, and even if the city was still dirty and overcrowded, it was nothing like what it used to be in the days before thaumaturgy became the energy standard.

Only, nobody wanted to remember it that way. Instead they chose to romanticize the past. They even sold "nouveau medieval" toys for children now, little windup cars with rubber wheels that drove around in circles on the floor, making engine noises and belching dark, "authentic" hydrocarbon smoke. Sick. It was one thing to blend the grace of twelfth-century clothing with twentieth-century fashion and call it nouveau medieval or renaissance punk, but what the hell was supposed to be medieval about a car, anyway? They were getting everything ass backwards.

The cab lurched suddenly, and the driver shook his fist and cursed in Spanish at the cab that had cut them off. "E'scuse me," the cabbie said, giving a nervous look in the rearview mirror.

"No problem," Wyrdrune said.

"My first day," the cabbie said, as if apologizing for his inexperience. "My first day on the job and I pick up a sorcerer." He shook his head. "Man, you talk about your pressure!" The cab lurched again. The driver swore and returned his concentration to his driving spell.

"It's all right. Just take it easy, you'll be fine," said Wyrdrune.

From the man's long white hair, full-length robe, and destination, the cabbie had assumed he was a sorcerer. It was a perfectly logical assumption. Most adepts wore their hair long; sorcerers wore it down below the shoulders. Warlocks wore monklike cassocks; wizards wore three-quarter-length capes; and sorcerers wore robes. It wasn't a rule, it was just tradition, but a well respected one. Aside from the fact that long hair and robes weren't fashionable and hadn't been for years, it was the way most people recognized sorcerers and wizards, and it was inadvisable to assume the appearance of a wizard if you were not even a lower-grade adept. You might meet a real one, and he might not be amused. As for mages, they generally wore robes in the functions of their office, but otherwise they dressed pretty much the way they chose. There were only five of them in the whole world, and they knew who they were. So it was logical for the cabbie to assume that Wyrdrune was a sorcerer, especially since he was on his way to Christie's, where the well-publicized auction of the Euphrates artifacts was to take place. But it was an incorrect assumption. Wyrdrune was not a sorcerer. He was not even a wizard. He was at best an undergraduate warlock, and one who had been kicked out of school, at that—a condition he hoped was only temporary. He was doing something about it at that very moment.

He imagined the police questioning the cabbie later, as they would be bound to. The cabbie would tell them that his fare had been a sorcerer. About sixty or seventy years old, he'd say—older, maybe, hard to tell. Long white hair and beard, green robe, slouch hat, about five foot five or six, walked stooped over. He'd tell them that he had picked him up at the Plaza Hotel and driven him to Christie's for the auction. They hadn't exchanged more than a few words. The sorcerer had given him a nice tip. Wyrdrune scowled at the thought of that tip. He could barely afford the cab ride, much less the tip, but there was nothing he could do about it, just as there had been no way to avoid tipping the doorman at the Plaza for getting him the cab. He had gone in and out of the hotel a number of times during the preceding day, so the doorman would see him several times and think that he was staying there. He wanted it to look as if the job had been done by a sorcerer from out of town, with money, perhaps backed by an organization. And once the job was done, money would no longer be a problem. He hated doing this, but he was truly up against it, and he just couldn't see any other way.

The cab pulled up behind a long black limo parked in front of Christie's. Some corporate sorcerer arriving in his company car. The guy got out and swept his robes out behind him with a flourish, midnight silk, very fancy, and then the doorman was opening the rear door of the cab and standing aside for Wyrdrune to get out.

"Good morning, sir," said the doorman.

Wyrdrune ignored him and headed toward the canopied entrance, walking slightly stooped over and leaning on his cane. A sign by the door read, PRIVATE AUCTION, EUPHRATES ARTIFACTS, 11:00 A.M., BIDDING LIMITED TO LICENSED MAGES, SORCERERS, AND WIZARDS OR THEIR BONDED REPRESENTATIVES. SORRY, NO CAMERAS PERMITTED.

The cameras that were not permitted inside the gallery were outside on the sidewalk by the entrance. The press was keeping a discreet distance while filming the arriving bidders. Politicians and celebrities were liable to get mikes shoved in their faces and be assaulted with a barrage of questions, but ever since an irritated sorcerer had made one newswoman's hair fall out, the press had been cautious around magic users.

And then he was inside. Getting in hadn't been a problem. Getting out again, however, could be a bit more difficult, especially if anything went wrong. There were a number of policemen stationed around the room, but security wasn't all that tight. Who in their right mind would try anything in a roomful of sorcerers? Nobody would. And that's just what Wyrdrune was counting on.

A bored-looking waiter approached him with a tray of champagne glasses, but Wyrdrune shook his head and waved him on. He was going to need all his wits about him, and he needed to keep both hands free. He edged around the room, avoiding eye contact, not wishing to be drawn into conversation. It was like a convention of magicians. The room was filled with a soft, conversational undertone and the rustle of capes and robes. Wyrdrune made his way around to the east side of the room and stood next to the heavy drapes just behind a marble column. The auctioneer, a tall, stylishly conservative man with a thin mustache and an artfully streaked geometric hairstyle took his place behind the podium and gave three sharp raps with his gavel on a small mahogany block.

"May I have your attention, please, ladies and gentlemen? We are about to begin." He waited a moment for silence. "Thank you. And good morning. I would like to welcome you all to the cooperative auction of the Euphrates artifacts, conducted by Christie Associates on behalf of the Annendale Corporation and the United Semitic Republics Department of Antiquities. Before we begin, I would like to remind you that bidding is limited to licensed mages, sorcerers, and wizards or their bonded representatives *only*. In order to avoid any embarrassment or inconvenience, I have been requested to inform you that you will be asked for your credentials when registering your purchase. All items up for bidding have been certified as prehistoric Mesopotamian antiquities by the Department of Archaeology of the University of Baghdad. These artifacts have been graded for thaumaturgical potential and certified by the International Thaumaturgical Commission's investigative committee, chaired by the honorable Sheik Rashid Ilderim Al'Hassan, Dean Emeritus of the Thaumaturgical College of the University of Cairo. We will begin with lot number forty-three, a matched pair of pagan statuettes carved in obsidian, possibly of Babylonian origin and believed to represent prehistorical deities. Bidding will begin at $25,000."

Amazing, thought Wyrdrune. Twenty-five grand for a couple of three-foot figurines carved out of black rock. Of course, an investigative board of sorcerers had determined that they possessed thaumaturgial potential, which meant that ancient trace emanations had been detected, suggesting they could be employed in some type of enchantment—*if* you could figure out the proper spell. Simple. Just punch up a search program on your corporate computer banks that would sort through all of the accumulated thaumaturgical data derived from thousands of ancient sourcebooks and archaeological records and *maybe*, if there was correlating information in the data banks, you might come up with something that would at least put you on the right scent. It was wildcatting for enchantments. You pays your money and you takes your chances. It must be nice to be rich, he thought. Or have a corporate sponsor. He didn't even have twenty-five dollars to his name, much less twenty-five thousand. But then, he wasn't planning on buying anything.

He watched from the far side of the room as the bidding progressed. The auctioneer stood behind an ornately carved podium on a dais. The items up for bidding were marked by catalog lots and brought up in no particular order that he could determine. They were exhibited briefly in front of the podium and then brought around behind it, to remain there in view of the audience until the high bid was reached. It was all done in a very proper, very classy style. Silent bidding, no crass shouting-out of prices. Heads deliberately nodded, fingers discreetly raised to indicate a bid, all very elegant and tony. All the better, thought Wyrdrune. The diversion would make more of an impact that way. At least, he fervently hoped so.

And on the opposite side of the room, someone else was hoping exactly the same thing.

A figure in a long, dark robe slowly moved forward, face concealed by a heavy cowl. The figure stopped by the marble column near the front of the room, opposite the one where Wyrdrune stood. Both arms were folded, hands tucked into long sleeves. The right hand withdrew slightly from the sleeve, and the hooded face looked down at a small black canister.

"I have seventy-five thousand, do I hear eighty? Seventy-five once . . . seventy-five twice . . . seventy-five three times, sold to the gentleman in the third row. Thank you very much, sir. May I have the next item up for bidding, please?"

Wyrdrune checked the folded newspaper article he had clipped from *The Times* last week, the one that had announced the auction and described several of the items up for bidding. He wondered about the items that the USR Department of Antiquities had decided to keep. Of course, there had been nothing in the papers about those. Perhaps, in due time, something would leak out as a result of industrial espionage or stock market transactions, but the most valuable thaumaturgical properties were always closely guarded secrets, especially in the United Semitic Republics.

The feature article about the recent discoveries in the Euphrates Valley had also profiled Sheik Al'Hassan, scion of one of the USR's oldest ruling families and one of the most powerful adepts in the world. Since his country had lost its oil wealth in the Collapse, it had struggled for years to recover from tumultuous civil wars. Although his nation was still poor, Sheik Al'Hassan had amassed a considerable personal fortune out of a grim determination to return to the style of life once known by Arab royal families. The same determination fueled his thirst for the old knowledge of his Pharaonic ancestors. He used his position on the governing council of the USR and his seat on the board of the ITC to good advantage.

He was one of only a handful of men who controlled access to archaeological sites and excavations in the USR, and it was rumored that a large part of his fortune had come from misappropriated funds from licensing contracts for archaeothaumaturgic expeditions. He was a controversial figure, a man who flaunted his wealth so blatantly that even the governing council of the USR could no longer look the other way. There was an investigation under way as part of a movement by the opposition to unseat him from the council, and there were even allegations of "thaumaturgical improprieties"—dangerous accusations indeed. It was political doublespeak, a thinly veiled accusation of practice in black magic.

This auction, conducted in cooperation with the USR Department of Antiquities and the Annendale Corporation, sponsor of the Euphrates expedition, was being held to raise funds for the badly depleted treasury of the USR, and there were a lot of people looking over Al'Hassan's shoulder. Yet he had managed to turn the entire affair into a public-relations coup, negotiating a widely publicized deal with the Annendale Corporation to "donate" their share of the profits to the USR in return for government bonds, unlimited access to the USR's Department of Antiquities archives, and future licensing considerations. Still, with the over-the-table bargaining so flamboyantly transacted, Wyrdrune could not help but wonder what went on behind the scenes, underneath the table. He knew a lot of other people would be wondering about it, too, and that could work to his advantage.

"Ladies and gentlemen, our next item is lot number twenty-five, three gems discovered in a cache at the Annendale Euphrates dig: runestones of unknown properties."

Wyrdrune tensed. This was it. He glanced down quickly at the newspaper clipping he held in his hand. He had underlined three lines describing a small bronze jewel box containing three roughly cut, unpolished stones that were incised with obscure, faintly visible symbols similar to cuneiform—a ruby, an emerald, and a sapphire. Highly precious stones. Small. Easy to conceal and carry. Even easier to dispose of. He crumpled up the clipping and dropped it on the floor.

"I have an opening bid of one hundred thousand. Do I hear one hundred and ten? Thank you, I have one hundred ten, do I hear one hundred twenty?"

Wyrdrune reached into the inside pocket of his robe and withdrew a small, soft leather pouch. Something inside the pouch was squirming.

On the opposite side of the room the hooded figure glanced furtively around and slowly brought out the black canister.

Wyrdrune opened the drawstring on the pouch, turned it upside down, and shook out a small lizard into the palm of his hand. He closed his fist around it and tucked the empty pouch back inside his pocket. Then, cupping his free hand over the one holding the salamander, he spoke a fire elemental spell under his breath. His hands began to feel warm. He opened them slowly and saw the salamander starting to emit a soft red glow. With a quick flick of his wrist he tossed the lizard onto the heavy drapes. It clung to the soft material, and as it glowed brighter, the drapes began to smolder. Wyrdrune started to move away from the marble column, slowly making his way to the far side of the dais.

The hooded figure on the opposite side of the room also moved forward, pulling the pin on the black canister.

The drapes suddenly erupted into flame.

"Fire!" shouted Wyrdrune.

"Stand back!" shouted a wizard in the crowd, raising his arms. "I'll blow it out!"

"No, a rain spell!" shouted someone else.

"I'll douse it!"

"Wait, look out!"

As the flames licked higher, a number of sorcerers threw their spells simultaneously, with the result that a gale-force wind suddenly ripped through the auction hall, accompanied by a small thunderstorm conjured up by someone else, which grew rapidly in intensity as it was joined by the force of at least six other rain spells. Robes billowed in the wind, thunder rolled and lightning crackled, water poured down in a deluge from roiling black clouds that suddenly appeared just below the ceiling, and everyone began shouting at once.

"Idiot! I said *I'd* get it!"

"I cast my spell first!"

"Will someone turn off the damn rain!"

Wyrdrune bolted toward the dais.

The hooded figure swore and stuck the pin back in the grenade, then ripped the cloak off and threw it to the floor, revealing a black-haired young woman in a leather and chain-mail jacket with a stand-up collar, skintight yellow breeches, and high black boots. She lunged toward the podium, shoving the auctioneer out of the way, and arrived there at the same time as Wyrdrune, both of them simultaneously grabbing for the box containing the stones. They both froze, staring at each other with astonishment.

"Thieves! Stop them!"

"Damn!" said Wyrdrune. He grabbed her wrist. "Come on—"

"Let go of my arm!"

She tried to jerk away from him, but Wyrdrune held on tightly. "No time—"

He spoke a teleportation spell, and they both vanished.

Wyrdrune reappeared inside his small apartment on East 4th Street with a slight popping sound as air was suddenly displaced by his manifestation. He dropped about a foot and a half to the floor and landed somewhat unsteadily. He felt dizzy. Teleportation spells were advanced-level thaumaturgy, and they always took a lot out of him. He had never fully mastered them. He swayed as the vertigo hit strongly and his vision blurred. The room seemed to be moving. He sighed with relief that he had made it and briefly shut his eyes, waiting for the room to stop spinning.

"*Whew*! That was close. Are you all right?"

There was no reply.

He opened his eyes. The girl was nowhere in sight.

"Where'd she go?" said Wyrdrune to himself, still feeling slightly disoriented. "*Uh-oh*." He bit his lower lip. He had prepared the spell for himself alone, to escape after the theft. If he had miscalculated somehow and she had materialized inside the wall—

There was a loud knock.

"Where are you?"

The knock was repeated twice.

The closet.

He walked over to the closet door, about five feet away from where he had materialized in the center of the room. He unlocked the door and opened it. She was standing inside the tiny closet, leaning with one arm against the inside wall. He had been holding his breath, and now he let it out in a heavy exhalation of relief as he stood aside to let her out.

"Boy, you had me scared for a minute," he said, peeling off his fake nose and taking off his wig.

As the white wig came off, shoulder-length, curly blond hair tumbled down from beneath it. He shook it out, brushing it away from his forehead, then peeled off the remaining latex rubber that had aged his features. Fifty years dropped away from him in an instant. He unfastened the robe and took it off. Underneath it he was wearing a short, tan, hooded warlock's cassock that came down to just below his waist, loose, multipocketed brown trousers, and high-topped red leather athletic shoes with blue lightning stripes on them.

"Another second and they would have nailed us," he said as he removed his disguise. "I can't believe it. I just can't *believe* it! I had it planned so well! There was no chance of anything going wrong. Well, hardly any chance, anyway, but—"

Her right fist connected with his jaw and sent him flying backward, to land hard on the floor. He fell on his back and lay there for a moment, stunned, then slowly got up to a sitting position. She was standing over him, glaring down at him with fury. He rubbed his jaw and stared up at her in astonishment.

"What the hell was *that* for?"

"For almost getting me stuck inside the wall, for starters," she said, "and for lousing up my job!"

"*Your* job?" he said angrily. "You mess up *my* heist, I save your ass from going to jail, and *this* is the thanks I get?"

"I had that place cased!" she said furiously. "All I had to do was set off a blackout bomb, grab the stones, and I would've been gone! And then *you* had to show up!"

Wyrdrune slowly picked himself up off the floor, still feeling weak and dizzy from the energy he had expended in teleporting. "A blackout bomb? A lousy smoke grenade? Your big plan was using a cheap dime-store magic novelty in a roomful of wizards? That's rich. You're lucky I came along."

"Who the hell *are* you, anyway?" she said.

"The name is Wyrdrune," he said.

"*Wyrdrune?* What kind of a name is that? Nobody's name is Wyrdrune."

"It's my magename, all right? Adepts have to be careful about revealing their truenames. *Broom!*"

She glanced around at the small apartment. It was a railroad flat, the rooms arranged one after another in a straight line, the entrance leading into the kitchen, a small alcove from the kitchen leading into the main room of the apartment, part of which had been walled off to accommodate the bathroom. A bedroom led off the living room, a small room hardly larger than a closet with a high wooden loft bed in it, a makeshift study with a tiny writing desk beneath the bed. Bookshelves were everywhere, crammed with volumes. Every square inch of space seemed to be taken up by something. The books had overflowed the shelves and were piled up waist-high on the floor, atop ratty-looking throw rugs and wooden crates. Various sculptures, cheap copies, stood atop wooden cable spools that served as coffee and end tables, and a number of fantasy art prints, inexpensively framed, hung on the walls. The place looked like the aftermath of an explosion in a novelty store.

"*Broom!*" he shouted again. "Where the hell are you? Make some tea!"

She walked over to one of the bookshelves and pulled out a volume bound in imitation leather. It was an elementary thaumaturgy text. She opened the book and saw a cheap printed bookplate pasted inside on the flyleaf. It read, "EX LIBRIS—Melvin Karpinsky."

"Melvin?" she said.

"Put that back," said Wyrdrune irritably. "I'll thank you not to touch my things, whoever you are."

"My name is Kira."

"Kira what?"

"Just Kira."

Her eyes grew wide as she saw a spindly-looking straw broom come walking in from the kitchen. It had rubbery, spiderlike arms with four fingers on each hand. It was carrying a small metal tray with a pot of tea, a container of sugar, and a cup and saucer on it.

"*Two* cups, stupid," Wyrdrune said. "I've got a guest."

"So?" the broom said. Kira had no idea where the voice was coming from. It had no face, much less a mouth. "It's not enough I should fetch and carry, I have to be a mind reader? What do I know from guests? I'm just a broom. It's not *my* fault you didn't tell me two cups. . . ."

Kira stared as the broom set the tray down on a cable spool, which served as a coffee table. Wyrdrune shut his eyes in silent suffering.

"*Why* can't I remember the spell to make that thing shut up?" he said.

"Two cups, he wants," the broom said, going back into the kitchen, grumbling under its breath. Assuming that it breathed. But then, how could it? "Two. I suppose he wants two saucers, right? Probably wants two spoons as well. What's next—coasters, maybe?"

Wyrdrune covered his face with his hand.

"You're not very good at this stuff, are you?" Kira said wryly.

She had hit a sore spot. "I'll have you know I studied under Professor Ambrosius, himself," he said.

"Who?"

He stared at her in disbelief. "You're kidding. Merlin Ambrosius? The legendary wizard to King Arthur? Subject of countless books, films, and a television miniseries?"

"Never heard of him. I don't watch TV."

The broom came back, carrying another cup and saucer. "Shall I be mother?" it said. "One lump or two?"

"You never *heard* of him?" said Wyrdrune.

"Hello?" the broom said. "Earth to warlock, I'm talking here. . . ."

"One," said Kira.

"Thank you," said the broom. "You're a good person." It poured her a cup of tea and handed it to her.

"He's the one who brought us out of the Collapse!" said Wyrdrune.

She shrugged.

"I don't believe it," he said. "Where did you go to school? Merlin Ambrosius is only the greatest archmage who ever lived! Before he came, there was nothing but darkness and despair."

"Darkness and despair?" she said, raising her eyebrows.

"Didn't you study about the Collapse? It was like the Dark Ages all over again. It was like the aftermath of a nuclear holocaust. And then Merlin came back."

"Came back from where?"

"From his entombment by Morgan Le Fay."

"Who's he?"

"*She.* She was a sorceress, half sister to King Arthur Pendragon."

She stared at him blankly.

"You're pulling my leg," he said. "You *really* don't know any of this?"

"So what are you telling me, she killed this guy and he came back from the dead to give you homework?"

"He wasn't dead, he . . . oh, the hell with it."

"No, go on, I want to hear this."

"What's the point?"

"You got something better to do? Go on. Finish the story."

He sighed. "Merlin Ambrosius was the mage who served King Arthur Pendragon of Britain. You ever heard of Camelot? The Knights of the Round Table?"

"I think we've established that my education's been neglected, okay?" she said. "I never even got as far as high school."

"Oh. I'm sorry. I didn't mean to—"

"Just get on with it." She put her booted feet up on the cable spool and leaned back against the cushions of the battered couch.

"It's a long story, but I'll try to make it short. It happened several thousand years ago. Arthur was the warrior king who united all of Britain, and Merlin was the mage who helped him do it. He gathered the finest soldiers of his time at his castle, Camelot, and formed the Knights of the Round Table. But his kingdom collapsed when his queen, Guinevere, and his best friend, the knight called Lancelot du Lac, fell in love and had an affair. Arthur had a son, named Modred, who was the child of Arthur and his half sister, Morgan Le Fay—"

"Sounds kinky."

"You want to hear this or not?"

"Sure, it's starting to get good."

"Modred found out about the affair and exploited it to bring about his father's downfall. It led to war and the end of the first thaumaturgic age. Morgan Le Fay knew that Merlin might have stopped it all. She wanted her son, Modred, to ascend the throne, so while she used him to bring down Arthur, she had one of her pupils, a girl named Nimue, seduce Merlin and place him under a spell. Then she had Merlin's body placed inside the cleft of an ancient oak tree and sealed up inside it."

"Why didn't she just kill him?"

"Because I guess she wanted him to die slowly. Only he didn't die. He was comatose, sort of like in suspended animation—"

"Suspended what?"

"A state similar to being asleep, only with all his life functions drastically slowed down. Like being in a trance. He couldn't break the enchantment that imprisoned him, but he used his powers to keep himself alive. And his powers kept the tree alive for all those years as well. Time passed. The old ways and the old knowledge became forgotten. The world changed. Technology was born, and no one believed in magic anymore. And as technology grew, the world began to die. Cities became bigger, and people started to choke in their own wastes. They polluted the oceans with their garbage, they choked the air, they buried their wastes in dumps and contaminated the aquifers, poisoning their own water supplies—"

"Right, I got that part," she said. "Darkness and despair. Get back to the guy in the tree."

"Okay. It was in the tenth year of the Collapse. A retired British sergeant-major named Tom Malory was out hunting for wood. It was winter and his kids were freezing. Unauthorized wood chopping was a felony. He knew where he could find wood, but it was in a protected area, all that was left of Sherwood Forest, nothing but a tiny grove of trees. He managed to get past the perimeter guards and over the fence. He wasn't sure if he was going to make it. He had no idea how he would smuggle the wood out past the guards, but he was desperate. Later on he couldn't say why he picked that particular tree, a gnarled, ancient oak that was at least ten times the size of any of the other remaining trees. It was huge. He knew it was crazy, one man trying to chop down a tree like that with nothing but an ax, but the moment he saw it, something in him snapped. Here everyone was freezing to death and burning whatever they could find to keep warm, the entire region had been almost completely deforested, and here was this one granddaddy of an oak tree, big enough to burn for years, standing there, as if mocking him. . . . He just lost it and attacked it with his ax. And suddenly there was a flash of lightning that came down and split the giant tree right down the middle. And Merlin was released. That was the start of the end of the Collapse. The beginning of the second thaumaturgic age. Merlin brought back the forgotten discipline of magic. He founded schools and put the world on a thaumaturgic energy standard. That was almost a hundred years ago. Merlin retired a couple of years back. He's Dean Emeritus of the Thaumaturgic College of Sorcerers in Cambridge, Massachusetts, now. He lectures all around the world. And I was one of his prize pupils."

"Some prize," she said.

The broom tapped Wyrdrune on his shoulder. "So are you going to drink your tea or what?"

He held up his cup so that the broom could pour. "All right," he said, "so I didn't complete the course. I needed money and I got a part-time job doing special effects for a band. Only, one of my fire spells went a little wrong and the concert hall burned down. They took away my scholarship and expelled me."

"You mean the fire at the Nazgul concert?" she said. "That was *you*?"

"It was an accident, okay? It could've happened to anybody. I was going to fence those stones so I could get the money to finish school. Guess I can forget about that now. Thanks for blowing it for me."

"What makes you think I blew it, warlock?"

She held out her hand. The three stones were resting in her palm.

CHAPTER
Two

CHAPTER
Two

Mustafa Sharif kneeled on the highly polished black marble floor, his head bowed, the soft folds of his best white kaffiyeh hanging down over his ears and covering his cheeks. He had prepared for this audience as if for a date with a beautiful woman, putting on his finest, most conservative custom-tailored suit, his best shirt, his blue silk tie, and his lucky obsidian-and-gold cuff links. He had polished his shoes until they gleamed, had had his fingernails freshly manicured and his mustache trimmed. Now he abased himself before his lord in the spacious presence chamber of the palace, and he trembled, afraid to look up and meet his gaze.

"I could not help it, Your Highness," said Mustafa, his voice amplified by the natural acoustics of the room, even though he spoke softly. "I was certain to have the highest bid, but the stones were stolen by a clever sorcerer—"

"You *allowed* them to be stolen?"

The deep, resonant voice was barely raised above a whisper, but it echoed in the arched ballroom with the vaulted, mosaic ceiling. It dripped with venom.

"There was nothing I could do, Your Highness! The room was full of sorcerers, and all of them were taken by surprise! There are no words to convey my profound chagrin over this most unfortunate—"

"Stop whining! Look at me when I speak to you!"

With a feeling of dread Mustafa slowly looked up at Sheik Rashid Ilderim Al'Hassan. He sat upon an ornate, jewel-encrusted throne placed on a dais, looking down at Mustafa with an unblinking stare. There was nothing overtly frightening about Rashid Al'Hassan. He was, in fact, a strikingly handsome man, dark, elegant, with chisled Egyptian features and a black, neatly trimmed, pencil-thin mustache. He was fifty-five years old, but he looked years younger. He was conservatively dressed in an expensive black suit with an extremely fine charcoal stripe, its cut making the most minimum concession to current fashion. His blue silk tie was impeccably knotted, and his white shirt was crisp and fresh. He wore diamond links in his cuffs, which had just a touch of lace around them, and a diamond ring on the third finger of each hand. On the little finger of his right hand he wore a gold-and-obsidian signet ring bearing his family crest. He wore a ruby scarab amulet set in platinum on a gold chain. His long kaffiyeh was the finest white linen, and it was held in place by a single band of gold with a small, emerald-eyed cobra's head rising from it. There was a single jewel set in the center of his forehead, a third eye, a tiny, dark, blood-red ruby. His eyes, sharply contrasting with his olive-colored skin, were the palest blue, so light that they almost seemed to glow. His gaze was magnetic, and it made Mustafa's skin crawl.

"I want those runestones found, Mustafa," he said. "And I want the thieves who had the temerity to steal them!"

Mustafa looked down, unable to meet that unflinching, snakelike stare. "They will be found, Your Highness! I swear it!"

"You know the penalty for failure, Mustafa," Rashid said softly. The tiny jewel set into his forehead began to glow.

Mustafa prostrated himself on the floor, trembling. "No, Your Highness!" he cried. "*Please,* I beg you. . . ."

"Look at me, Mustafa."

"Your Highness, I *implore* you—"

"*Look* at me."

Sweat beading on his upper lip, Mustafa slowly raised his head. The jewel in Rashid's forehead blazed, and an intense beam of white light shot from it, striking Mustafa in the head.

"*Pain,* Mustafa."

Mustafa screamed, wreathed in the aura of the beam, his features twisted in agony.

"This is only a brief taste of the agonies you'll suffer if you fail me," said Rashid.

Mustafa had never felt such searing pain in his entire life. He could not stop screaming. It seemed as if his eyes were melting from their sockets.

"There are worse things than death, Mustafa," said Rashid. "Remember."

The room went dark, lit only by the burning braziers that stood along the walls. Dark shapes seemed to writhe out of the shadows, undulating, reaching for him. . . .

"*Noooo!*" Mustafa screamed.

"Remember," said Rashid softly. His voice became a ghostly echo, reverberating throughout the chamber. It seemed to bounce around inside Mustafa's skull. "*Remember . . . remember . . . remember . . .*"

The pain stopped suddenly, and everything went dark. Mustafa huddled on the ground, shivering, sweat pouring off him. Thin tendrils of smoke rose from his body. He found himself lying facedown in a refuse-strewn alley somewhere in New York City. Several feet away from him, a cat arched its back and yowled, frightened by his sudden appearance out of thin air. Like a blind man, he groped his way along the ground, slowly rising up to his hands and knees. His heart was fibrillating, and ever single nerve synapse in his body was thrashing violently. He seemed to see the spectral afterimage of Rashid's face before him, receding into the distance. He raised his head. His features had become those of a very old man, deeply lined and pale. His hair had gone completely white.

"Remember..."

Wyrdrune and Kira walked together down the sidewalk of Third Avenue. He had the hood of his cassock up. Her hands were thrust into her pockets, and she walked with the jaunty swagger of a tough street urchin.

"We split sixty-forty and that's final," she said.

They stopped before the steps leading down to the entrance of a basement-level pawnshop with the traditional three balls mounted over the window.

"*I* do the talking, understand?" she said.

Wyrdrune grimaced. "Who'd get a word in edgewise?"

They went down the steps and through the door, causing a small brass bell to tinkle as they walked through.

The place looked like a tiny warehouse. Every available inch of space was taken up with rows of shelving carrying everything and anything that could possibly be pawned—books, musical instruments, magical requisites, art objects, items of jewelry, and clothing. The place resembled an exploded cornucopia of bric-a-brac. A large paragriffin sat on a perch behind the counter, a creation of thaumagenetic engineering with brilliant gold plumage and metallic scales. It sqawked loudly as they came in.

"Can I help you? Can I help you? *Aarrp!*"

A huge man came through some drapes behind the counter. He must have weighed well over three hundred pounds, and he was almost perfectly round. His jowls were heavy and sagging, and his eyes were deeply set, beady, like a pig's. He breathed laboriously, as if the slightest movement were an effort. He was wearing a white suit and a dark red, tassled fez. He wore an amulet around his neck the size of a small saucer, a representation of the worm Ouroboros eating its own tail with the Eye of Horus in the center.

"Well, well," he said, huffing and puffing and rubbing his hands against his chest, "if it isn't my old friend, Kira. Who's your friend? And what can I do for you today?"

"Maybe we should go in the back, Fats."

"Certainly, my dear, certainly. If you and your friend will kindly follow me?"

He raised up a portion of the counter so they could go through and indicated the drapes leading to the back room. "Watch the store, Rick," he said.

"Sure thing, Fats," said the paragriffin. "Gotcha covered. *Aarrp!*"

"Is he a sorcerer?" whispered Wyrdrune.

"Fats?" said Kira. "No. But I'm not too sure about the bird."

It was dark in the back of the store. It was a small room, lined with shelves full of junk. There was a small round card table covered with green baize standing in the center of the room beneath a large hanging lamp made of multicolored stained glass. A small TV set was on, the sound off. It was tuned to a game show. Wyrdrune glanced at it sourly and wondered about going to school for at least four or five years in a thaumaturgic college, sweating through hours of mind-numbing course work and studies, writing a thesis and submitting to both the lengthy written and oral examinations just to earn the right to take the still more complicated certification tests, with additional exams for each succeeding level of advancement in adept certification, and finally getting a job with the Public Service Works as an engineer adept, maintaining the spells that kept the old power stations functioning just so people like Fats could sit around drinking beer and watching game shows. He wondered if this was what Merlin really had in mind when he brought back the old knowledge.

"Well," said Fats, slowly lowering himself into a large armchair, "I assume you've come to discuss business. What do you have for me?"

He kept his eyes on Wyrdrune, leaving it to Kira to come to the point so that he could claim entrapment just in case Wyrdrune was a cop. She reached into one of the pockets of her black leather jacket and withdrew the leather pouch Wyrdrune had given her. She loosened the drawstring and dumped the runestones out onto the table. They seemed to glow softly, like embers in a fire, beautiful and strange.

Fats stared at the stones for a long time before reaching out and touching one tentatively with a meaty index finger.

"So what do you think?" said Kira.

"Very nice," Fats said slowly. "*Very* nice, indeed." He took a jeweler's loupe out of his pocket and started to examine the stones carefully. "This wouldn't be the gallery job, by any chance, would it? The so-called 'daring heist' at Christie's?"

"We don't ask questions, Fats, remember?" Kira said. "Do we do business or don't we?"

Fats removed the jeweler's loupe, sat back, and folded his hands over his large stomach. He smiled faintly. "Well, my dear, I believe it's possible that we might come to an arrangement. . . ."

"How much?" said Kira.

Fats pursed his lips, considering. "Well, now, let me see. . . . Mmmm. Yes. I should think about . . . five thousand."

"*Five thousand?*" Wyrdrune said. "Are you kidding? The *low* bid on those stones was—"

Kira elbowed him in the side. "Try again, Fats."

"Come, come, my dear," he said. "Let's be realistic. We're old friends, you and I—"

"We were never friends, Fats. I don't do business with friends."

"Well, then, we are old business partners—in a sense. We have always done reasonably well by each other. Surely you'll admit that I've never cheated you."

"You'd cheat your own mother if it meant a profit," she said. "Don't insult my intelligence, okay? You know damn well they're worth a sight more than a measly five thousand."

"Well, perhaps that's so," said Fats, "but on the other hand, there is a certain question of heat involved, wouldn't you say? This isn't exactly our usual form of transaction, now is it? You seem to be moving up in the world. Personally I find that highly encouraging. I'm always the first to support personal enterprise. However, what we have here are the ill-gotten gains of a rather highly publicized enterprise, if you get my meaning. I'm going to have to take some extra special pains, go to some rather extraordinary lengths to, ah, find the appropriate client with whom to negotiate the sale of these little baubles. It will be a far more complicated matter than the usual sort of snatch-and-grab or cat burglary you've specialized in in the past. It's not unreasonable that I should expect to be compensated for my efforts on your behalf."

"If you're going to be making efforts on *my* behalf," said Kira, "then how come I'm not getting a percentage of the final sale price? Come on, Fats, stop wasting my time. Either make a reasonable offer or we'll take our business elsewhere."

He raised his eyebrows. "Indeed? Have you been soliciting new distributors behind my back? I'm truly disappointed in you, Kira. Whatever has become of loyalty? However, if you genuinely believe that you can obtain a better deal elsewhere, I certainly won't stand in your way."

"Fine. It's been nice, Fats."

She reached for the stones, but his hand snaked out with

deceptive speed and came down on top of hers. "Let's not be hasty, now," he said. "Surely you won't begrudge an old man the simple pleasures of haggling? Let me see if I can't sweeten the pot somewhat, purely for old times' sake. What would you say to eight thousand?"

"No deal. These stones are easily worth ten times that."

"Ten times? I hardly think so. Still, I'll entertain a counter offer. What did you have in mind?"

"At least twenty thousand."

"Ridiculous, my dear. Out of the question. I'd be cutting my profit to the bone. Make me a more realistic offer."

"All right, then, fifteen."

"No, no, really, that would never do. I'll go as high as nine."

"You'll go ten."

Fats sighed. "Very well, ten, but not a penny more. Take it or leave it. This sort of ingratitude is highly painful to me."

"We'll leave it," Wyrdrune said.

"We'll take it," Kira said simultaneously.

"Well, which is it to be, then?" said Fats, looking up at them with raised eyebrows.

She pulled Wyrdrune by the arm and drew him away several feet. *"What do you think you're doing?"* she hissed at him.

"Are you crazy?" he whispered. "Ten thousand dollars? The bidding on those stones went as high as a hundred and twenty thousand, and it was going even higher! You're letting this guy steal us blind!"

"Listen, warlock," she said, "let me tell you a few facts of life. With stolen merchandise, especially stolen merchandise that's really hot, you're not going to get anywhere *near* actual market value, much less street value. Fats is going to be the one taking all the risks disposing of the goods. He's one of maybe a handful of people in the city set up to fence this kind of stuff. If I walk out on him now without cutting the deal, it's going to hurt our relationship, and frankly I can't afford that. I don't have time to educate an amateur, all right? I'll make a deal with you, I'll go fifty-fifty with you if you'll just keep your damn mouth shut, but if you queer this for me, you're going to have a *real* problem on your hands. Now what's it going to be?"

Wyrdrune sighed. "All right, all right. But if you ask me, we're being had."

"Maybe, but it's still going to be the easiest five thousand dollars you ever made. Take what you can get and don't bitch about it." She turned to Fats. "It's a deal."

"I'm so very glad," he said. He stood, picked up the stones, and dropped them back into the pouch one at a time, then turned and rummaged among some shelves until he found a metal box. He opened it with a tiny key and withdrew a packet of bills. "There you are, my dear," he said, handing the bound bundle to her. "It's all there. You may count it if you wish. A pleasure doing business with you. Do come back again. And bring your friend."

Outside in the street, Wyrdrune shook his head. "I guess I shouldn't complain, considering the way things might have turned out. I suppose it wasn't all that bad."

"It was too easy," Kira said sourly. "He was really flush this time. I should've hardballed him. I bet we could've gotten more."

He stopped and stared at her. "*What?* After all that back there, now you're saying—"

"Keep your voice down, will you? All right, maybe I was wrong. He seemed just a bit too pleased with himself. Forget it. What the hell, we came out all right. It's like you said, it could've been much worse. Now—"

Wyrdrune made a quick pass with his hands, mumbled something under his breath, and they both suddenly vanished. He reappeared with a pop back inside his apartment on East 4th Street.

"No point in carrying all that money around in *that* neighborhood," he said. "I figured I'd—" He looked around and saw that he was alone. "Kira?"

There was a knock at the door of his apartment. He ran to the door and looked through the peephole, then unlocked it quickly. She was standing in the hall, arms folded across her chest, a scowl on her face.

"What do you say next time we take the bus?"

"I'm sorry. I could've sworn I got it right that time—"

"I don't want to hear about it," she said, walking past him into the apartment. "Do yourself a favor, warlock, and take a few more magic classes or something. You're dangerous." She quickly counted out some bills and stuffed them in her pocket, then tossed the rest of the bundle to him. "Here's your cut."

"You don't mind if I count it," he said. "It's not that I don't trust you—"

"Maybe you want to search me, just to make sure I didn't steal anything when you popped me in your closet before?"

"I didn't mean—"

"Fine, go ahead and count it. I got my cut right here," she said, reaching back into the pocket of her jacket. "You can count that too. I wouldn't want to—"

As she pulled the bills out of her pocket a small leather pouch fell out onto the floor.

"What the hell is that?" she said.

Wyrdrune bent down and picked up the pouch. It looked uncomfortably familiar. He opened up the drawstring and shook the runestones out into his hand. He glanced up at her.

"Hey, I don't know where that came from," she said, seeing his look. "If you're trying to pull some kind of fast one here—"

"Not me," he said. "This is cute, Kira. Real cute."

"I'll say," she said. "I sell 'em and you magic 'em right back. Not smart, warlock. Not smart at all. You've really done it now. That's once fence I won't be able to do business with anymore. And Fats is a bad man to cross."

"What are you talking about?" he said. "I didn't—"

"Wait a minute," she said, snapping her fingers. "Just hold it right there. You know, this has possibilities. Sure. I've got lots of contacts. We could make a hell of a big score here. We could just resell the stones over and over—"

He sat down at the table, staring at the stones.

"—we could hit out-of-town fences so my contacts around here wouldn't dry up," she said. "I could ask around, make a few calls. If we moved fast, with one job, we could clear maybe ten, twenty times as much—"

"You don't seem to understand," said Wyrdrune. "I didn't *do* this!"

She stopped and looked at him, frowning. "I suppose the stones just jumped back into my pocket by themselves. I don't get it, warlock. What's your angle?"

"Uh-huh," he said, nodding. "I think I see. And I'm not buying it, either. I may not be very street-smart, girl, but I'm not stupid. I've seen people with fast hands before. If you think you can run this kind of scam and then turn around and put the blame on me, you'd better think again."

Her eyes narrowed. "Oh, I get it. Fats has no idea who you are, so what've you got to lose, right? And if it gets back to you, you turn it all around and pin it on me, is that it? Well, I'm not falling for it. A con like that could get you killed, warlock."

"The name's Wyrdrune, and you're right. I'm not going for it. We're getting rid of these things right now. This time we sell the stones and they *stay* sold, you understand? And then this so-called partnership gets dissolved for good. I've had about enough."

She watched him suspiciously. "Yeah," she said, nodding. "Sure thing, warlock. Anything you say. The sooner the better."

"That suits me just fine. And you'd better not try to hustle me again or I may lose my temper. And I wouldn't recommend making a wizard angry, you get my drift?"

"Wizard, huh? What are you going to do, dropout, sic your broom on me and have it *nudzheh* me to death?"

"That's enough! I don't want to talk about this anymore. Let's get it done, all right? The sooner I'm rid of the stones *and* you, the better I'll like it. You're the one with all the connections. What's our next stop?"

She stared at him for a long moment, then nodded. "Okay. Forget it. I shouldn't be wasting my time with amateurs, anyway. We'll hit Rozetti's."

"Rozetti's?"

"He operates out of a bar on Christopher Street. Nice deal, huh? So now you'll have two fences you can connect up with. Only I got news for you, warlock, if you try any more parlor tricks and go pinning it on me, remember, I'm the one who's got the good faith built up with these people and I know where you live. Need I say more?"

"Just shut up, all right? Let's just do it. You handle the deal and then that's it for us. I don't care what you do or where you go. But if you try setting those people on my tail, I've got some news for you: You'll be buying into more trouble than you'll know how to handle."

"Now you just look here for a second—"

"No, *you* look here! I said I don't want to talk about this anymore! All right? Just drop it! Come on, we're going to Christopher Street! Right now!"

"Fine! We'll take the *bus*!"

They came out of the bar together, each of them another ten thousand dollars richer. The money had done a great deal to soften their disposition toward each other. They stood outside the bar, looking at each other warily. She grinned.

"Satisfied now?" she said. "You were watching me like a hawk in there. I really have to hand it to you, warlock, you don't let up for a minute. You still won't admit that—"

"Will you drop the game already?" he said. "It's done. If

you lifted those stones again after we sold them, you must
be a better magician than I am."

"That isn't saying much," she said. "Just remember what
I told you. Here's your cut."

From inside the bar a voice shouted, "They pulled a fast
one! Stop them!"

Her jaw dropped. "I don't *believe* it! *How could you be so
stupid*—"

"I didn't—"

Several large men came running out of the bar.

"*Damn* you, warlock, you're going to get us killed!"

He grabbed her arm. "Not if I can help it!"

One of the men leapt at them, intending to bring both of
them down in a flying tackle. Instead he landed hard on his
chest on the sidewalk, and the wind whistled out of him.

"Where the hell did they *go*?" one of the others said.

They reappeared in the midst of a flock of pigeons peck-
ing up bread crumbs beneath the arch in Washington Square
Park. The birds took off in a flurry all around them, and they
had to cover their faces as several of the pigeons struck them
in their flight. The arch was covered with cabalistic graffiti
and words written in Spanish. About twenty-five yards
away, a crowd was gathered around a turbaned fakir doing a
snake-charming street act with a creature that was half dog,
half cobra. A number of outlandishly dressed street people
were plying the crowd, and one little eight-year-old kid was
deftly lifting wallets out of back pockets.

"I think I'm getting motion sickness," Kira said, leaning
against the arch.

"We've got a problem," Wyrdrune said.

She looked at him furiously. "You're telling *me*?"

Wyrdrune started walking toward a nearby park bench,
shaking his head. Kira followed him.

"Where do you think you're going? Now I've got *two*
fences on my tail! Do you have any idea what you've done?

You've been nothing but trouble, warlock! Real *bad* trouble! I ought to—"

"I thought *you* were the one who wanted to keep selling the stones over and over again?" said Wyrdrune, spinning around to face her.

She gritted her teeth. "Hell," she said, "in spite of everything, that still may not be such a bad idea, but I didn't want to do this on my own turf, damn it! These people *know* me!"

Wyrdrune pursed his lips and sat down on the bench. "There's something funny going on here."

"Notice I'm not laughing," she said.

He reached into his pocket and took out the pouch. He stared at it. "It's got to be the stones," he said. "*They* must be doing it."

"Oh, come on! You expect me to believe that?"

"I don't care what you believe. I know you didn't have a chance to lift them, and I sure as hell didn't do it! There's no other explanation."

He shook the stones out of the pouch, put the pouch back into his pocket, and tossed the stones over his shoulder into the bushes.

"*What are you doing?*"

"Performing an experiment," he said. "Come on."

He got up and started walking quickly away from the bench. She stared at where he had tossed the stones, then looked after him, then back at the bushes once again, bewildered, uncertain what to do. "*Wait!* Where're you going? You're crazy, you know that?"

"So humor me," he called back. "Come on."

She glanced desperately at the bushes once again, then at him, then back at the bushes, then she swore and ran after him. She caught up to him and grabbed him by the arm, spinning him around. They stood in the middle of a walkway, near a sign that read, MAGIC CARPET RIDES. A heavyset man standing underneath the sign was collecting money from several parents while their children jumped up and down excitedly, watching several other kids riding round in a circle on a couple of rugs flying about two feet off the ground.

"They're enchanted runestones," Wyrdrune said. "Unknown properties, remember?"

"So you just threw them away?" she said with disbelief. "You're out of your mind! I'm going back there before somebody picks them up!"

"Okay," said Wyrdrune, "but check your pockets first."

"Right," she said, reaching into her pockets. "I suppose they came back all by them"—she pulled the pouch out of her right-hand pocket—"selves?"

Wyrdrune stood before her, arms folded. "I rest my case."

She looked up at him. "Very funny."

"Laugh if you like," he said, "but *I* didn't do it. And I don't care if you believe me or not. We can sell them, but they won't stay sold. I don't know why and I don't care. I've had enough. You stole them, looks like you're stuck with them. Take them. And go away. Preferably very far away."

He turned and started walking away from her.

"Wait a minute!" she said. "I don't understand what's going on here! What do you mean, I'm *stuck* with them?"

He kept on walking. "They keep coming back to you. I'm going to quit while I'm ahead. The way I see it, it's not my problem."

"Hey! Hold on! You can't just walk away!"

"Watch me."

She chased him and caught up with him, grabbing his arm and spinning him around again. She held the stones up. "Look, you, I want an explanation! You got me into this, now what *is* it with these things?"

"*I* got you into it? Funny, that's not how I remember it."

He took the stones out of her hand and dropped them back into the pouch. "You wanted the stones? Okay, fine." He took her right hand and slapped the pouch into it. "Now you've got 'em."

He turned and walked away. She glared after him for a moment, then took a deep breath and let it out. "Well, that suits me! You're not the only hotshot wizard in town, you know. I'll find out what these things are for myself! They're probably worth a fortune!" She turned away and started walking in the opposite direction. "Great. Just means more for me. Who needs you, anyway? Damn amateurs. I'll just—"

She came to a dead halt, her hands in her pockets.

She spun around. "*Hold it!*"

Wyrdrune stopped.

"Not so fast, warlock!"

He closed his eyes. "Don't tell me . . ."

He reached into his pockets. His right hand pulled out the pouch. He looked at it and sighed. "This just is *not* my day."

CHAPTER
Three

"... and when I turned around, they were gone. Honestly, that's really all I know," said Fats, wiping his face with a large handkerchief.

"And the ones who brought them to you?"

"A girl named Kira," Fats said, unable to take his gaze away from the old man. "About eighteen or nineteen years old, slim, dark, five foot five or six, stylish in a tough sort of way. You know the type, hair combed back along the sides, sort of an angular fall down over the eyes, mailed leather jacket, boots, that sort of thing. A street person, a young hustler. Though not in the sexual sense, you understand. I mean, she's the sort who'd try her hand at almost anything involving a certain amount of risk if there was money in it. Cat burglary, snatch-and-grab, running a con. Strictly third-rate, really. Frankly I was surprised—well, shocked, to put it bluntly—when she brought me the stones. Not really in her league at all, but I took a chance. After all, she'd never burned me before. I can't imagine what she must have been thinking. That young man she was with must have put her up to it."

"Describe him."

"I never heard his name," said Fats, unable to stop talking. He was seized by a compulsion to tell this old man everything. Whatever it would take to get him to leave and not come back again. "He was young, as I've already mentioned. Long hair, thick, blond, and rather curly, a warlock's cassock—"

"A *warlock's* cassock? Not sorcerer's robes? Are you certain?"

"Yes, quite certain. I've seen them before, you know. Of course, that doesn't necessarily mean anything. It might have been only a costume, but she called him 'warlock.' I'm quite certain of that. I swear, mister, that's all I know."

Fats fought to free himself from the old man's gaze, but he couldn't look away. Those eyes were loathesome, terrifying. Where the pupils should have been there were two dark, grinning skulls. Contact lenses, Fats told himself, they had to be, but still . . .

"You will let me know if you encounter them again," Mustafa said, putting his sunglasses back on.

"Certainly. Anything you say."

"If you can lead me to them, rest assured that I shall make it very worth your while," said Mustafa. "If not . . ."

Fats swallowed hard. "I'll ask around. See what I can find out."

"Good," said Mustafa. "We seem to understand each other. Here is my card." He held up his right hand. It was empty. A second later a business card appeared between his index and middle fingers. It gave his name and the number of the USR's embassy on First Avenue. "Call anytime. If I am not in, you may leave a message that you called and I will get back to you."

Gingerly Fats took the card, as if afraid that it might burn him. As the old man left, Fats sagged, as if he were a marionette whose strings had been abruptly cut.

"No sale, no sale!" said the paragriffin as the door closed behind the old man with a brief tinkle of the bell.

"Shut up, Rick," said Fats.

"*Aaarp!*"

"No sale, indeed," said Fats. "Well, we'll have to see what we can do about that." He picked up the phone and dialed a number.

A voice on the other end answered with a simple, "Yes?"

"You know who this is?" said Fats. "You recognize my voice?"

"Yes."

"I have a job for you," said Fats.

"We'll talk."

There was a click on the other end of the line as the other party hung up. Fats knew he would get in touch in his own way, at his own time. He was a very careful man. And a very lethal one.

They sat together at a corner table in the darkened bar of the restaurant, the pouch containing the runestones between them in the center of the table. They both had drinks before them, strong ones, and they sat with their elbows on the table, chins resting on their palms, staring at the pouch. At the other end of the bar a musician was improvising lyrics to the accompaniment of an enchanted harp zither that played itself. He merely made token passes over it with his hands, pretending a skill he didn't have.

"I don't know why," said Wyrdrune, "but I've got a very bad feeling about all this."

"What's to worry?" said Kira. "We've got some enchanted runestones on our hands that we can't seem to get rid of, we're wanted for grand theft, we've burned two fences, and they've probably put contracts out on us by now. Apart from that, we don't like each other very much. So far I'd say this has been a heck of a relationship."

"Yeah," said Wyrdrune. "I just can't wait for our second

date. We ought to celebrate. What the hell, why not? We're loaded."

He made a pass in the air with his left hand, and a bottle of imported champagne appeared in an ice bucket on their table, along with two wineglasses.

"Hey, I saw that!" shouted the bartender from across the room. "That'll be fifty bucks!"

"You mind change?" said Wyrdrune, raising his voice to be heard over the musician.

"Long as it's fifty bucks," said the bartender.

"Good," said Wyrdrune, gesturing again.

A shower of nickels appeared over the bartender's head, raining down on him. He yelled and ducked down behind the bar as the change pelted him like hail.

Kira looked at Wyrdrune with shock. "You can make money appear out of thin air and you *steal*?"

"I can't create matter," Wyrdrune said. "And counterfeiting by enchantment is one of your more serious federal crimes. That wasn't real. I just temporarily transmuted some ice cubes from his freezer."

"*That does it!*" shouted the bartender, unsteadily rising to his feet behind the bar. The coins had reverted back to water, and he was drenched from head to toe. "*Pay up and get out!*"

A man the size of a redwood tree suddenly appeared beside their table. His voice was incongruously soft and pleasant.

"I think perhaps you'd better pay your check and leave, sir," he said, looking apologetic. "I really don't want any trouble. I've just got a job to do. You know how it is."

The mark of a good bouncer was the ability to do his job without making it a challenge to the customer. This one knew his business, and Wyrdrune found himself feeling sympathetic. He nodded and started to count out the money for their bill.

"What the hell," said Kira, "I don't really like champagne, anyway."

"I'm sorry I got aggravated back there," Wyrdrune said as they left the restaurant. "I'm just feeling really bothered by this. I tried teleporting the stones away, but they . . . resisted."

Neither of them noticed it, but they were being followed.

"Look, if we're stuck with them," said Kira, "why not just make the best of it? We can run the con with a few more fences, then split up and leave town."

"I like the splitting-up part," Wyrdrune said, wryly, "but then which one of us will the stones wind up with?"

"What difference does it make?"

"I don't know," said Wyrdrune, "but magical events do not transpire without a reason. And I just can't figure any of this out. Something very strange is happening."

"Tell me about it," she said, with a sarcastic look.

"No, I mean, something strange is happening to *me*. I don't know if you noticed, but the first time I teleported us back to my apartment from Christie's, it just about knocked me out. Teleportation spells are advanced-level thaumaturgy. I never did finish my training, I'm just a bit too naturally gifted for my own good. At least, that's what Merlin always used to tell me."

"So?"

"So the last several times I teleported us, I barely even broke a sweat. I mean, it was easy!"

She shrugged. "Maybe it's like exercise and you're just getting stronger the more you do it."

"That's just it, it doesn't work like that. At least, not exactly. A full-fledged mage can teleport about as easily as you can blink, but I'm only at the warlock level. And magic always exacts a price. You have to maintain a delicate balance when you're using natural forces thaumaturgically. I should be feeling the strain of it, but I'm not. It's as if I were getting strength from somewhere. I think the runestones may be responsible. Nothing else has changed."

"So? Why complain if they're making you a better wizard?"

"Because I don't like not knowing things. In thaumaturgy, what you don't know can hurt you."

"Well, why not—*look out!*"

She shoved him hard, and he fell sprawling on the sidewalk. The knife slashed through empty air where he had been a second earlier. Kira brought her leg up hard, bent at the knee, and drove her kneecap into the assailant's groin. The air whooshed out of him and he sagged to the ground.

There were four of them. The other three were on her at once. She blocked a knife thrust and drove her fist hard into one man's face, then pivoted sharply, avoiding another thrust from the third man, and continued the movement by bringing her leg up high in a spinning back kick, the heel of her boot connecting with the fourth man's temple as he lunged at her. The second man came back at her and she trapped his knife hand, twisted sharply, and he cried out as she disarmed him, but she had to let him go to deal with one of the others as he grabbed her from behind. She brought her foot up and stomped down hard on his toes, then drove her elbow back into his stomach. He let her go, doubling over with pain, and she spun around to face the next threat.

Wyrdrune mumbled quickly under his breath and made several quick passes with his hands. Kira spun around again, her hands upraised in a fighting stance.

All four men were gone.

"Where'd they go?" she said, bewildered.

"I guess you scared them off," said Wyrdrune, repressing a smile. "You handle yourself well. That was pretty impressive."

"I can take care of myself," she said.

The four assailants, three of them still brandishing their

weapons, suddenly reappeared in a police station several blocks away. The desk sergeant looked up and smiled.

"Well, well. What have we got here?"

The four men looked around, eyes wide. One of them said, "Guido—"

"Shut up," said Guido. "Just *shut up*!"

Wyrdrune and Kira climbed the steps to the front door of his apartment house.

"Those were Rozetti's men," she said. "I recognized a couple of them. They know where I live."

"Great," said Wyrdrune. He sighed. "Just great. Well, I guess you can stay at my place until we figure something out."

She gave him a sidelong look as he opened the front door.

"Relax," he said. "I'll take the couch. You're not all that irresistible, you know."

"Yeah, well don't do me any favors, okay? I'll take the couch. Just don't get any ideas."

As they opened the door to his apartment, the broom was standing there with its spindly hands on its hips—or at least the place where its hips would have been if it had hips.

"Well, I hope you're satisfied," the broom said. "Dinner's just *ruined*. I slave over a hot stove all day and does anybody care? You could have called, but *noooo*...."

Wyrdrune flopped down on the couch and closed his eyes. "Just make us some coffee, Broom."

"Coffee, he wants," the broom said. "I've got a quiche that looks like a potato chip and he says, 'Just make us some coffee.' Fine. What do *I* care? Just stand me in a corner, I don't count for anything...."

Kira sat down in the reading chair and put her feet up on a wooden crate. "Well," she said, "I can't say it hasn't been interesting."

"The sooner we get rid of these damn stones *and* each other, the better I'll feel," Wyrdrune said. "There's an aura about them I find highly disturbing."

"There's an aura about *you* I find highly disturbing," said Kira. "Trouble just seems to have a way of finding you."

Wyrdrune shook the stones out of their pouch and stared at them. "There's something very powerful about these stones. I can *feel* it going right through me. I have a nasty feeling that our trouble's just beginning."

Sheik Al'Hassan entered the dark underground chamber. He was wearing a flowing black silk sorcerer's robe. His black silk kaffiyeh was held in place by the cobra-headed circlet. The blood ruby set into the skin of his forehead was glowing.

So much time and effort and the stones had been snatched right out from under his nose! *Years* spent in the dusty archives of the Department of Antiquities, searching through ancient tomes and scrolls, experimenting with a long succession of forgotten spells, taking incredible risks, and finally he had stumbled upon the one clue that had led him to the secret tomb buried deep in the Euphrates Valley, hidden for millennia.

There had been no way to unearth the tomb without attracting a great deal of attention, so that was exactly how he had done it. He had used contacts gained through the International Thaumaturgical Commission to place the right information with influential sources in the Annendale Corporation headquartered in Boston, allowing their researchers to make the "discovery." He had felt magical trace emanations vibrating up from deep beneath the ground, but those fools had felt nothing, not even their archaeothaumaturges, who had merely examined the information he had provided them with and conceded that there might indeed be thaumaturgical artifacts in the ruins buried there.

The corporation had applied for an archaeothaumaturgic excavation license, and he had swayed the Department of Antiquities into granting it to them. It hadn't taken very much persuasion. Even with his position on the board be-

coming more and more precarious as allegations of miscon-
duct mounted, even with the movement to unseat him from
the ITC, they had agreed. They could not afford to reject the
Annendale Corporation's application, and he had known that
from the start. The government was broke. There was a fam-
ine in the African nations of the USR, and refugee camps
were already being formed. The USR did not have the resources to finance an expedition, which might take years to
complete its work. The hard-liners at the Department of Antiquities insisted that any archaeological treasures discovered
within the boundaries of the USR belonged to the USR and
had to remain there. However, the governing council knew
that they could realize their value far more quickly if they
put them up for auction instead of taking a chance and hoping that after years of tests, experiments, and investigative
research, some of those artifacts might produce badly
needed revenue.

It was an opportunity to strengthen his position in the governing council by being the man who brought millions in
desperately needed revenue into the treasury without any
compensation for himself. He made arrangements with the
Annendale Corporation to use their public-relations department to generate maximum publicity for the discovery and
the expedition . . . and, not coincidentally, for himself.

While the expedition was still being formed, the Annendale Corporation's media machine had gone to work, and
Rashid soon found himself on the covers of several international magazines. He was written about extensively, for the
first time with his approval, and he was inundated with re-
quests for interviews. His face was everywhere. He was the
subject of a biography that detailed his life from his boyhood
in Egypt—as the last male heir of an ancient ruling family
that had been forced to sell off everything they owned—to
his student days in America, when he had studied with Merlin Ambrosius himself, his tuition paid by a government that
needed him to bring back thaumaturgic knowledge. The bi-

ography traced his rise to prominence in the government of the USR and his appointment to the board of the ITC, but it downplayed his notorious excesses, rationalizing them as the overindulgence of a boy who had grown up in abject poverty and suddenly found himself a man wealthy beyond his wildest dreams.

His frequent junkets abroad, paid for by the government treasury, were described as noble, self-sacrificing efforts on his country's behalf, attempts to conclude valuable trade negotiations and to make political associations, to form social connections that would help to bring his country back to its former place as a modern world power. His harem of five hundred wives was described as part of his effort to bring his country back to the traditional Islamic ways by setting an example and attempting to stimulate others into doing something about the rapidly falling birthrate. He was portrayed as a man who educated and provided shelter to young women who otherwise would be destitute. It was the same with his male "retainers"—no mention of the word *slave*—young men he helped by providing jobs for them, using his personal fortune to assist those who had nothing. His "playboy reputation"—in the authorized biography those words were always printed in quotation marks—was merely the result of the magnetism of a wealthy, powerful man whose ability to keep so many wives was like an open challenge to women all over the world. And while the expedition proceeded with the excavation in the Euphrates Valley, Rashid was having his image transformed into that of a dedicated thaumaturge, humanitarian, statesman, and philanthropist.

Still, there were a lot of people who weren't fooled by it. He had made many enemies, and they weren't shy about giving interviews themselves. In recent years his life had become a morass of intrigues, investigations, libel suits, and publicity, corporate, and governmental power struggles. He rode the wave at its very crest, driven by an obsession to rediscover the forgotten magic of the ancient ones and be-

come the greatest mage who ever lived, greater even than his
old teacher, Merlin Ambrosius.

Then the day came when the excavations were completed
and he stood, late at night, within the subterranean chamber
that he stood in now, feeling the incredibly powerful emanations all around him, amazed that the corporation's people
were unaware of them. The musty air in that dank, ancient
cave *throbbed* with them. It was a force more powerful than
anything he had ever experienced. It seemed to pull at him,
to draw him toward the lower sections of the cavern, beyond
the place where the excavators dug, to a mammoth wall of
solid rock. Whatever the source of the power was, he knew
it was behind that rock, buried behind tons and tons of
stone.

He reached out to touch the rock wall, and a surge of heat
passed from it and through his fingers and up into his arm,
bathing his entire body in an incandescent aura. He stood
there, riveted to the rock wall, his screams echoing in the
excavated chamber, his body thrashing, and then the contact
was broken abruptly and he was hurled across the chamber,
landing hard on his back, tendrils of smoke curling up from
his body.

He got up slowly to his hands and knees, moaning, searing pain lancing through his forehead as if a hot iron spike
had been driven deep into his skull. He touched his hands to
his forehead and felt blood trickling down, and something
that had not been there before. Something hard and smooth
had sprouted through the skin of his forehead, over his "third
eye." It burned. It burned like white phosphorus. Holding
his hands to his head, he staggered around the chamber,
gasping with pain, and then he saw the rock wall glowing
with blue fire. As he stared at it with disbelief he felt himself
being drawn toward it. He fought the pull, but there was no
resisting it. He came up against the flaming rock and somehow passed right through it into the cold blackness of a
chamber hidden on the other side.

It was freezing cold in there, a deep, biting chill that penetrated to the bone. He couldn't see anything. Wind plucked at his clothing. How could there possibly be a wind inside a chamber sealed in solid rock? Torches blazed up on the walls around him, illuminating a cavern even larger than the one the excavations had revealed. It was big enough to hold a small town, a subterranean valley shaped like a perfect circle, with huge bronze braziers marking the points of a gigantic pentagram of obsidian and gold mosaic inlaid into the cavern floor. At the center of the pentagram was an altar carved out of a stalagmite the size of a small building. Steps ascended to the top of the altar, curling around the stalagmite like a serpent.

The wind drove him toward the altar. He crossed the boundaries of the pentagram and the wind grew stronger. It lifted him above the ground and blew him toward the steps, lifting him to the top of the stone altar, where he was set down above the yawning chasm of a shaft that reached deep down into the earth. It was like the ritual shafts found in Druidic ruins, only on a gargantuan scale. Its circular mouth was ringed by a mosaic of obsidian and gold, the tiles forming runes and spelling out a message in some long-dead language. The shaft seemed to be bottomless, and directly over it, on the lip of a stone ledge, was a rune-encrusted chest of solid gold.

Rashid edged onto the narrow ledge until he reached the golden chest. He tried to move it, but it seemed welded to the rock somehow. No matter how he tried, he couldn't force it open. He felt the jewel that had appeared in the center of his forehead suddenly grow hot, and then his neck snapped back as a sharp beam of dazzlingly brilliant light lanced out from the gem and struck the chest, like an industrial laser cutting around the perimeter of the lid. The gold flowed as it melted and obscured the runes carved into the chest. The lid sprang open.

Rashid slowly reached inside the smoking chest and took

out a small box, the only thing the chest contained: a simple
jewel box cast in bronze. He opened it. Three little runestones were lying inside it, roughly cut, unpolished gems—
a ruby, a sapphire, and an emerald. He closed the lid of the
little jewel box and then looked down over the lip of the
stone ledge and into the pit.

And he knew what was at the bottom.

It took all his strength to carry that tiny jewel box down
the steps carved into the stalagmite and past the boundaries
of the pentagram. The little box had grown heavier and
heavier; it seemed to sap his strength till he could no longer
lift it and was forced to push it inch by inch across the
cavern floor, sweat streaming from his face, but as he felt
his strength failing him, something came to reinforce it and
make him stronger until he finally managed to push the little
box out past the boundaries of the pentagram. And then the
mysterious weight of the jewel box disappeared, and he
stood, lifting it easily in one hand, his chest heaving from
his exertions. He walked toward the rock wall again, and it
burst into blue flame as he passed through it and into the
outer chamber that had been discovered by the excavators.

He stood there, drained, utterly exhausted, yet wildly ex-
hilarated.

"Are you all right, Your Highness?"

Two of the corporation security guards entered the
chamber, and the beams from their flashlights struck him.
He started to recoil from them, but caught himself.

"Yes, yes, I'm fine," he said, breathing hard, barely able
to stand. He was dizzy and on the verge of collapse.

"You were down here so long, we started to get worried,"
said the other guard. "We didn't want to disturb you, but
you'd really better come back up now. It can be dangerous
down here. The air's not very good."

"Yes," said Rashid, breathing hard and nodding weakly.
"Yes, perhaps I'd better."

His vision blurred and he collapsed.

"Watch it!" They picked him up and braced him, the first guard holding Rashid's arm across his shoulder.

"What's that he's got there?" said the second guard. He picked up the jewel box.

"Hey, look at this!" he said. "He found an artifact the others must have missed."

"We'd better get you back up right away, Your Highness," the first guard said as Rashid moaned. "Just take it easy and relax, you'll be okay."

It was a full day before his strength returned and he was able to walk on his own again, but by then, the runestones had been placed with the other artifacts to be examined by the ITC certification board. And with everyone watching him so closely, there had been no chance to get them back. If he had tried to teleport them magically, their theft would have been discovered instantly and the other mages might have sensed his use of power. Nevertheless, just before they were due to be shipped out to the States for the auction, he tried to steal them thaumaturgically. And they had resisted.

No matter, he had thought. He would simply purchase them at auction. With his immense personal fortune, it was unlikely that anyone would be able to outbid him, unless some corporation discovered his interest in the runestones and decided to bid against him, thinking he might know something they didn't. To prevent that, he had employed Mustafa as a proxy to go to America and buy the stones. And the fool had bungled it. He had allowed them to be snatched out from under his very nose. Well, he had given Mustafa a lesson in the penalties of failure. Mustafa would not forget. Every time he looked into a mirror, he'd see that Rashid had taken over half his life away and know that he could do far worse if he failed him again. Mustafa would not fail him. Soon, the runestones would be back in his possession. And then it would begin.

He walked through the blazing wall and stood inside the sealed chamber as torches ignited all around him. He crossed the boundaries of the pentagram and felt the power coursing through him. He went up to the altar and walked out onto the stone ledge. Freezing wind blew up from the pit and bathed him in an icy chill.

"Soon, My Lords," he said, his deep voice echoing in the cavern. "You've waited for over two thousand years, and now the time is near. Soon you shall be free!"

CHAPTER
Four

Wyrdrune lay stretched out in his loft, watching the morning news and talk show on a small portable TV suspended in midair above his bed.

"And now for an update on the latest news," the pretty cohost said. "We'll go to Bill Foster in the newsroom."

"Thank you, Jane," said Foster. "Police are still looking for leads in the daring robbery that took place at the auction of the Euphrates artifacts at the Christie Gallery early yesterday. Stolen was a set of three runestones of unknown properties—a sapphire, a ruby, and an emerald—rough-cut, unpolished stones which aside from their undetermined thaumaturgical worth, have an estimated street value of over two hundred and fifty thousand dollars."

"Two hundred and fifty—" Wyrdrune sat up, striking his head on the ceiling. He winced. "Those damn bastards ripped us off!"

"You mean we ripped *them* off," Kira said, coming into the room. "We've still got the stones, remember?"

"Quiet, I want to hear this."

"Police are still questioning the sorcerers who were in attendance at the auction," said the newsman. "Eyewitnesses were able to provide them with several descriptions, from which police artists have made these composite sketches."

A graphic slide showed drawings of an old man with a large, hooked nose, a long white beard, and long white hair —Wyrdrune in his old sorcerer's disguise, though unrecognizable from the picture—and a remarkably close likeness of Kira.

"Oh, great," she said.

"Police are seeking two suspects," said the newsman. "The older man believed to be between sixty and seventy years of age, about five foot six, a hundred and forty pounds, alleged to be a sorcerer, last seen wearing dark green robes and a wide-brimmed hat. The younger man is described as being—"

"What do they mean, the younger *man*?" said Kira.

"Ssh!"

"—about seventeen or eighteen, dark-haired, Hispanic, about five foot five and one hundred and twenty pounds, last seen dressed in a neo-medieval black leather jacket and high boots. Both men are presumed to be highly dangerous. Police have established a special line to call—you should be seeing the number on your screen—and Sheik Rashid Al'Hassan, USR governmental liaison to the Annendale Expedition, has offered a reward of $50,000 for information leading to the arrest of the perpetrators and the recovery of the runestones. An additional reward of twenty-five thousand dollars has been offered by Boston Mutual, the agency insuring the artifacts."

"Oh, terrific!" Kira said. "Now we'll have every two-bit snitch in town—"

"*Will you be quiet?*"

"On the international front, controversy continues over the ITC investigation into the activities of board member Sheik Rashid Al'Hassan, of the United Semitic Republics. Amid allegations of—"

Wyrdrune waved absently at the TV, and the volume went down. "Well, I don't see what you're so worried about," he said. "Nobody's going to recognize me from that picture, and they think you're a guy."

"A *guy*?" she said. She stripped off her leather jacket and threw it on the floor angrily. She was wearing a tight white tunic, very sheer, with the nipples of her breasts clearly visible through it. "Do I look like a guy to you?"

Wyrdrune cleared his throat uneasily. "Must be the way you dress," he said.

"What's *wrong* with the way I dress?"

"Nothing," he said quickly. "But you've got to admit that it isn't very . . . well, feminine."

"Feminine? What's that mean, *feminine*? What am I supposed to do, wear one of those floor-length, poopsy-doopsy Lady of the Lake skirts with the plunging neckline and the little droopy gold waistband pointing down at my crotch?"

"Poopsy-doopsy?" he said.

"You know what I mean! Just because I don't choose to dress like some adolescent male's sex fantasy—"

"Wait a minute, settle down—"

"—doesn't mean I—"

"*Chil*dren, *chil*dren!" said the broom, swaying into the room. "Enough, already! Are you coming in to breakfast or are you going to stand there making like two yentas at the Automat while my omelets turn into hockey pucks? You ever eat cold omelets? It is to *varf*, believe me."

"How'd you like to be made into a toothpick?" Kira said, shooting her hand out and grabbing the broom around its handle, lifting it up off the floor.

The broom started to make choking sounds.

"Put it down," said Wyrdrune. "Please."

She let go of the broom.

"Such hostility!" the broom said. "Enough *tsuris* I've got with Melvin the Magician, he has to bring home a homicidal S&M queen! *Vey is mir*, I haven't got enough troubles—"

"That's it," said Kira. "I'm tossing this mop right out the window!"

"Mop?" the broom said. "*Mop*? Are you ready for this? Don't you touch me! Don't you *dare* lift your hand against me! Melvin, are you just going to lie there and let me be insulted like this?"

"If you don't shut your mouth, wherever in hell your mouth *is,* I'm going to stick you in the sink and grind you up in the garbage disposal!" Kira said.

"Will you listen to yourself?" said Wyrdrune. "You're arguing with a *piece of wood,* for goodness sake!"

"Well, I like that!" the broom said. "I don't have to listen to this! Obviously I'm nothing but a servant around here! You work your fingers to the bone, sweeping out, cooking and cleaning, scrubbing floors and chasing cockroaches, and this is the thanks you get? *Fine.* Get your *own* damn breakfast. If you want me, I'll be in the closet, eating my heart out!"

"Eating my heart out?" Kira said.

Wyrdrune started to chuckle. A moment later they were both laughing.

"Where on earth did you find that thing?" said Kira, wiping the tears from her eyes.

"It belonged to my mother," said Wyrdrune. "I animated it during my first year in thaumaturgical college so she'd have something to take care of her while I wasn't around. It's a real pain, but it's sort of nice to have around, and it reminds me of her."

"She still around?"

"No. She died three years ago."

"Oh. I'm sorry. What about your dad?"

"I never knew him."

"That's rough. I never knew my parents, either."

"Not at all?"

She shook her head. "I grew up in foster homes. I ran sway when I was twelve. Been on my own ever since."

"Since you were twelve? How did you live?"

"Pretty much the same way I'm living now. You do what you can. You grow up in the streets, you learn how to survive. It can be tough, but it's like they say, whatever doesn't kill you makes you stronger."

"You know, I don't think I've ever met anyone quite like you."

"Yeah, well . . ." Their eyes met briefly, and both of them looked away quickly. "Come on, let's go eat breakfast before those eggs get cold."

"Uh . . . you mind waiting in the other room? I'm not exactly dressed."

"Oh. Sure. Sorry."

Several minutes later he came into the kitchen. Kira was pouring them coffee. She jerked her head toward the closet.

"It's still in there, sulking. I tried apologizing to it, but it won't come out."

Wyrdrune grinned.

"What's so funny?"

"Nothing. I was just picturing you standing in front of that closet door, apologizing to a broom."

"Just sit down and drink your coffee. I don't know how you take it."

"Cream and sugar."

"On the table. Okay, warlock, so what's our next move?"

He sighed. "You've got me. If your underworld friends know where you live, then obviously you can't go home. They'll be watching for you. We'll be safe here for the time being, but the sooner we find out what the story is with those stones, the sooner we'll know what to do about them."

"How do you figure on doing that?" she said.

He shook his head. "I don't know. I was up pretty late last night, going through all my books, but then it occurred to me that there wouldn't be anything in the books about them; otherwise, the expedition people would've known what they were, and they didn't. They were certified as enchanted runestones of unknown properties. And I simply don't have enough skill or knowledge to divine their function."

"So who does?"

He pursed his lips. "Only one person I can think of, but I don't know if he'd even see me after all that's happened."

"Who's that?"

"My old professor up in Cambridge."

From the bedroom there came a loud crash as something fell to the floor and shattered.

"What the hell was that?" said Kira.

Wyrdrune covered his face with his hands. "Shit. My TV. I forgot I left it hanging."

She grimaced. "Do me a favor, okay? If we're going to go to Boston, what do you say we take the train?"

Lieutenant Dominic Riguzzo hung up the phone and rubbed the bridge of his nose. Across from him, sitting at the desk butted up against his, Detective Sergeant Allan Cleary lit up another in a long succession of cigarettes. Riguzzo made a face and waved away the smoke that billowed toward him.

"Damn it, Al, do you have to smoke those awful things in here?"

"If they bother you so much, why don't you trade desks with somebody?"

"Are you kidding? Who'd trade? You think I haven't asked? Besides, those cigarettes of yours stink up the whole squad room. A hundred and sixty cops in this damn precinct, and I have to get a desk next to the only one who smokes. You're going to poison me."

"They're herbal, Dom. Noncarcinogenic."

"Tell that to my lungs. Anyway, they stink."

"All right, all right," Cleary grumbled, stubbing out the cigarette in a glass ashtray. "There! Satisfied?"

"Yes, thank you very much."

"What was that call? Did you come up with anything?"

"Nothing, just more harassment," said Riguzzo, grimacing. He took a sip of his cold coffee. "Seems like everybody and his mother-in-law's getting in on the act. You ready for this? That was the Honorable Ambassador Plenipotentiary of the USR legation, no less, Ahmad Pasta Fazool or something, one of those names that sprains your larynx if you try to say it, wanting to know if we'd made any progress in our investigation and making all sorts of demands about recovery of the gems and extradition of the perpetrators to the USR."

"Extradition?" said Al Cleary. "What extradition? The crime was committed in our jurisdiction."

"You tell him, okay? I'm tired of arguing with these people. Next thing I know, I'll have the State Department on my ass."

"You know what they do with thieves over there?" said Cleary.

"Tell you the truth, Al, I don't really care."

"They chop their arms off, that's what they do. Ask me, it's not a bad idea. Cut down on repeat offenders." He gave a barking laugh. "Cut down, get it?"

"Sure, Al, sure."

He stared down at a crumpled piece of newspaper that he had straightened out on his desktop. An article clipped from *The Times*. Several sentences were underlined. Lines describing the stolen goods.

"Doesn't make sense," he said.

"What doesn't?" said Cleary, looking up from his paperwork.

"There's something bothering me about this," said Riguzzo, frowning. "We may be going about this thing all wrong."

"How's that?"

"Well, because the heist was accomplished with the aid of magic, we're assuming that whoever stole the gems did it to use them in some kind of spell. Maybe a corporate crime.

Like maybe they knew something about the stones nobody else did. But aside from the fact that the perpetrators escaped by magic, we've really got nothing to support that theory."

"I don't understand. What are you getting at?"

"This newspaper clipping we found crumpled up on the floor at the crime scene."

"Yeah, what a mess it was in there. What'd they say, a hundred and fifty thousand dollars of water damage?"

"Yesh, well, some of the ink ran on it, but you see where these lines are marked?"

Cleary got up and came around the desk to stand beside him, looking down at the clipping spread out on the desktop. "So?"

"So this. Everybody who was invited to that auction received a prospectus. One of these things," he said, holding up a printed brochure of color photographs. He opened it and leafed through the pages. "Here," he said, spreading the brochure out on the desk and pointing to a photograph of an open bronze jewel box containing the stones. There was a short paragraph of copy underneath it, describing the item.

"Yeah?" said Cleary. "I still don't get it."

"That's just the thing," Riguzzo said. "Neither do I. You got here a picture of the stolen goods and a detailed description. Why didn't we find one of *these* things with the copy underlined or circled or something? Why a torn-out newspaper clipping? These brochures were sent out in advance to every major corporation and independent sorcerer registered with the BOT. And they were also available upon request. The newspaper article didn't even have a photograph.

"You're thinking the perp wasn't an adept registered with the Bureau of Thaumaturgy?" Cleary said. "How do you figure that? You can't get a license to practice magic without filing with the bureau."

"Exactly. Why would somebody tear out this article and underline the part about the gems unless they found out about the auction and the items up for bidding *from the papers*? We may be looking for suspects in the wrong group of people."

Cleary shrugged. "Unless it was the kid who spotted the piece and tore it out and then got a wizard to help him make the heist."

"Only why would a wizard need the kid? Why not just pull the job himself? No, I don't like it. It just doesn't fit. I'm thinking maybe we should be looking for somebody who took their thaumaturgical exams and failed to get certified. Someone who knows enough about magic to be dangerous but doesn't have a license to practice."

"But would somebody like that be walking around with long hair and dressed in sorcerer's robes?" said Cleary. "That would be asking for a lot of trouble."

"It would if they really did that," said Riguzzo. "But what if the long hair and the robes were only a disguise meant to make us *think* a sorcerer did it? I mean, look, we traced this guy through the cabbie back to the Plaza Hotel, where the cabbie picked him up. Just the old man, not the kid. The doorman remembers seeing the old man coming in and out of the hotel several times during the previous day, but the desk clerks have no recollection of him, and nobody saw the kid or anyone answering to his description. We've checked out every other adept who was registered at that hotel and they're all clean."

He shook his head. "No, I'm telling you, it stinks." He tapped his nose. "This thing is telling me we're on the wrong track. And I don't like the combination of an old man and a street punk. I mean, what did the kid do, plan the job and bring his grandpa in on it?"

"You're thinking it was two young snatch-and-grabbers making the big score, one of them disguised?" said Cleary. "Why not both of them disguised, then?"

Riguzzo shook his head. "I don't know. Maybe something went wrong. Maybe the kid was never supposed to make the snatch and he was only a backup. Remember, none of the

witnesses saw anyone answering the kid's description coming in, right? What does that suggest to you?"

"That the kid was also disguised when he came in," said
Cleary.

"Right. It was a big auction, large crowd; no one was
checking credentials at the door, only at the purchase desk.
They were just concerned about keeping the riffraff and the
cameras out. So anybody could've walked in if they looked
right. You know what I think? I think they stole the stones,
not to use them but to fence them."

"Yeah, could be," said Cleary. "It makes sense. What do
you say we go visit some of our less reputable local mer-
chants?"

"I'll get my coat," said Riguzzo. "Let's go shake a few
trees and see if anything falls out."

CHAPTER
Five

Porfirio Rozetti was having linguine with clam sauce when the two detectives walked into the restaurant. He saw them and rolled his eyes.

"Guido, go see what they want."

A man who looked like a Neanderthal got up from the table, wiped his mouth with the napkin tucked into his shirt collar, and walked quickly toward Riguzzo and Cleary as they approached the table. The napkin was still tucked into his shirt.

"What can I do for you, gentlemen?" he said, his voice deep and guttural, thickly laced with a Brooklyn accent.

"You can get out of the way, Guido," said Riguzzo. "You're blocking out the sun. I came to see your boss."

"Mr. Rozetti's having lunch."

"I'll try not to make him lose his appetite," Riguzzo said, brushing past him and heading toward the table in the corner.

Rozetti heaved a deep sigh, crumpled up his cloth napkin, and tossed it on the table. He looked up with extreme annoyance at Riguzzo.

"Whattaya want, Riguzzo? Can't a man eat his meal in peace?"

"Hello, Pony," said Riguzzo. "How's the fix down at the track?"

"Hey, there's no call for that, all right? I done my stint, I don't fool with the horses no more. I'm rehabilitated, haven't you heard? I'm a respectable businessman now."

"Sure you are. Mind if we sit down?"

"Hell, take a load off. Guido, Louie, Mark, go get a drink at the bar or something."

The three heavyset men left the table, making room for the two detectives. Riguzzo and Cleary sat down across from Rozetti.

"So what can I do you for?" Rozetti said. "You guys want some linguine?"

"Thanks, I'll pass," Riguzzo said. "Actually we just dropped in for a chat."

"A chat? What's that, a chat? You guys getting lonely down at the precinct? What the fuck do you want?"

"I want to clear some paperwork from my desk," Riguzzo said. "I thought maybe you could help us out."

"What do I look like, a secretary? What kinda paperwork?"

"It has to do with the job at Christie's the other day."

"Oh, yeah? What makes you think I'd know anything about that?"

"Let's cut through all this, okay?" Riguzzo said. "What we've got here is what's called a 'sensitive issue.' A theft involving a major corporation and a foreign nation. A lot of people are upset. In other words, it's a real headache for me."

"I'm sorry to hear that. You want some aspirin?"

"Yeah, actually, I wouldn't mind. You got some?"

Rozetti shouted out toward the bar. "Hey, Guido! Get the detective here a couple aspirin!"

"How long have we known each other, Pony?" Riguzzo said.

Rozetti shrugged. "I don't know. Twenty, thirty years?"

"About that. Have I ever not played straight with you?"

"No. No, I'll give you that, *paisan*. For a cop, you've always been all right. Okay, square business. What's on your mind?"

"I'm prepared to do a little horse trading here, Pony," said Riguzzo. "Figure you'd know all about that."

"Right, cut with the jokes already. Get to the point. What kinda deal you offering?"

"I can get you full immunity—for starters," said Riguzzo.

"Assuming I've done anything I need immunity for, that's not so bad—for starters."

Guido brought the aspirin and a glass of water. Riguzzo took the pills and washed them down.

"Thanks, Guido. Go kill a mastodon or something." He turned back to Rozetti. "I can also set it up so you'll collect the rewards being offered for the recovery of the stones and the arrest of the perpetrators. It comes to a total of some seventy-five thousand dollars. That's not so bad for sitting on your ass and dropping a few hints between mouthfuls of linguine, is it?"

"No. No, it's not so bad. But assuming I even knew anything about this situation to begin with, why would I need you to guarantee that? What's to prevent me from going direct to Boston Mutual and droppping a few hints, like you say?"

"I see you already know something about this situation," Cleary said. "Looked into it, have you?"

"*Irish* cops I don't talk to," said Rozetti. "So? Like I said, what's to prevent me?"

"Absolutely nothing," said Riguzzo. "If you really think Boston Mutual's just going to hand over twenty-five thousand dollars to a man with your record without finding some convenient excuse to disallow you, go right ahead. And you can call the United Semitic Republics embassy while you're at it and try for the fifty thousand dollars, but at the moment, they're very hot on trying to arrange extradition of the perpetrators, before we've even apprehended them. If they should happen to get some sort of idea that you were somehow involved in the job, they might not take it very kindly. Granted, they've got no jurisdiction, but then, Sheik Al'Hassan is a very wealthy and influential man, and I hear he bears grudges."

"You wouldn't want Sheik Al'Hassan to think you had anything to do with this, would you, Rozetti?" said Cleary. "Gorillas like Guido wouldn't even make him break a sweat."

"*You*, I don't like," Rozetti said, pointing his index finger at Cleary. "All right," he said, turning to Riguzzo, "so make your pitch. You're saying you get me full immunity, just in case there might happen to be any stray charges floating around, and you arrange to collect the money on my behalf as an informant who wishes to remain anonymous, is that it?"

"That's it. What do you say?"

Rozetti rubbed his chin. "No strings?"

"No strings. You scratch my back, I'll scratch yours. And maybe, just *maybe*, I'll do you a favor sometime, if it's not unreasonable."

"Yeah?"

"Yeah. How about it?"

Rozetti rubbed his chin some more. "Okay, Riguzzo, you got a deal."

They shook hands across the table.

"First off," said Rozetti, "you guys aren't even looking for the right people. Those reports I saw on the news? Forget it. You're way off. You're not looking for an old sorcerer and a young guy. You're not even looking for two *guys*. You're looking for a coupla kids, one male, one female."

"Are you saying a couple of *kids* pulled this job?" said Cleary.

"You going to listen or what?"

"Go ahead, Pony, I'm listening," said Riguzzo.

"I even got a name for you. Kira. The picture your guys drew was a pretty good one, only she's a she, not a he. Granted, you can't hardly tell because of the way she dresses, but take my word on it."

"What's her last name?"

"Don't know. Never heard it, but she's been around before. Strictly small-time stuff, burglary, snatch-and-grab, nothing heavy. Nothing like this job. It's way out of her league if you ask me; but she's the one that pulled it off, I'm telling you."

"And the other one?"

"Never saw him before. Young kid, mid- to late-twenties maybe, long curly blond hair, about five nine or ten, one sixty-five or so. She called him warlock."

"Warlock? What's that, a street name?"

"Got me. But I'd say no. She called him that like I call you *paisan*, like it's just something she calls him."

"They came to you with the stones," said Riguzzo, prompting him.

"Full immunity, you said?"

"That's what I said. If you cooperate, I won't even mention your name if I can help it."

"That's good enough for me. Yeah, they came to me with the stones. I knew what they were right away."

"And you turned them away?" said Cleary.

"What, are you kidding? Stuff like that? I bought the damn things! Paid twenty thousand for 'em."

"You *have* them?" said Riguzzo, leaning forward.

"Don't I wish! Listen, if I had the stones, you think we'd be talking here? They took me. Warlock, or whatever his name is, pulled a fast one and zapped 'em away, right out of my damn pocket. I sent the boys after them, but they blinked out who knows where. I'm out twenty thousand, and I'm not very happy about it."

"I don't suppose you'd know where we could find this Kira?" said Riguzzo.

"I can tell you where she lives, but don't waste your time. If she was there, believe me, I'd have the stuff *and* my money back."

"Stay out of it, Pony," said Riguzzo. "I don't want to start tripping over your boys. And if you've got a contract out on them, call it off. *Now*."

"Yeah? And what happens to my twenty thousand?"

"Cost of doing business," said Riguzzo wryly. "Declare it as a loss on your next income-tax report."

"Very funny. But I'll tell you something, *if* I had a contract out on them and *if* I decided to be a nice guy and write it all off to experience, they're still in a pile of shit. Word is I'm not the only one they pulled this hustle with. I can't guarantee what somebody else might or might not do."

"I'm just asking you to guarantee what *you* do, Pony," said Riguzzo. "I'm not kidding. Call your people off. And I want that address."

"Third and Delancey," said Rozetti. "Here, I'll write it down for you. But I'm telling you, you're wasting your time. They're either holed up somewhere else or they've skipped town."

As they left the bar-restaurant, Cleary glanced at Riguzzo, who was scowling.

"I never knew you and Rozetti went back so far," he said.

"We grew up together," said Riguzzo. "Sort of together, anyway. We lived on the same block, went to the same school, but that was about it. We had different interests, different friends."

"How about that?" Cleary said. "I never knew that about you. You and Pony Rozetti, king of the bookmakers."

"That's not how he got the name Pony, you know," said Riguzzo. He grinned. "He likes to put it around that he got the name from scamming in the race game, but he got the name because when he was ten years old, he took his first and last ride on a merry-go-round. It scared him so much, he hung on to the wooden horse's neck for dear life and it took three people to pry him off."

"Really?"

"Yeah," said Riguzzo, smiling.

"You believe what he said back there?"

"Yeah, I believe him," said Riguzzo. "And I also believe that he's got a contract out on those kids and he's not about to pull it. He was always meaner than a junkyard dog, even as a kid. I made a deal with him, and I'm going to have to stick with it, but he's going to be trouble. He always was."

"There's nothing that says you have to stick to that deal," said Cleary.

"We shook hands on it."

"So? What does that mean, with a guy like Rozetti?"

"It means that because I stick to deals I make with guys like Rozetti, we've got our first solid lead in this damn case," said Riguzzo. "If you want to make lieutenant, it'll pay you to remember that."

"Well, it's a pretty sad state of affairs when you have to cut deals with scum like Rozetti," Cleary said. "He actually sat there and confessed to receiving stolen goods, and we can't even use it against him because you gave your word."

"That's right," Riguzzo said, "but I'll tell you a funny thing about these people. They've got a code of conduct all their own, especially people like the Pony. It's a matter of pride with them. You cut a deal with someone like Rozetti and he gets caught not living up to his end while you do, he comes out looking bad and he knows he'll never get a break from you again. On the other hand, if you live up to your part of the bargain and he lives up to his, he can sit around over linguine and Chianti, bragging to his cronies about how he cut a deal with the cops and came out of it ahead. It raises his stature. Gives him power. And he'll play reasonably straight with you because it's worth it to him. He knows he's built up some credit, and because he brags about it, word gets around that you're a cop who plays by the rules but that you're flexible. If you get a little, you'll give a little. And that's worth a lot more in information in the long run than busting someone like Rozetti and having him walk out three hours later."

"Well, I guess I never thought about it that way," Cleary said. "I can't argue with your results. At least now we've got corroborative testimony for the ITC. It's one less headache for us. Now that we know for sure that there was an adept involved, we can turn the case over to them."

"Not on your life," Riguzzo said.

"What? Why not?"

"Because it's my case and I intend to see it through. Besides, who do you think's been stalling the ITC? Me, that's who. And it hasn't been easy. They've been leaning hard, trying to get jurisdiction in this case because magic was involved, and it's all I've been able to do to keep them out of it."

"I don't understand," said Cleary. "Why?"

"Think about it, Al. Who's on the executive board of the ITC and has also offered a reward for information, et cetera?"

"Well, Sheik Al'Hassan has . . . oh."

"Yeah, oh. The only way I've been able to keep them out of it is by insisting we don't have any real proof that sorcery was involved in the theft. As far as I'm concerned, it could have been a simple snatch-and-grab and the perpetrators escaped on foot during all the confusion. They don't like it; they know it's a stall, but about the only way they can horn in on the case without our requesting their assistance is by getting a sworn deposition from a certified sorcerer that the thieves used magic to effect their escape. And they're not willing to do that because it would be bad politics. It's like I told Rozetti, it's a sensitive issue. They'll lean hard, but they'll only push so far."

"You really think Al'Hassan would use an ITC investigative team as some kind of vigilante squad?"

"I wouldn't put it past him," said Riguzzo. "And I'll tell you something else I think. I think he's probably got some independents sniffing around over here already. There's nothing I can do about that, but I'll be damned if I have to open up my files and grant legal jurisdiction to a bunch of assassins from the USR who are functioning under the protective cover of an ITC investigative team. I'm not going to stand for extradition in this case, and I won't stand for any legally sanctioned homicides, either. I'm bringing those two in myself, and they're going to stand trial, by the book and by the numbers. Now come on, let's take a look at the girl's apartment."

"I feel like a damn idiot in this getup," Kira said. She was dressed in a clinging, sheer white neo-medieval shift with a gold braided cord encircling her hips and light, graceful, embroidered high-heeled slippers. The dress had a deeply plunging neckline, and it hugged her curves. It flattered her figure and her dark coloring. "I just can't see spending that kind of money for a flimsy, cutesy little thing like this. I feel like a Park Avenue hooker in it."

"Well, you don't look like one," said Wyrdrune, tossing his bag down on the hotel bed.

"What's *that* supposed to mean?"

"It was meant as a compliment, believe it or not," he said. "It actually makes you look very nice."

"Well, you've obviously never seen a Park Avenue hooker, either," she said. "They look very nice, too, but they're still advertising. That's the whole point of these stupid shoes," she said, kicking them off and opening her bag. "They make you arch your back and stand on tiptoe, so you've got to thrust your hips forward when you walk. Catch-me, fuck-me. That's why you like it so much. It's the I'm-available-and-ready look."

"You know, I try to say something nice to you and you always manage to turn it all around somehow," said Wyrdrune. "I didn't mean anything at all like that. I just meant that you looked nice, period. Oh, the hell with it. And as for the way you walk, I've got news for you, even in those shoes, you still manage to stomp around as if you were looking for a fight. The way you were scowling at that desk clerk, it looked as if you were about to punch him out."

"That's because the son of a bitch was leering at me and staring at my tits," she said. "He's probably down there right now, fantasizing what we're doing up here. Mr. and Mrs. Karpinsky." She shook her head. "You really think he bought that?"

"It doesn't matter if he bought it or not," said Wyrdrune. "What matters is that you look as little like that police artist's sketch as possible. And if he thinks we're a couple of young kids checking into a hotel for a high-style dirty weekend, so much the better. There's nothing unusual about that, and no reason for him to give us a second thought."

"Well, okay, you've got a point there," she said, "but did we have to pick such an expensive hotel? There must be a thousand places in Boston cheaper than this."

"That's right, and cheaper hotels aren't as secure or as respectful of the privacy of their guests," said Wyrdrune. "And if the police were looking for us, they'd probably look in the cheaper places first—I think."

"You're becoming a regular criminal mastermind, aren't you?" she said with a grin. "What the hell, we've got plenty of money. We might as well enjoy ourselves. When are we going to see this Merlin character?"

"*We* are not going to see 'this Merlin character,' " said Wyrdrune. "*I'm* going to see him. That's if he'll even see me. I'm not exactly one of his favorite people these days. And I shudder to think what he'd make of you. You don't just drop in to see an archmage, plop down in his chair, and ask him, 'How's tricks?' A certain amount of respect is called for."

"Oh, I see. You think I'd embarrass you, is that it?"

"Frankly yes, I do. He's . . . well, he's extremely old-fashioned. A bit eccentric too. He's several thousand years old, after all, and while he's made some concessions to the modern world, he doesn't exactly live in it, if you know what I mean."

"No, what do you mean?"

Wyrdrune sighed. "Well, it's kind of hard to explain. He's . . . he's not even human, exactly."

She raised her eyebrows. "What is he, an extraterrestrial?"

"I wouldn't be surprised," said Wyrdrune. "According to legend, at any rate, he's the son of an incubus, a sort of spirit being. He doesn't really talk about his past very much. He especially doesn't like being asked about King Arthur and his knights. It's a bit of a sore subject with him. And he's not especially fond of women, after what happened to him."

"Yeah, well, if it went down like you said, he wouldn't have been in that mess if he'd kept it in his pants."

"That's *exactly* what I mean," said Wyrdrune. "God, I can just imagine you saying something like that to him! You'd wind up spending the rest of your life as a guppy in a fishbowl on his desk or something. Believe me, you're better off staying here at the hotel while I go see him. And don't go wandering around, please, whatever you do. Have a meal sent up, some wine, take a bath or something, but just please stay in this room."

"I've managed to take care of myself pretty well before you showed up, you know," she said sourly.

"I'm just asking you, as a favor, *please* don't go out, okay? I'd . . . I'd worry about you."

She started to say something, then stopped herself. She smiled. "All right, warlock. If it'll make you feel better, I'll stay right here, okay? I promise. At least it'll give me a chance to get out of this dumb skirt. But don't be gone too long. I don't like being cooped up. It makes me nervous."

"I'll get back as soon as I can," he said. "And you really do look very nice in that dumb skirt."

She tossed a pillow at him. "Go on, get out of here."

The phone rang once and stopped. A moment later it rang again. Fats picked it up.

"The bar across the street," the soft, crisp voice on the other end said. "Now." And he hung up.

Two minutes later Fats was sitting at a table in a darkened corner of the seedy bar, opposite a neatly bearded man of average height with a compact, trim build. His hair was a dusty blond color, and his eyes were hazel. He wore gold-rimmed tinted glasses, and he was dressed in a well-tailored, though nondescript, dark suit with just a conservative touch of lace at his throat and cuffs. There was nothing particularly noteworthy about the suit, save for the fact that Fats knew he had them custom-made to conceal the bulge of a shoulder holster. Except for the glasses, which were an eccentric touch and gave him the look of an antiquarian, he would not have stood out in a crowd unless one were to look closely and notice that he filled out his suit with solid muscle. The glasses made him look studious, almost clerical. They gave him a thoughtful look and he was, indeed, a thoughtful man; but the sort of things he often thought about would have made most people extremely uncomfortable.

"There are complications," he said. "You didn't tell me there were other interested parties involved."

"Is that a problem?" Fats said.

"It's always a problem when I haven't been given all the relevant information. Especially when the police are involved. The police are aware of the young woman's identity; and they've searched her apartment, which had already been rather thoroughly examined by Porfirio Rozetti's people.

And there's a vehicle with diplomatic plates that's been parked across the street from her apartment since yesterday evening. I don't suppose you would know anything about that?"

Fats took a deep breath and wiped his forehead with a handkerchief. "About the police I did not know," he said. "I give you my word. I had no idea they'd discovered her identity. At least, not until they came to see me earlier this afternoon."

The man sat silently waiting.

"As for the others..." Fats shifted in his seat uneasily. "I do not make a habit of comparing notes with Pony Rozetti. He is, after all, the competition. And he has no style, no couth whatsoever. I imagine they must have cheated him in the same manner that they cheated me. It would not surprise me if he was the one who put the police onto Kira. It is precisely the sort of thing he would do if he thought there was something in it for him. I imagine they offered him a deal, similar to the one they offered me. However, I feigned total ignorance and told them nothing. Cooperating with the authorities is not good business practice. Word gets around, and the better class of people become somewhat hesitant to call on you. However, that would not stop Pony Rozetti. He would deal with anyone. The man has no discrimination, none whatsoever."

"And what about your diplomatic friends?"

"Yes, well," said Fats, mopping his forehead once again, "that is another matter entirely. The gentleman came to see me—he was most persuasive...quite threatening, really—and gave me this card." He took Mustafa's card out and passed it across the table.

The soft-spoken man examined it briefly and gave it back to him. "The USR," he said. "Al'Hassan's people. You should have told me. This complicates things."

"If you want more money—"

"That depends," he said, "on what you want me to do."

"Nothing has changed, as far as that's concerned," said Fats. "I still want them taken care of. And I want those stones."

"Then it will cost you more. If I have to compete with the police and with Rozetti's people, that poses no great problem, but the sort of people Al'Hassan can bring in raises the risks considerably. I will require adequate compensation."

"I will not have it get around that I was taken by a couple of young amateurs," said Fats vehemently. "I have a reputation to protect. I have no wish to alter our arrangement. Very well. How much more do you want?"

"The sum we originally agreed on, plus expenses, plus twenty-five percent of what you realize on the sale of the stones."

Fats' jaw dropped. "That... that... really, my dear friend, that is *highly* extravagant! Be reasonable! If you will allow me to make a counteroffer, might I suggest—"

"I'm not one of your clients, Fats. I do not haggle. That is my price. Take it or leave it."

Fats mopped his forehead once again and grunted. "You drive a hard bargain. Very well, I'll take it. It is a matter of personal pride. But I trust that you will at least try to keep your expenses reasonable."

"Whatever they are, you will pay them."

"Yes, of course, I was merely expressing—"

"I'll be in touch."

He got up and left. Fats remained at the table, twisting his handkerchief in his hands. He signaled the waiter for another drink. "A most disquieting man," he mumbled to himself. "*Most* disquieting."

Walking across the quad gave Wyrdrune a sharp pang of nostalgia. It hadn't been so very long since he had been a student here, living in a tiny apartment over in Brookline and taking the bus to Cambridge every morning to attend classes. University life had always appealed to him. There was a secure sense of community about it, a sense that one was working toward large and important goals, a stimulating atmosphere of intellectual activity and culture. He missed it terribly. After he had lost his scholarship and been expelled, it felt as if the rug had been pulled out from under him. All things considered, he had been fortunate to avoid a civil suit over the damages, but without a scholarship there was no way he could complete his education. It rankled. He had been at the top of his class, dean's list every semester, and because of one stupid lapse in judgment, he had thrown it all away.

Ever since his childhood he had wanted to be a wizard. He could not remember ever wanting to be anything else. When he was nine years old, his mother took him to a circus. It was a small, traveling tent show on its last legs. They never had much money when he was a boy, and his mother could not afford much in the way of entertainment for them, so the circus was a real treat, even though the audience was small and the clowns seemed somehow listless and the animals looked old and tired. But the highlight of the experience for him had been the sideshow, where he had seen The Great Goldini.

There hadn't been more than five or six people watching his performance, and the magician had not captivated them, although he had tried hard. He made doves appear and disappear, did tricks with cards and coins, and a pickpocket act with a bored-looking volunteer from the audience. He had known that he was losing them, but he had noticed the little boy who watched him so intently, and at the end of his performance he had beckoned him over.

"Did you enjoy the show?" he had said hesitantly.

"Oh, yes! Very much! It was magic!"

"Regrettably it was not really magic, but it was magic of a sort," The Great Goldini had said.

"How did you make the coin walk across your hand and disappear?"

"Would you like me to show you?"

"Oh, yes, *please!*"

The Great Goldini had looked up questioningly at Mrs. Karpinsky with his big, sad brown eyes. "You would not mind, missus?"

"No, of course not," his mother had said.

"Come, missus," said Goldini, whose real name was Nathan Goldblum. "Would you maybe like some tea and halvah while I speak with your young man?"

"Some tea and halvah would be very nice, thank you," his mother had said, pleased with Mr. Goldblum's manners, and Wyrdrune—then just plain Melvin Karpinsky—had been filled with pride at being referred to as a "young man."

The old stage magician had taken them to his trailer, where he made a pot of tea and carefully cut up some chocolate halvah and arranged it nicely on a chipped china plate. His mother had sat in a chair with the plate on her lap, holding the teacup carefully and sipping from it slowly while Goldini sat down in a folding wooden chair and beckoned Wyrdrune over. Inside his trailer, with his cape off, he did not look anywhere near as impressive as he had looked on stage. Without his tall hat, Wyrdrune could see that he was almost completely bald, with just a fringe of hair around his head, and he needed a shave. He was thin, and up close he looked a great deal older.

"Watch," said Goldini, and he took a coin out of his pocket and made it walk across his fingers. And then, suddenly, it disappeared!

"It's a magic coin!" said Wyrdrune.

"No," said Goldini. "It isn't really, you know. You can do it, too, with a great deal of practice. See, watch very carefully, I'll show you."

And he had done the trick again, very slowly, so that Wyrdrune could see how it was the deft motion of his fingers that made the coin appear to walk. Then Goldini showed him how he palmed it at the end, so that it never really disappeared but was only hidden.

"Oh," said Wyrdrune. "I see how you did it. It isn't really magic, is it?"

"No, it isn't," said Goldini with a sigh. "Are you very disappointed?"

"Oh, no, sir," Wyrdrune had said. "It's a wonderful trick. Do you think I could try?"

"Certainly," Goldini said, and handed him the coin.

He couldn't make it walk. He kept dropping it.

"It's hard," said Wyrdrune, frowning with concentration as he tried to make his fingers do the same thing he had seen Goldini's do.

"Yes, when you first try to learn the trick, it's very hard," Goldini said. "But if you practice every day, you get much better at it. It's just like real magic that way. You have to practice very hard. It's called sleight of hand, and it's a very old sort of trick, though not as old as *real* magic, of course. You see, young man, there was a time, many years ago, when there wasn't any real magic. People had forgotten about magic, and because they had forgotten how to do it, they stopped believing in it. They thought it was just a fairy tale, a story. But it was real. And there were still some people left who really believed in magic, but because no one remembered how to do it anymore, they couldn't do it, either. There was no one to teach them how, you see. Still, they wanted to keep the memory alive, and so they learned how to do a sort of magic—magic that wasn't *really* magic, you understand, but looked as if it were. Tricks just like this one."

"Were you one of those people?" Wyrdrune said.

"My grandfather was," Goldini said. "And my father after him. They were called stage magicians, illusionists, and sleight-of-hand artists, and they did shows for people just like the one that I just did. They made people disappear and they sawed beautiful women in half and they took rabbits out of a hat and they made people seem to float straight up into the air, only they didn't *really* do it. All those things were only tricks to make it *look* as if they'd really done it, but they were fooling people. It was a nice kind of fooling, though. Everybody knew it wasn't really magic, but they came to watch because it looked like magic and because they could appreciate the skill with which the tricks were done. They knew it wasn't easy, and it took a lot of practice. A lot of them would try to figure out how these tricks were done, but there were others who didn't really care. For a little while they would pretend they didn't know those things were really tricks. Just for fun, they would pretend to themselves that what they were seeing people like my father and my grandfather do really *was* magic. And in that way the memory was always kept alive."

Goldini sighed. "But these days, magic is much more than just a memory. The great Merlin Ambrosius, the most wonderful magician who ever lived—and he's a *real* magician, you know, not just a man who does little tricks like me— brought back the old knowledge, and it isn't very interesting for people to see me do my act when they can see real magic all around them every day. When I was a little boy, just about your age, my father taught me how to do magic tricks. As a matter of fact, the very first thing I learned was how to make a coin walk across my hand. It was that very same coin that you are holding now. My grandfather gave it to my father, and my father gave it to me, and I practiced every day. My father taught it to me because it was all he knew, you see, but even then there was already real magic in the world and no one cared very much about the sort of tricks my father did when they could see the real thing. Still, I've always felt that what my father and my grandfather did was really quite important, because it had kept the memory of real magic alive. It was a dream. A wonderful, magical dream. And it finally came true. Always remember that, young man. If you have a dream, and you hold on to it, and you continue to believe in it when everyone else around you has long since stopped believing, then one day it will come true."

Wyrdrune had nodded solemnly and held the coin out so that Goldini could take it back.

"No, you keep it," said Goldini. "And remember, practice every day. Who knows, perhaps someday you will become a *real* magician. In the meantime this magic coin will help you hold on to your dream."

Wyrdrune reached into his pocket and took out an old, worn fifty-cent piece. He held it in his hand for a moment and stared at it wistfully, then deftly walked the coin across his fingers, up and around his hand, made it "disappear," palming it expertly, then snapped his fingers and made it "reappear," flipping it up into the air and catching it between his index and middle fingers.

"What happens when you lose your dream, Mr. Goldini?" he asked softly. "What happens when you almost make it and it's taken away from you?" He stared at the coin and sighed. "What happens then?"

He looked up at the administration building. There was an archway over the entrance, and carved into stone over the archway were the words EX TENEBRAS AD LUCE. From the darkness, into light. He took a deep breath and went inside.

CHAPTER
Six

The penthouse apartment overlooked Fifth Avenue. It was decorated elegantly. The deep carpeting was a rich, dark blue, and the furnishings were exquisite pieces of mahogany and zebrawood, not a sign of glass or chromed steel anywhere. Built-in bookcases held rare volumes dealing with history, science, philosophy, and archaeology, books about primitive tribes, books about weapons, books about military campaigns, and works of fiction arranged on the shelves in careful groupings according to subject. Several impressionist paintings graced the walls, originals by Monet, Cézanne, and Van Gogh. A large wooden cabinet housed a collection of wines, the bottles all arranged horizontally in wooden racks. On top of the polished mahogany bar in the corner of the living room was a burnished silver tray holding a crystal wine decanter and several crystal wineglasses.

The bearded man in the gold-rimmed glasses unstoppered the decanter and poured himself a glass of port. He sipped the wine, savoring it, pausing first to sniff its full-bodied bouquet and observe the delicate sheeting action on the glass.

"Apollonius, we have work to do," he said.

With a soft humming sound, one of the bookshelves slid aside into a recessed niche in the wall, revealing a sophisticated console of electronic equipment and several monitor screens. Several soft red indicator lights came on.

"Working," said the computer.

"I require an open line to the Bureau of Thaumaturgy," he said. "We're going to tap into their data base. We are looking for candidates for first-level thaumaturgical certification examinations held over the past five years."

"Working," said the computer. Several moments later it said, "I have those records accessed. Do you require a printout?"

"No, not yet," he said. "First search the data base and eliminate all female candidates. Then eliminate all candidates who passed their certification exams. We are looking for males who failed their exams, between the ages of eighteen and twenty-five . . . no, better make that eighteen and thirty, to be on the safe side. Blond, blue eyes, approximately five foot nine or ten, weight about one hundred and sixty pounds."

"Working," said the computer. It took a little longer this time. He sipped his wine and waited. After a short while the computer said, "I am ready with that information."

"How many names are there?"

"One thousand, one hundred and sixty-eight," said the computer.

"That many? Hmmm. Stand by."

He went over to the coffee table and opened the briefcase he had lying there. He took out a videocassette that Fats had given him, a recording from his pawnshop security system.

"*Warning!* There is a safeguard program attempting to lock in on me," said the computer.

"Block it."

He opened the case for the cassette and inserted it into a slot on the console.

"Play this cassette for me," he said.

"Working," said the computer. The cassette was drawn into the slot, and a moment later the images appeared on one of the monitor screens. The concealed camera had been mounted in the far corner of the pawnshop, shooting down over the counter.

"Fast forward."

The images sped up.

"Hold it," he said.

The images froze on a picture of Wyrdrune and Kira entering the shop.

"Resume normal speed," he said.

He watched as the tape resumed running, then said, "Hold. Zoom in. Hold. A little to the right. Hold. Zoom in again. Hold."

The picture was a tight close-up of Wyrdrune's hooded face.

"Can you enhance to eliminate the shadows?"

"Working," said the computer. The image started to lighten.

"Hold. Compare that image against the photographs in the BOT files for a match."

"Working," said the computer.

He waited. After about a minute and a half he frowned.

"Is there a problem, Apollonius?" he said.

"There is no match in the BOT data base," said the computer.

"Are you certain?"

"I have state-of-the-art software, and my hardware contains half a million dollars in thaumaturgically etched and animated chips," said the computer. "I am always certain."

He smiled faintly. "My apologies, Apollonius. However, we seem to have a problem. If our warlock passed his certification exams, he would be registered with the BOT as a licensed wizard or sorcerer, and he is not. If he did not pass his exams, his application should still be on file with the

BOT. And it is not. All of which seems to suggest that he never even applied to take his first-level certification." He frowned. "But why?"

"Perhaps he did not complete the required schedule of courses to qualify for certification," said the computer.

"Excellent, Apollonius. Very good, indeed."

"Thank you."

"You are quite welcome. You may disengage from the BOT line."

"Disengaged."

"I trust we successfully avoided the lock-in of the safeguard program?"

"Of course."

"Good. Let me see . . ." He sipped his wine. "What we need is some sort of central data base for students of thaumaturgy. Does such a thing exist?"

"One moment, I will check my encyclopedic data base," said the computer. "Yes, there is a central transcript file of all applicants accepted into accredited university-level thaumaturgy programs maintained at the Thaumaturgical College of Sorcerers in Cambridge, Massachusetts. Do you wish me to access that data base?"

"Yes, but let's avoid the normal channels, shall we? Let's tap an open line and sneak in quietly."

"Working," said the computer. It took about two minutes. "I am inside," it said. "I have accessed the transcript files."

"Good. Follow the same procedure as before. Let's see if we can find our young warlock in the university files."

The computer hummed softly as it conducted a search program. "*Warning!* I have a safeguard program attempting to lock in on me," it said again.

"Block it, please, and continue."

"Working." Another few moments passed. "I have a match," said the computer.

"Put it up on the screen, please."

A second later Wyrdrune's transcript, accompanied by a photograph, appeared on the monitor screen.

"The subject's name is Karpinsky, Melvin; magename: Wyrdrune; accepted into the Thaumaturgical College of Sorcerers in Cambridge, Massachusetts, in the fall of 2219. The subject was granted an Ambrosian Scholarship and completed the required courseload up to his junior year with honors but was expelled at the beginning of his—*Warning!* I have detected another break-in. Someone else is attempting to access this data base."

"Can you trace the source?"

"Working," said the computer. "I have locked in and initiated source search. One moment . . . I have that information now. The source of the break-in is the embassy of the United Semitic Republics in New York City, located on—*Warning!* There is a safeguard program attempting to lock in on me."

"Block it."

"Working . . . *Warning!* I am unable to block the safeguard program! *Warning!* Safeguard program has locked in!"

"Disengage!"

"*Warning!* Source search has been initiated!"

"Disengage immediately!"

"*Warning!* I am unable to disengage!"

"Shut down, Apollonius! Shut down at once!"

"*Warning! Override! Override!*"

"Shut down! Shut down!"

"*Warning! Warning! No! No! Aahhhhhhhhhhhhhh!*"

He shielded his face with his arms as his computer system suddenly exploded, sending shrapnel flying across the room. The shock wave picked him up and threw him back into a wall. Black smoke billowed out from the console, shot through with electric sparks. A voice came out from inside the cloud.

"*Who are you?*"

He raised himself to his hands and knees. Blood streamed from several cuts in his scalp, running down his forehead and into his eyes. His hands were bloody from shielding his face. "You go to hell!" he said.

The cloud roiled and the voice said, *"Do not meddle in things that do not concern you. Let this be a warning."*

A horizontal pillar of fire shot out of the cloud, like molten liquid exploding from the nozzle of a flamethrower. It streamed across the living room and struck the opposite wall, igniting it. A fortune in original oil paintings burst into flame.

"No!" he screamed.

He got up and ran toward the paintings, but the entire wall had quickly turned into a solid sheet of flame, and the heat was such that he could not even get near it. The sprinkler system was set off, as well as a fire alarm, but it was too late. He staggered through the smoke, behind the bar, and raised up a concealed trapdoor that hid a floor safe. He opened the safe, eyes streaming from the smoke, and removed a metal strongbox that contained, among other things, his bank records and his multiple passports in several different names from a variety of nations. He tucked the strongbox under his arm and stood there helplessly amid the smoke and fire as the water from the overhead sprinkler system rained down on him, drenching him, making the flames sputter and filling the room with even more smoke. He had lost everything.

He still had his bank accounts in Switzerland and Latin America and the Caribbean, but that was only money. It could not replace the van Gogh and the Cézanne and the Monet, which had survived for centuries, carefully preserved in museums and private collections, now gone forever. It was an agonizing loss. Money would not replace the rare books. Even if anything could be salvaged, it would be lost to him because he had to leave quickly now, before the fire department and the police arrived. There was virtually nothing in the penthouse apartment, save for the documents inside the strongbox, which would give anyone the slightest idea who had lived there. His life was a carefully constructed web of aliases, and now he would have to start all over somewhere else, find a new base of operations, establish an elaborate new system of security that would allow his clients to reach him without ever knowing where he was. It would all take a great deal of money, perhaps all that he had left, but it was not the money that mattered. It was the incredible barbarity of such a callous act of destruction, such monstrous vandalism, that filled him with cold rage.

He staggered toward the door through the smoke and flames, pausing to take a last look at all that was left of the things he cherished. He was full of raging fury, a fury unlike anything he had ever known in a life of cold, emotionless professionalism. Now, for the first time, it was personal. He turned and fled down the fire stairs.

The worst part of it was that the department secretary did not even remember him. His face meant nothing to her; neither did his name. Perhaps it was just as well. If she *had* remembered him, she might have been a great deal more difficult about arranging an appointment with his old professor. As it was, he gave his magename, which Merlin himself had bestowed on him, partly in jest and partly as an accurate description of his overeagerness to master spells far above his level and invariably getting them all wrong. The secretary assumed he was an alumnus come back to visit his old alma mater.

"Oh, yes, of course," she said, pretending to remember his name. "Do you have an appointment, sir?"

"Actually, no, I don't," he said, "but it's regarding a matter of considerable urgency, and I'm sure that Professor Ambrosius would wish to see me."

"Dean Ambrosius is no longer teaching a regular schedule of classes at the university," she said, "but he is still a very busy man, you know. There are tremendous demands upon his time. Perhaps if you could tell me what it was about . . . ?"

"I'm sorry, Ms. Soames, I'm afraid I couldn't really do that," he said. "It's a matter of some delicacy, and it's quite important that I speak to him about it personally. Professional ethics, you understand."

"Oh, I see," she said, obviously not seeing at all and not caring a great deal, either. "Well, as it happens, Dean Ambrosius had an interdepartmental staff meeting earlier today, and it's possible that he might still be on campus. I'll buzz Archimedes and see if he's in his office and available to see you."

"Archimedes?" Wyrdrune said, but she was already on the phone.

"Hello, Archimedes? This is Betty Soames. I have one of our graduates here in the office with me, an alumnus who's anxious to see Dean Ambrosius. He says it's quite important."

She paused a moment while Wyrdrune wondered who Archimedes was.

"Wyrdrune," she said into the phone, then paused a moment. "Yes, that's right. Okay, I'll send him over." She hung up the phone and looked up at him. "Dean Ambrosius has a faculty luncheon to attend at noon, but he can see you for a few minutes. His office is—"

"Yes, I remember," Wyrdrune said. "Thank you."

He went past her desk and down the hallway that led to the private offices of the department chairman and the senior professors. At the end of the hall there was a large oak door with an engraved brass nameplate on it. It read, simply, M. AMBROSIUS. He took a deep breath and knocked on the door.

"Enter," said a querulous voice from within.

He opened the door and walked in.

It was a small, windowless office, not even half as large as the department chairman's. The walls were completely obscured by bookshelves containing scores of ancient tomes

bound in old, cracked leather covers. There were books
everywhere, from floor to ceiling. The floor was covered by
a beautiful, well-worn Persian carpet, and there were a couple of large comfortable leather reading chairs on either side
of the large carved mahogany desk. The desk was cluttered
with stacks of papers, scrolls, an appointment calendar, a
skull with the top of its cranium removed so that it could
hold an ashtray, a wooden pipe rack holding half a dozen
curved, large-bowled briars, a humidor, and . . . incongruously, a personal computer. There was no room on the walls
for any artwork because of all the books, but there were
several small sculptures placed around the room, among
them a foot-high bronze of Gandalf the Sorcerer from the
classic Tolkien stories, and a small sculpture of a winged
dragon sitting on a glass ball on one corner of the desk.
There was a large stuffed owl on a perch in front of one of
the bookshelves, and, completely out of place, a six-foot-tall
cigar-store Indian stood in a corner of the office.

Merlin Ambrosius sat in a high-backed chair reading a
newspaper. With his feet up on his desk and his unkempt
white hair haphazardly trimmed to just above his shoulders,
he looked less like an archmage than a disreputable coffee-
house poet. His snow-white beard was full, but he no longer
wore it long. It was cut in the style of a Gloucester fisher-
man, wide and flaring. He was dressed in a brown herring-
bone-tweed jacket, a white knitted crewneck sweater, and
worsted wool trousers. He wore suede desert boots, and an
Irish tweed walking hat was hung on a large hook screwed
into the side of his chair. He was smoking a deeply curved,
large-bowled briar pipe packed with his usual peculiar blend
of tobacco, a sorcerous concoction that smelled different
with every puff. It filled the office with a pungently piquant
mixture of scents: a touch of latakia and perique; a whiff of
brimstone mixed with the smell of macaroons baking in an
oven; a faint tang of cherry; and the odor of Scottish heather
after a spring rain.

Merlin put down his newspaper and squinted at Wyrdrune from beneath his huge, bushy white eyebrows. His mouth was almost obscured by his luxuriant beard, and his eyes were an amazingly youthful, periwinkle blue.

"Hello, Professor," Wyrdrune said, standing before him, ill at ease. "Thank you for seeing me."

Merlin grunted. "What have you burned down this time, Karpinsky?" he said. "Don't tell me you've managed to get yourself readmitted."

"No, sir, I'm afraid not," Wyrdrune said, "although I still have hopes of finishing my studies."

"So? What do you want from me, a recommendation?"

"No, sir, I honestly don't feel I've earned that. However, I'm faced with a rather serious problem, and I was hoping you could give me some advice. I frankly didn't know where else to turn. I'm in a lot of trouble."

"Somehow that does not surprise me," Merlin said, taking his feet down and using his thumb to tamp down the tobacco in his pipe. "Very well, what is it? What have you done this time?"

"Well, it's a rather long and complicated story, sir—"

"It would be," Merlin said wryly, putting his elbow on the desk and propping his chin up on his palm. "Do you think you could manage to abbreviate it somewhat?"

Wyrdrune took a deep breath and let it out slowly. "Well, I don't know if you've heard about the jewel theft in New York, at the auction of the Euphrates artifacts—"

"You didn't."

"Uh, yes, sir, I—I'm afraid I did."

Merlin shut his eyes and gave out a soft groan. "Ohh, Karpinsky," he said, shaking his head. "*Why* are you telling me this?"

"Sir, I was desperate," he said. "I was behind on my rent; I couldn't get a job; I just didn't know what else to do."

"So you robbed the most prestigious gallery in New York City?"

"I know it was crazy. I can't explain it. I honestly don't know what made me do it. Something just came over me. I'm not a thief. Really, I'm not. I've never stolen anything in my entire life. Well, there was that time I tried to lift a copy of the midterm exams, but—"

"Karpinsky," Merlin said, "there are times when I truly think you are a punishment from God. I've managed to enjoy four blessed years of uninterrupted academic boredom, and now you come back like some neurotic poltergeist to complicate my life. Why couldn't you simply be content to work hard and apply yourself to your studies? Why must you always look for shortcuts?"

Wyrdrune couldn't think of anything to say.

Merlin sighed. "You were my most promising student," he said. "I haven't met anyone so naturally gifted since Le Fay. Regrettably, that was not all you had in common with her. You were both equally irresponsible, equally impatient. You know, if you had possessed but an ounce of his dogged determination, you could have been another Al'Hassan. I had hoped that a few years would give you some maturity, some proper perspective. When I heard you were waiting outside in the office, I thought that perhaps you might have learned your lesson and were ready to try again. I was even prepared to intercede with the Dean of Admissions on your behalf, but instead I'll have to intercede with the police. I don't know what I'm going to do with you, Karpinsky. You're an emotional basket case, just like that young fool, Lancelot." He picked up the phone. "Betty? Cancel my luncheon, will you? Give the chairman my apologies. And hold all my calls, please."

He hung up the phone.

"I imagine you're going to need a lawyer," he said. "I suppose you'd better tell me all about it."

"Well, I guess it started when I picked up a paper to look at the want ads," Wyrdrune said. "I was going to try to find a job, *any* job. All I wanted was to pay my rent and try to get some money set aside for groceries and maybe start saving up for my tuition. I really was going to try to come back and do it right this time, I swear."

"Yes, yes, go on. Get to the point."

"The article about the auction of the artifacts just seemed to jump out at me," said Wyrdrune. "I started reading it, and when I got to the part about the runestones, I don't know what hit me, but all of a sudden I just knew I had to have them. I suppose it may sound strange, but there was never a question in my mind about it. I saw that if I could steal the stones and sell them, I could pay off all my bills and have enough money left over to go back to school and complete my studies, do it right this time, but those all seemed like secondary considerations somehow. I forgot all about the want ads. I clipped the article and read it over and over again, and the desire just kept on getting stronger. It wasn't even a desire, really, it was more like a compulsion. I knew I had to do it. I just *had* to. Nothing else seemed to matter. So I figured out a plan where I'd disguise myself as an old man, a sorcerer, and steal the stones during the auction by creating a diversion, a fire—"

"Naturally," said Merlin wryly.

"And everything went right according to plan until I actually tried to grab the stones. It turned out that someone else had the very same idea. A girl. She tried to grab the stones at the same time, and we both just barely managed to get away."

"But you did steal the jewels?" said Merlin.

"Yes, she grabbed them while I teleported us out of there," said Wyrdrune.

"You *teleported*?" Merlin said, raising his eyebrows.

"I know, I really wasn't ready for teleportation spells, but I figured it was worth a chance, you know, just to escape . . . funny thing, though, I've been getting much better at it. It doesn't even make me tired anymore. And I think I know why too. I think the runestones are responsible."

"What makes you think that?" said Merlin, frowning.

"I just can't see any other explanation," Wyrdrune said. "They were certified as enchanted runestones of unknown properties, and there's no doubt they're enchanted. That's part of the problem. Kira and I—that's the girl who stole them with me—we've been trying to sell the stones, well, that is, we *have* sold them several times, only they keep coming back to us. We just can't seem to get rid of them. And we can't seem to get rid of each other, either. We don't exactly get along too well, but it seems as if we're stuck together somehow, and it's almost as if the stones don't *want* us to be apart. And lately I've had the strangest feeling that it wasn't even really my idea to steal the runestones. Now, I know this is going to sound crazy, but I'm starting to suspect that the stones *wanted* me to steal them, that I never really had any choice in the matter. I know that sounds as if I'm trying to make excuses, but I'm not. That's really how I feel. Frankly, sir, I'm scared. There are people after us, not only the police, and I've been getting some very strange sensations lately. I don't know what's happening to me. I seem to be getting stronger somehow. Part of me wants to get rid of the damn stones, just throw them away or something, and part of me wants to keep them. And I don't know why. On top of that, I'm starting to have these strange dreams where people are talking to me in a language I can't even understand—"

"Where are the runestones now?" said Merlin.

"Right here," said Wyrdrune, reaching into his pocket and taking out the pouch.

"Give them to me."

He handed the pouch across the desk to Merlin.

"Sit down, it looks as if you're on the verge of a nervous breakdown," said Merlin. He frowned, holding the pouch. "What in heaven's name have you got here?" he said. "I haven't felt such power since . . ." His voice trailed off.

He shook the stones out onto the desktop and stared at

them, then he reached into his jacket pocket and took out a pair of square, steel-rimmed glasses. He put them on and held the stones up one at a time, squinting at the barely discernible runes carved into them.

"I don't recognize this language," he said slowly. "I have absolutely *no* idea what it is. Unless . . . no, that's not possible. Archimedes . . ."

The computer on the desktop came on with a soft chime. "Yes, Professor?" it said in a young male voice with a clipped British accent.

"Take a look at this and see what you can make of it," said Merlin. He held up one of the stones in front of the screen. "Damned useful things, these computers," he said.

"I never thought I'd see you break down and get one," Wyrdrune said.

Merlin shrugged. "The department bought it for me. Frankly I can't imagine how they make them work. I understand how they use alchemy now to make plastics in the absence of petroleum, and I naturally comprehend the animating principles that give life to those little things they call chips, but beyond that, it's all a mystery to me. I've got a book here somewhere that supposedly explains it all, but I can't make any sense of it."

"I have nothing like that in my memory, Professor," Archimedes said.

"What about the university library?" said Merlin.

"I've already checked with the library computer," said Archimedes. "It might as well be Greek. Of course, if it was Greek, then we could read it, couldn't we?" The computer chuckled. "Sorry."

"Never mind, Archimedes. Thank you just the same."

"Wish I could be of more assistance, Professor, but I'm only as good as my input, you know. Will there be anything else?"

"No, that will be all for the moment."

"Jolly good."

Merlin grimaced. "Ridiculous expression," he said. He pursed his lips and stared at the stones. "Whatever these things are," he said, "they are immensely powerful. And I find myself feeling a strong affinity for them."

"So you believe me, then?" said Wyrdrune.

"I believe what you've told me," said Merlin. "I also believe that you've stumbled onto something of very great significance. And I am concerned that I cannot read these runes. They are either some made-up language, someone's personal thaumaturgical code, or else it's a language that predates even me, and considering where these came from, I am inclined to believe the latter. And *that* is very worrisome. Very worrisome, indeed."

"What do you think I should do, sir?" Wyrdrune said.

"Well, obviously the police will have to be called in," said Merlin, "and you're going to need a damned good lawyer, but before we do that, I want to find out what these are. I'd like to take them home with me. Have you a place to stay?"

"Yes, sir, we're at—"

"Come to think of it, I'd rather you didn't tell me," he said. "That way there can be no question of my harboring a fugitive, either directly or indirectly. Personally I couldn't care less, but the university administrators would howl if I brought them any adverse publicity." He shook his head. "There was a time when I never would have concerned myself with such things." He sighed. "I must be getting old. Anyway, let me see what I can make of these. Come see me tomorrow. We'll do lunch."

"Sir, one thing . . ." said Wyrdrune.

"Yes?"

"I'll gladly leave the runestones with you, but I really don't think they'll *stay* with you."

"Oh, I think I can manage to hold them," Merlin said. "Does anyone else know you're here?"

"No, sir. Well, that is, Kira knows, of course, and then there's Ms. Soames——"

"Don't worry about Betty," said Merlin. "She'll forget your name completely by this evening, if she hasn't forgotten it already. The woman has the attention span of a mayfly. No one else knows you've been to see me?"

"No, sir, no one."

"Fine. Perhaps we had better keep it that way, at least until we decide how to proceed. In the meantime, do you need any money?"

"Oh, no, sir, we've got quite a bit, actually."

"Oh, yes, of course, from having fenced your ill-gotten gains," said Merlin. "I gather it would have been awkward to return the money. Well, I wouldn't go on any wild spending sprees if I were you. Getting yourself out of this mess is liable to be expensive."

"I want you to know that I really appreciate this, sir," Wyrdrune said. "I know I've been a disappointment to you, and it's very kind of you to help me out like this after the way I've let you down."

"Kindness has nothing to do with it, Karpinsky. This is going to cost you. There's no such thing as a free lunch, you know. From now on you are going to do exactly as I say. Rest assured, I'll find some appropriate tasks for you to perform in exchange for my help, but first things first. Let's find out just what sort of mess it is you've gotten yourself into. Go on now and stay out of trouble, if that is even remotely possible for you. I'll see you tomorrow."

"There is a call for you, *Effendi*," said the consular attaché with a respectful bow. "A Mr. Rozetti. He insists that he will speak only with you."

"Thank you, Hakim," said Mustafa without turning around. He was standing by the large plate-glass window, staring out over the city. "I will take it in here."

The attaché bowed once more and left the room. Mustafa
went over to the large, lustrously polished cherrywood desk
and picked up the phone. "Yes, Mr. Rozetti?" he said.

"This phone safe?" said Rozetti.

"All of the telephones in the embassy are protected by
safeguard spells against eavesdroppers," said Mustafa. "You
may speak freely, Mr. Rozetti."

"Yeah, well, a man can't be too careful these days, know
what I mean?" Rozetti said.

"I know precisely what you mean, Mr. Rozetti. Kindly
get to the point of your call."

"I've found them," said Rozetti.

Mustafa paused a moment to make sure his voice was
steady. "Where are they?"

"Not so fast, Mr. Sharif," Rozetti said. "First I'm going to
require some, what you call, assurances."

"What sort of assurances?"

"First, my name is kept out of it. Completely. I never
even called you. Second, your boss, Sheik Al'Hassan, is
made to understand in no uncertain terms that I didn't have
anything to do with this. Those people came to me, and I've
been cooperating one hundred percent from the word *go*.
You make sure he understands that. Okay?"

"Agreed," Mustafa said.

"Wait a minute, I ain't finished yet. The reward. I got that
comin', right? And that money the insurance people have
put up. I mean, I've had a lot of my people on this, know
what I'm saying? I feel I should be compensated. That's fair,
right?"

"If your information leads me to the thieves and to the
runestones, then you will be, as you say, compensated," said
Mustafa. "And your identity will not be revealed. Is there
anything else you require in the way of assurances?"

"Yeah, one other thing," Rozetti said. He hesitated.
"Look, uh . . . don't take this the wrong way, but I'd really

like for you not to come around no more. After this we're quits. I got a business to take care of. Just send someone over with the money. Preferably cash."

"As you wish. Now, where are they, Mr. Rozetti?"

"Boston."

"What do you mean, Boston? Boston is a rather large place."

"They took the train to Boston earlier today. I figured they'd probably try to skip town, and I had my people covering the train stations and the airports, just in case. And we got lucky. These two are real amateurs. They were spotted at Penn Station, getting on the train to Boston. I called ahead as soon as I heard and had some people I know pick them up and follow them when they arrived there. They're staying at the Copley Plaza."

"These friends of yours in Boston," said Mustafa, idly staring down at the cobra in the glass terrarium on his desk, "do they know why they are watching these two thieves for you?"

"Yeah, because they ripped me off," Rozetti said.

"What I meant was, does anyone else besides yourself know of my interest in this matter?" said Mustafa.

"What? No, I kept it confidential, just like you said. Besides, why should I give anybody else a cut of the reward money? This business is just between you and me, right?"

"Indeed, Mr. Rozetti," said Mustafa. "And I am pleased that we were able to conclude it so successfully. Would you mind holding on a moment, please?"

He took the phone away from his ear and placed the receiver down inside the glass terrarium. He softly mumbled a few words in Arabic and made a languid, beckoning gesture at the snake. The cobra slowly writhed toward the receiver, then it passed *through* the mouthpiece until it had disappeared completely into the phone.

Mustafa could hear Rozetti's voice on the other end as the

receiver lay in the terrarium. "Sharif? Sharif, you there? Hello? Hello, Sha—what the—" There was a gasp, followed by a high-pitched scream.

Mustafa reached inside the empty terrarium, picked up the receiver, and, with a smile, replaced it on its cradle. Now only one loose end remained.

CHAPTER
Seven

Riguzzo had another headache. He stared at the body of Pony Rozetti and wondered why he didn't feel anything except the headache. They had, after all, known each other for a very long time. They never had been friends, certainly, but the ties of the old neighborhood had meant something—not a great deal, perhaps, but it had always been a link of sorts. He thought that he should feel something, sorrow or pity, a sense of loss over a life wasted, but he felt none of those things. Perhaps, he thought, it was because he had so long ago resigned himself to the fact that something like this was bound to happen sooner or later. His mother had known it years ago. He remembered her cautioning him about Rozetti and his wild friends. "You stay away from the Porfirio Rozetti and his bunch," she had told him when he was only twelve years old. "They're nothing but trouble. That boy will come to a bad end, you wait and see. I feel sorry for his poor mother."

Guido came up to him and handed him a paper bag. "This was what done it, Lieutenant," he said. "I put it in a bag because I figured you might want to analyze the thing or something."

Riguzzo looked inside the bag. It held a dead snake. A cobra.

"I killed it," said Guido. "We heard the boss scream, and Louie and me came runnin' in. He was right there like you see him, with the snake all coiled up on the desk, standin' up and hissin' at us. I bashed it with the chair."

The broken chair was still lying on the floor, and there were marks on the desk where Guido brought the chair down several times, hitting the snake. Riguzzo handed the bag to one of the other officers.

"Give this to the lab boys," he said.

"I figure someone must've put it in his desk," said Guido. "He was on the phone, and he must've opened the desk up to get something and the son of a bitch jumped out and bit him."

Riguzzo walked around behind the desk. "The drawers are all closed," he said.

Guido shrugged. "Maybe he closed the drawer with his chest when he fell forward on the desk."

Riguzzo nodded to himself. It could have happened that way. He stared at Rozetti's body, slumped over the desk. The telephone receiver was lying on the floor, dangling from its cord.

"Who was he calling?" he said.

"I don't know, Lieutenant," Guido said. "But I figure you can find out easy enough."

Riguzzo nodded. "You didn't touch anything?"

"Only the chair, when I killed the snake with it," said Guido. "But you'll find my prints all over this office. I was in here a lot. Mark and Louie too."

"Was anyone else in this office, someone who might have left the snake here?" said Riguzzo.

"Not since yesterday," said Guido. "We had a poker game in here last night. The boss, Mark, Louie, me, and Anthony.

We played till about one o'clock in the mornin', and we locked up when we left. Nobody's been in here today except me and the boss. And *I* sure as hell didn't leave that snake there. Afraid I can't prove it, though."

"I don't think you did it, Guido," said Riguzzo. "But I don't suppose there'd be much point in asking who would want him dead."

Guido snorted. "Are you kiddin'? I can think of maybe a dozen guys right off the top of my head."

"So can I," Riguzzo said wryly, "but somehow I can't see any of them using a snake to do it. That's not really their style, is it?"

He went out into the restaurant. Cleary was just hanging up the phone in the bar. "That was Hellerman," he said, referring to another detective on the squad. "Are you ready for this? Guess who else was just found dead? Our old friend, Fats."

Riguzzo frowned. "When?"

"Early this morning, around six A.M. There was a fire in his pawnshop. Place went up so fast, he never had a chance to get out. Fire department found him burned to a crisp. They say it looks like arson."

Riguzzo pursed his lips. "Just a coincidence, I suppose, Fats and Rozetti going at almost the same time."

"Yeah, like the fire at Christie's was a coincidence," said Cleary. "And the fire at that penthouse on Fifth Avenue. The home of the mysterious John Roderick, who's dropped clean out of sight. A million-dollar penthouse goes up in smoke, and he doesn't even show up to file an insurance claim."

"You think there's a connection?" said Riguzzo.

"You tell me," said Cleary. "Hellerman can't find any record of a policy on that place, and he's checked with all the major underwriters. What's more, he can't find any record of John Roderick, either. Nothing but window dressing. All he's got is a checking account and cash reserve at First City, amounting to a little under a hundred and fifty thousand, and just one credit card account. Petty cash, looks like, for someone with a place like that. No life insurance, no major medical, no stock portfolios. . . . The guy paid taxes, though. According to the IRS, Roderick was self-employed as an art appraiser. Which means he'd know all about galleries and auctions. Made forty-five thousand last year. And he lived in a million-dollar penthouse. But here's the kicker. Hellerman smelled something and he got ambitious. He traced the birth certificate Roderick used to get his social security card. John Roderick was born on December 20, 2205, in Providence, Rhode Island, which should make him forty years old. Only it seems there's also a death certificate on the same John Roderick, listing him as having expired on January 23, 2206.''

The water was running in the bathroom when Wyrdrune came back to their hotel room. Kira's clothes were thrown haphazardly on the bed and floor, and there was a room-service tray holding a bucket of ice and a bottle of expensive Scotch. The bottle was about a third empty. There were also the remains of a large bowl of tortilla chips and a dish of hot red salsa. Scotch and *salsa*? Wyrdrune's stomach churned. The TV was turned on, but the sound was off and the radio was tuned to an oldies station, filling the room with the driving, pounding, cybersounds of The New Romancers.

"Kira!" he shouted over the noise.

"That you, warlock?" she called from the bathroom.

"And what would you do if it wasn't?" he said.

A knife thudded into the wall about two inches from his left ear. Kira came out of the bathroom, wrapped in a white hotel towel. Her wet, black hair was combed straight back and it was dripping on the carpet. She folded her arms and glanced at him with raised eyebrows.

"I had to ask, didn't I?" he said. He pulled the knife from the wall. "The hotel's just going to love that." He fingered the gash it had made in the wall. He examined the knife.

The long, slim, nine-inch blade was shiny and razor-sharp. The bone handle added another four inches to its length. It was not suitable for a survival or a hunting knife. It was designed for just one thing. Killing people. He hefted it in his hand. "You mean to tell me you actually had this in the shower with you?"

"Never out of my reach," she said, taking it back from him.

He turned the music down. "We're not exactly on a holiday, you know," he said. "With the music up like that, someone could have slipped the lock and gotten inside without your hearing him."

"Oh, I see," she said. She took the knife and flipped it up into the air, caught it by its point, and twirled it expertly. "Guess you're right," she said with mock seriousness. "I should be more careful."

He grimaced, picked up a glass, poured himself a shot of Scotch, neat, and tossed it down. Then he poured himself another.

"I don't suppose you thought to pack a hair dryer," she said.

Wyrdrune snapped his fingers and made a gun at her with his thumb and index finger. A blast of warm air struck her face, and she gasped in surprise as her hair seemed to writhe of its own volition and style itself into her usual exaggerated back-at-the-sides and fall-over-the-eyes geometric cut. It took less than a couple of seconds.

"Hey!" She turned around and checked her reflection in the mirror, making minor adjustments. "Not bad," she said. "You could make a nice living doing that."

"Unions wouldn't like it," Wyrdrune said. "There are some jobs adepts are not supposed to take. It would be unfair competition. But I used to do my girlfriend's hair like that."

"You never told me you had a girlfriend," she said.

"*Had* is the operative word," he said. "She left me for a

young corporate wizard from L.A. A tanned beefcake with a chauffeured limo, custom-made silk robes, open-necked shirts with half a dozen magic amulets on ropy gold chains, and enough money to keep her in the style to which she desperately wanted to become accustomed."

"So how did the meeting with the old man go?" she said, changing the subject. "Did he see you?"

Wyrdrune cleared his throat again and took another drink. He tried not to stare at her, sitting back in a chair with her legs curled up underneath her. It was not a deliberately provocative pose, which made it all the more provocative. She had, he noticed for the first time, truly spectacular legs, long, shapely, and muscular. "Yes, he saw me," he said. "We had a long talk. I told him all about it and he's going to help."

"What did he tell you about the stones?" she said.

"He said he could feel that they were very powerful, but he couldn't read the runes carved into them. He's going to try to figure out what they are. He asked to hold on to the stones, and I'm supposed to go back and see him at his place tomorrow—"

"You *gave* them to him?"

"Of course I gave them to him," he said. "How else are we going to find out what they are? He said he could hold them, keep them from returning to us while he studied them. Besides, you don't just say no to the most powerful archmage in the world. We're lucky he's even bothering to help us. He didn't have to do it, you know. He can help us get a lawyer and intercede with the police—"

"The *police*! Are you crazy? I thought this guy was a friend of yours!"

"Will you just relax, please?" Wyrdrune said, trying not to notice how the towel was slipping slightly. "Look, we're in way over our heads. We've gotten mixed up in some sort of an enchantment, and we don't even know what the hell it is. I know how you feel. I didn't really want to give them to him, either. I had to force myself. Those stones are doing something funny to us, and we'd better find out what it is before something starts happening that we can't stop."

She bit her lower lip and nodded. "I'm sorry," she said. "It's just that I've been feeling jumpy ever since you left. I started feeling a bit crazed all alone in here. I . . . I guess I was really worried about you."

He looked down and took another drink. "About me or about the stones?" he said.

"About you," she said, grimacing. "You may have had a lot of schooling, but you don't seem to know your way around too well."

He smiled wryly. "Thanks for the vote of confidence."

She shrugged. "It just felt kind of strange not having you around. I started feeling nervous. They've got a gym here for the guests, so I decided to have a workout, take some of the edge off. Would you believe it, I benched a hundred and sixty pounds, ten reps. The most I could ever do before was a hundred and twenty, and that was only once or twice. Some of the guys were looking at me as if I were from Mars or something. I've never felt so strong. I must have a lot of excess energy or something."

"I wouldn't be surprised if it was the stones," he said. "They've had some sort of an effect on us, that much is certain. Maybe they're ancient talismans of some sort that increase your power."

"What's wrong with that?"

"Nothing, except that I've never known magic not to exact a price of some sort, and I don't like not knowing what that price could be. According to Merlin the kind of thaumaturgy we practice nowadays is kid stuff compared to the sort of spells the ancients used to mess around with. And for that matter, we don't even know what kind of magic it is. We're assuming that it's white—the odds are probably in favor of that—but what if it's black magic?"

"You're saying that it could be something really nasty?" she said.

"I don't know much about black magic," he said. "It's against the law to practice it these days, but I do know that most of it was very nasty stuff. And it could turn on you just like that." He snapped his fingers.

A leather pouch appeared nestled in his palm.

He stared at it. "Oh, no. . . ."

"What did you do?" she said.

"I didn't do anything!" he said. "At least, I don't *think* I did."

"I thought you said Merlin could keep them from returning to us," she said.

He hefted the pouch in his hand, and even though he already knew what was inside it, he opened up the drawstring and checked. The knowledge confirmed, he shut his eyes briefly and sighed. "That's what he said. I'm just hoping that he put them in his briefcase and forgot to do anything about it. Becuase if he put a holding spell on them and it didn't take . . ." He got up. "I'd better go back and see him right away."

She got up from her chair and stood before him, blocking his way. "No, you don't," she said. "I'm not about to spend all night cooped up in here alone, not knowing what's going on. It'll keep until tomorrow." She took his hand, the one holding the pouch, and covered it with both of her own. "Just take it easy. Don't let these damn things make you crazy."

Her towel fell.

She made no move to pick it up or cover herself. She just stood there looking at him with her hands cupped over his.

He swallowed hard. It was as if he could feel her heartbeat through her hands. Neither of them spoke for a long moment, and then she flowed into his arms and their lips met in a long kiss.

She fumbled with his clothes, practically tearing them off

him, kissing him hungrily all the while. They fell back together on the bed, all else forgotten as a desperate, overpow-
ering need for each other washed over them. She straddled
him on the bed, bending over him, holding his face between
her hands and kissing him deeply.

"I've been wanting you so bad," she said between kisses.
"I've been fighting it, but I just can't help it anymore."

It's crazy, he wanted to tell her, *we don't even* like *each
other,* but even as he thought it, he knew it wasn't true. He
put his arms around her tightly, crushing her to him, wanting
to meld his body with hers and become a part of her. Later
they lay slightly apart, staring at each other, feeling a cur-
ious mixture of affectionate contentment and puzzled embarrassment.

"What's *happening* to us?" he said.

"I think it's called falling in love," she said, smiling.

"I know," he said, "but what I meant is . . . what if it isn't
us?" He picked up the pouch containing the runestones and
dumped them out onto the sheet between them. "How do we
really know?"

"What difference does it make?" she said. "I've never felt
this good before. So what if it doesn't make any sense? I'm
not complaining."

"Sexual rituals were often a part of the magic of the
ancients," Wyrdrune said.

"Is that all you think it was?" she said. "A sexual ritual?"

"I don't know what to think," he said. He reached out and
stroked her cheek. "How do you feel right now?"

"Terrific," she said. "But I'll admit I'm also feeling a bit
shook up. It just sort of happened, didn't it?"

He nodded. "Rather conveniently, too, the moment the
runestones came back to us."

"So what are you saying," she said, an edge in her voice,
"the *runestones* made you do it? That's why you made love
to me?"

"It wasn't exactly a case of me making love to you," he said. "You practically attacked me."

"Yeah, well, maybe I need to get my ears checked, but I didn't hear you crying rape," she said sarcastically.

"I'm not saying I didn't enjoy it, for crying out loud," he said.

"Well, that's damn decent of you!" she said, sitting up in bed. "I'd hate to think you suffered through it!"

"I didn't mean it that way!" he said, sitting up and throwing back the sheets. He got out of bed and started getting dressed. "Why do you always have to turn everything around?"

"I'm *not* turning anything around!" she said. "You make it sound like it was all one-way! Well, excuse *me,* but I wasn't the one shouting, 'I love you, I love you' loud enough to wake up the entire floor!"

"Don't be crude."

"Crude?"

"All right, I didn't mean that, it's just that it's not fair to throw something in my face that I said in the heat of passion! It's . . . it's not dignified!"

"Dignified! What the hell does *dignity* have to do with anything? What do you usually do, screw in a tuxedo?"

"You're being ridiculous."

"I am *not* being ridiculous! We make love together—and don't tell me it wasn't terrific for you—and then you turn around and say some magic pebbles made you do it! Talk about a cop-out! I ought to let you have one right in the jaw!"

"Oh, I see, you love me, so now you're going to beat me up to prove it."

She jumped out of bed, her hands clenched into fists. "You drive me *crazy,* you know that?"

He gently took her by the shoulders. "You drive me crazy too," he said. "I'd just feel a whole lot better about it if I knew for sure it wasn't magic."

She grinned. "I thought it *was* magic."

"You know what I mean. Doesn't it worry you that . . . that something might be manipulating you?" he said.

She stopped smiling. "You're serious, aren't you? You *really* think that's what it is?"

"Kira . . . I just don't *know*. And it's like I told you before, when it comes to magic, what you don't know *can* hurt you. I know I'd be hurt if I found out that the only reason this happened was because we were both under a spell."

"I thought that's how it was supposed to happen," she said.

He smiled. "You're a romantic. Somehow I'd never have expected it of you."

"There are a few things about you I wouldn't have expected, either," she said. "But I think I understand what you mean. I wouldn't have thought we'd wind up together like this. It just sort of sneaked up on us. But maybe that's just the way it happens."

"Maybe," he said. "But what if it's not? Wouldn't you want to know?"

She licked her lips and shook her head. "No," she said softly, shaking her head again. "No, if something could make me feel that way when I didn't really feel that way, no, I don't think I'd want to know." She sighed and looked away. "I mean, I would, and then I wouldn't. I wouldn't want it not to be real and I'd want to know if it wasn't, but at the same time I wouldn't want to know that we'd been had that way. Hell, I'm all mixed up now." She paused, thinking. "Anyway, how does anybody ever know for sure?"

He frowned. "What do you mean?"

"The only way we're going to find out is to just go with it," she said. "And that's all anyone can ever really do, isn't it? Just take a chance. Hell, warlock, don't you think it's worth it? I'll take a chance if you will."

He started to say something, then stopped. He picked up

the stones from the bed and put them back into the pouch. "I'd better go see Merlin right away."

She stared at him. "You're leaving *now*?"

"Yes, I think I'd better."

"I don't believe it. You're really worried about this, aren't you?"

"Aren't *you*?"

She shook her head and shrugged. "I don't know. All I know is that something really nice happened between us, and it's as if you're trying to find excuses for it."

"All *I* know," he said, "is that the fact that I'm worried about this means I care enough about what happened to *want* it to be real. And for somebody as hard-nosed and streetwise as you just to accept it at face value and not want to know for sure seems out of character to me, and that worries me too."

She frowned. "That was a very nice thing you said. Sort of."

He sighed. "I'll see you later. Don't go out, okay?"

He closed the door.

She stood there, unclothed, hands on her hips, staring after him. "I've got to be crazy," she said to herself, "falling for a guy like that. Maybe it really *is* the stones." She took a deep breath and let it out slowly. "Now he's got *me* doing it. I need a drink."

She reached for the half-empty bottle of Scotch.

And the lights went out.

Merlin lived in a large, gabled dinosaur of a Victorian mansion on Beacon Hill, with mullioned windows and carved cornices; heavy, arched, iron-reinforced wooden doors that looked as if they had been taken off some Norman barbican; balconies and gingerbread moldings and shingles that looked as if they had been designed by Hieronymus Bosch. The house perched like some giant bat on a promontory, a biblical rendition of a demon by Doré—dark, fore-boding, and ominous.

Incongruously the lawn in front of it was peopled by ceramic gnomes, three-foot-high statuettes painted in bright enamel colors wearing tall, pointed caps in green and red and blue, holding lanterns, sitting on mushrooms, waving cheerily at passersby or scowling with their arms folded across their chests. There were dozens of them standing on the grass, crouching in the garden, hunkering down by the front steps, hiding in the bushes.

As Wyrdrune opened the black wrought-iron gate and started up the walk, he thought he caught a flicker of motion out of the corner of his eye, and he turned quickly, but it was just one of the ceramic gnomes standing in a jaunty pose and grinning like an idiot, holding one finger up in the air, as if emphasizing a point he was making in a speech. Wyrdrune made a face and turned away, then thought he heard a slight movement and spun around again. He frowned. He could have sworn the gnome had only been holding up one finger before. Now he was holding up two, making a *V* for victory, only the back of the hand was facing out, which made it not a *V* for victory, but another old British gesture of altogether different significance.

Wyrdrune stared hard at the ceramic gnome for a moment, then turned and continued up the walk. He heard a rustling behind him and spun around again, but this time the gnome was gone. He glanced around at the other figures on the lawn, all of which seemed to be looking right at him, faces frozen into expressions of ceramic imbecility.

Scowling, he walked up the front steps and approached the heavy, arched, wooden front door. There was a huge, ornately carved iron knocker on the door, a demonic visage of some sort, and the knocker itself was the distended, lower part of the demon's jaw. Wyrdrune grabbed it and swung it hard three times against the knocker plate. As he released it, the eyes on the iron knocker opened wide and stared at him.

"Who is it?" said the knocker.

Wyrdrune backed off from it a pace. "It's me, Wyrdrune," he said. "Karpinsky."

"Oh, it's you," the knocker said. "Well, I suppose you'd better come in, then."

The door opened by itself with a loud, protracted creak, and Wyrdrune entered the dark hall. The door closed behind him and bolted itself. Two small fixtures mounted on either side of the door blazed up, illuminating the foyer. He stood on a carpet runner that led across the foyer to a wide, carpeted stairway. The stairway branched off to the left and right from the landing, leading to the upper floors. To the left of the foyer was an arched entry to the living room; to the right, through a pair of open wooden doors, was the library.

It was difficult at first to tell one from the other, because both rooms were filled with books, arranged in floor-to-ceiling mahogany bookshelves, but after a moment Wyrdrune realized that the room to the right was the living room because it had a large fireplace with a flagstoned chimney, a long couch, and several upholstered chairs placed around a long coffee table, while the room to the left held, in addition to all the bookshelves, a writing desk, a leather reading chair, a table, and a sideboard with an old gasogene, a bottle of whiskey, and a glass decanter. It was obviously a library and a study, a place where Merlin spent much of his time.

As he stood there wondering which way to go, Merlin came down the stairs, followed by a large, round-topped, iron-banded wooden chest, the sort of chest a pirate might have buried his treasure in. The chest was floating down the stairs about three paces behind him. He saw that Merlin had changed into a dark blue brocade smoking jacket and matching carpet slippers. He was still wearing the same woolen slacks and smoking his ever-present pipe. At the moment it was sending out clouds of strong Turkish tobacco, emitting an odor reminiscent of burning peat. Wyrdrune wrinkled his nose, but he knew the smell would probably change momentarily, and sure enough, it did, to a gentle whiff of chestnuts roasting.

"I was just up in the attic, looking through some of my old things," Merlin said, gesturing at the chest floating in midair behind him. "I gather you're here because the little buggers have returned to you. I didn't miss them until I got home and opened up my briefcase. I take it you brought them with you?"

"Yes, sir," Wyrdrune said, reaching into his pocket for the pouch. "I've got them right here. I guess you didn't have a chance to put a holding spell on them."

"What do you take me for," said Merlin irritably, "some doddering, absentminded, old tree-hugger?" He always referred to the Druids as tree-huggers. He had little regard for them and was contemptuous of the fact that legends alleged him to have been one. He had even less regard for trees, which was, perhaps, understandable. "Of course I put a holding spell on them," he said. "The trouble is, it didn't seem to work."

Wyrdrune swallowed hard. If Merlin couldn't hold them, then who could? Merlin seemed to read his thoughts.

"It really is rather annoying," he said. "If *I* can't bind the bloody things, then we may have a serious problem on our hands. I've spent the entire afternoon and evening going through most of my old books and records, all to no avail. I've looked through everything except the scrolls and message stones in this old chest. Maybe there's something in there that could give us a clue. I haven't looked through any of this stuff since Arthur's time."

"Since King Arthur's time?" said Wyrdrune with disbelief, staring at the chest. Merlin almost never talked about those days.

"Yes," said Merlin sourly. "I had a premonition that there could be trouble with Le Fay and that young delinquent,

Modred, so I took the trouble to safeguard my most important talismans and records in the crystal cave." He snorted. "Astonishing that they all survived, all things considered. I found all manner of horrors above them when I came back and excavated them. At one time or another, a housing development was built over the site, and before that, a stadium of some sort—I found several concrete slabs covered with those modern runes you call graffiti, something about 'West Ham United' and 'Footballers Forever' or some such nonsense, obviously a later perversion of the old Roman circuses, which were considerable perversions in themselves. . . ."

As he rattled on, he went into the living room, followed by the floating chest. He waved absently at the fireplace and ignited several large logs stacked on the grate, which erupted into a considerable conflagration. He waved absently again at the coffee table, and several stacks of books and papers went flying to the floor, as if swept off the table by an invisible hand. Then he gestured with waggling fingers in the general direction of the library, from which, as if suspended from an invisible conveyor belt, a train of heavy, leather-bound books with gilt lettering on the covers started to float into the living room. He sat down in a large, bat-wing wooden chair with deep purple velvet cushions and started to pull the books out of the air as they danced past him, opening them, rifling the first couple of pages, grunting and shaking his head and tossing them away with apparent unconcern. As he drew the books aside, they went spinning across the living room in a wide arc, through the archway and across the foyer, into the library, and back into their proper places on the shelves.

"I was vaguely conscious in a torpid sort of way while I was trapped inside that tree, sticky with sap and tickled by acorns, which several generations of disrespectful squirrels insisted on storing in a cache they'd gnawed out right be-

neath my nose. Detestable, lousy, yammering creatures. I
followed the so-called progress of the ages. In their time,
Lancelot and the rest of those young braggarts could
be rather trying, but I wonder what they would have made
of the likes of Richard III, Cromwell, Henry Morgan,
Beau Brummel, Disraeli, Bernadette Devlin, and Maggie
Thatcher, to name only a few. I watched the empire rise and
crumble, haul itself up out of the ashes of the German
bombing, and go all to pieces once again before the inevitable Collapse. I thought Le Fay's enchantment would last for
a millennium or so, but the bitch laid a proper corker on me,
and it took much longer than I thought."

He shook his head, grumbling as he scanned the books,
then stopped for a moment and looked off into the distance.
"More was lost with Avalon than I can ever say," he said
wistfully. "The world forgot the old ways and grew up an
orphan, unsupervised and neglected like an unwanted bastard child. I tried to set men back on the proper course, but
sometimes I wonder if it's not too late. There's virtue in
simplicity, but men have enshrined the complex and the bur-
densome, and the new beliefs die hard. I've had to learn to
compromise. There was a time when I didn't even know the
meaning of the word."

He glanced at Wyrdrune and sighed. "I must sound like a
babbling, senile old woman," he said.

"No, sir, not at all," said Wyrdrune. "I love to hear you
talk about the old days. The truly old days, that is, not the
pre-Collapse years that everyone seems to be so fascinated
by today. Frankly I don't understand it."

"Don't you?" Merlin said. He snorted through his beard.
"It's quite simple, really. The past always seems infinitely
more attractive than the present or the future. The present is
a constant struggle for survival, and the future is either a
hoped-for dream or a dreaded nightmare, depending on
one's disposition. But the past . . . it always represents secur-

ity, no matter how dismal it may have been. One thinks back upon the past like an old soldier remembers well-fought battles of his youth or an old woman whose children have all grown thinks back upon the hopes and dreams of girlhood. The past always represents a simpler time, hopes for a future brighter than the one that came to pass, and one remembers it not necessarily the way it was but the way it seems to be, seen through the gauzy filter of advancing years." He shrugged and grimaced wryly. "If I were to be truly honest, I'd have to admit that Camelot had its drawbacks too. It was a glorious time, perhaps, but it could have done with indoor plumbing, central heating, and deodorant soap."

He grunted, snapping himself out of his reverie. "See what happens when you start rummaging through old things in the attic? You start to daydream, and the next thing you know, you're getting all wistful and maudlin, like some old grandmother who's found her trousseau buried in a trunk beneath a pile of old socks." He bent down over the books again and finally found what he was looking for. "Ah, here we are," he said, stabbing his forefinger down at the open book. "Away with you," he said, waving his hand in a gesture of dismissal, and all the other books trooped obediently back into the library.

"Forget the damned spell I used to safeguard this old relic," he said, indicating the chest. "I had to look it up."

He gazed hard at the chest, raised his right hand, and muttered several phrases rapidly in an ancient Celtic dialect. Nothing happened. Merlin raised his eyebrows and grunted, then repeated the spell, again with no apparent result. He frowned and gave the chest a kick. The lid sprang open.

"Must've been stuck," said Merlin grumpily. "Now, let's see what we have in here that might put us on the right track."

He raised his arms over his head, and the contents of the old chest rose up, as if borne up by an invisible fountain—

papyrus scrolls encased in gold and silver tubes; clay tablets incised with cuneiform; Egyptian cartouches, amulets, and scarabs; cylinder seals carved from semiprecious stones; fragments of stone bearing inscriptions from Sumerian temples; and ancient syllabaries engraved on ivory and carved into alabaster and obsidian. The artifacts all swirled in arabesques above the chest, then came down and neatly arranged themselves, spread out on the coffee table, as the lid of the chest slammed down.

Merlin waved his hands in front of his face, coughing from the dust that came up from inside the chest. He reached into the pocket of his smoking jacket, took out a handkerchief, and blew his nose loudly, then wadded up the hanky and stuck it back into his pocket.

"Now, then," he said, "let's have those stones of yours."

Wyrdrune handed him the leather pouch, and Merlin shook the rune stones out into his hand. He held one of them up close to his face and squinted at the runes carved into it, then bent down over the coffee table and started scanning the artifacts arranged there, humming softly to himself.

"The devil of it is," he said, "it seems to me that there's something uncomfortably familiar about all this, as if I've encountered it before somewhere, long ago, only I can't quite recall what . . . hello! What have we here?"

He picked up an irregular fragment of sleek obsidian about the size of a dinner plate, bearing an inscription written in some long-forgotten language. The characters that had been incised into the stone were filled with gold, so that the message stood out bright and sharp against the jet-black stone.

Merlin examined the stone fragment intently, frowning, comparing the gold-filled characters with the runes cut into the three gemstones. They were unquestionably similar. His eyes seemed to glaze over and, as if in a trance, he started to recite:

"Three stones, three keys to lock the spell,
Three jewels to guard the Gates of Hell.
Three to bind them, three in one,
Three to hide them from the sun.
Three to hold them, three to keep,
Three to watch the sleepless sleep."

Wyrdrune stared at him, fascinated, as the glazed look in Merlin's eyes went away and he seemed to focus once more on the fragment of obsidian with the gold characters inscribed on it. His lips moved soundlessly for a moment, and his gaze traveled from the ancient inscription to the runestones.

"Yes," he said, as if speaking to himself. "*Yes,* I remember now! The number three, six lines to the incantation, the number three occurring nine times in the spell . . . multiples of three . . . the living triangle. There are five small triangles in a pentagram, containing fifteen points . . . five multiplied by three, and the five larger triangles that make up a pentagram, each adding three more points for a total of fifteen . . . again five multiplied by three, for a total of ten triangles in the pentagram, thirty points . . . ten multiplied by three . . . the ten triangles of the pentagram multiplied by the six lines of the incantation and the nine recurrences of the number three equal three hundred and sixty, the degrees of the eternal circle . . . of course! *Of course!*"

"What *is* it?" said Wyrdrune.

Merlin slowly sat back in his chair. "An enchantment from the dawn of time," he said. "An incantation containing the most powerful symbols of thaumaturgy—the living triangle, the warding pentagram, and the eternal circle—as indicated by the strongest of the ancient chains of numerology. A binding spell of incalculable power." He picked up the runestones. "And these must be the keys. The three-in-one, the living triangle. And the warding pentagram, from which these stones must have been taken, is the lock. And the eternal circle is the prison.".

He looked at Wyrdrune with alarm. "For the binding spell to be secure, the keys must be inside the lock, the multiples of three, the living triangle within the pentagram. Only now the keys have been removed and the eternal circle can be broken."

"But . . . I don't understand. What does that all mean?" said Wyrdrune.

Merlin sat silent for a long moment. "A catastrophe that will make the Collapse seem insignificant. Indeed, the Collapse prepared the way for it."

"For *what*?" said Wyrdrune.

"The release of the Dark Ones," Merlin said. "And as unbelievable as it may seem, of all people, Karpinsky, *you* are the one who holds the key."

CHAPTER
Eight

She was lying naked on a cold stone floor, in the middle of a large chamber. She could see little of her surroundings. The only light came from several braziers standing near her, illuminating the large room dimly, throwing garish, dancing shadows on the walls.

She crouched on the floor, waiting for her eyes to become accustomed to the dim light, her mind racing. A moment ago, or at least it seemed as if it had been a moment ago, she had been in their hotel room. Wyrdrune hadn't been gone a minute when she felt an icy blast of wind and everything suddenly went black. She felt dizzy, disoriented. She had been with Wyrdrune long enough to know what being magically teleported felt like, only this was worse, the effects magnified, as if she had been transported a much greater distance.

She felt the strong blast of icy wind again. It blew briefly through the shadowy chamber, and she raised a hand to her face and shut her eyes against it as it blew past her, then, just as abruptly as it had started, it was gone.

"Stand up, girl."

The deep voice echoed in the darkened chamber. A dark figure sat on a large chair placed on a dais before her. She stood and faced him, not making any attempt to cover her nakedness. She felt confused and frightened, but she was determined not to show it.

"Your body is well made," the man in the darkness said. "You would bear many strong sons. But you should not stand unclothed in the presence of a king."

The man in the shadows raised his hand, and suddenly she was dressed in a long, loose-flowing gown of black velvet embroidered intricately with gold thread.

"Better," he said.

"Who are you?" she said, feeling afraid, but summoning up her nerve. "What am I doing here? And why are you hiding in the dark?"

Two braziers standing on either side of the dais blazed up suddenly, illuminating him. He sat casually on the gem-encrusted throne, wearing an elegant, dark, custom-tailored suit with a generous amount of lace at the throat and cuffs. A long black kaffiyeh was held in place on his head by a gold circlet with a cobra on it. The blood ruby glowed softly in his forehead.

"I am Rashid Ilderim Al'Hassan," he said, "and I do not hide from such as you. You have stolen something that belongs to me. I want it back."

"Sorry," she said. "I didn't exactly have anything on me when I arrived."

"Where are the runestones?"

"Drop dead."

The jewel set in his forehead blazed, and a bright bolt of light shot out from it, striking her right between the eyes. She cried out and fell to her knees, bringing her hands up to her face.

"The last woman who spoke to me in such a manner amused my retainers for three weeks before she died," he said. "It would serve you well to remember whom you are addressing. Obviously, since you do not have the rune-stones, your young warlock companion does. Where has he gone with them?"

"I don't know," she said.

The jewel in Rashid's forehead blazed again, and this time a bright, sustained beam lanced out from it, striking her and bathing her in its searing, incandescent aura. Her scream echoed off the walls. After a moment that seemed like hours, the beam was cut off, and she collapsed to the floor, holding herself in agony.

"I can bring you pain that is a hundred times worse," said Al'Hassan.

"And if I tell you what you want to know," she said, gasping, "I suppose you'll just pat me on the head and let me go, right?"

"Perhaps, if it amuses me," he said. "But, on the other hand, there are many ways to die. The choice is yours."

"I don't think so," she said, breathing heavily. "You'll have to come up with a better offer."

Al'Hassan smiled in spite of himself. "You are not what I expected," he said, getting up and descending the steps of the dais to the floor, approaching her. "You are afraid, yet you find courage in your pride. I find that a worthy attribute." He stood over her. "I might consider making a place for you in my harem if you were to cooperate."

"That's a better offer?" she said. "I think I'll pass. I could never marry a man who wears more jewelry than I do."

Al'Hassan bent down and lifted her easily with just one hand, holding her off the floor by the throat, choking her. "You insolent little guttersnipe," he said. "I could—" The breath whistled out of him as she suddenly struck out with her foot, kicking him hard in the solar plexus. He doubled over, releasing her, and she followed up the kick with a hard right cross to his jaw. He staggered back and fell. Kira turned and ran, but before she could get ten yards, she was again bathed in the burning radiance of the beam from Rashid's "third eye," and she felt her feet leaving the floor as she rose up into the air, writhing and gasping with pain.

She floated higher, almost to the ceiling of the presence chamber, as Al'Hassan stood beneath her, the blinding beam of force shooting out from the brightly glowing gem set in his forehead. The pain was unbelievable. It felt as if her skin were being torn off. She screamed.

He held her high in midair for a moment, then cut the beam off and allowed her to fall to the black marble floor. She landed hard, like a sack dropped from a height, and lay on the floor, stunned, whimpering, unable to move.

"I could have your hands cut off for that," Al'Hassan said coolly. He wiped the blood away from the corner of his mouth with the back of his hand and looked at it, unable to believe she had actually struck him.

"Yeah," Kira gasped, "I had you figured for a freak."

He grasped her by the hair, pulling her head back sharply, turning her face up to him. "No doubt you think yourself clever," he said. "Yet you do not even begin to comprehend what you have done. You have meddled in something far greater than you could ever imagine. Something that makes your life of very little consequence."

He yanked her by the hair and pulled her to her feet. She swung at him with all her might, but her fist stopped inches from his face, as if it had struck an invisible wall. Suddenly, she couldn't move.

Al'Hassan smiled. "You will not catch me by surprise a second time," he said. She stood immobile, frozen like a statue in the act of trying to strike him. He stroked her cheek with his forefinger. "There is a primitive rage in you I find rather appealing. Submissive women bore me."

Her vocal cords were paralyzed.

He ran his hand along her jawline, smiling at the expression of loathing in her eyes. "What, nothing to say?" He touched her lips gently. "You will speak soon enough. I may decide to keep you, after all. Wild creatures are always the most difficult to tame. And half the reward is in the effort."

As he got off at his floor, the blond man came out of the elevator right behind him, and Wyrdrune suddenly felt the point of a sharp knife against his side, just over his kidney.

"Don't make a sound. Not even a whisper."

A strong hand on the back of his neck, fingers pinching hard just below the base of the skull, propelled him forward, the knife point urging him on.

The blond man pushed him toward the stairway exit, through the door, and face up against the wall on the landing. He pressed him hard against the wall and quickly frisked him.

"What do you—" Wyrdrune began, but the point of the knife pressed against him only slightly, yet enough to shut him up at once.

"Not a word, young warlock. Don't even blink your eyes unless I tell you to." He lifted the leather pouch containing the runestones out of Wyrdrune's pocket. "Now turn around slowly, spread your arms, and press your hands flat against the wall behind you. Pretend you're crucified."

Stunned, Wyrdrune did as he was told, turning around slowly, putting his back to the wall and placing the palms of his hands flat against the wall behind him, arms spread out slightly.

He had barely even noticed the man before, just one of several people who had gotten on the elevator with him in the lobby. Now he saw that he was blond and bearded, of average height and weight, dressed in a conservative, well-tailored suit with just a touch of lace at the throat and cuffs. He wore gold-rimmed eyeglasses, and at first glance he looked for all the world like a well-groomed accountant or lawyer, someone who would never really stand out in a crowd. But then, on closer examination, one noticed the eyes behind the tinted glasses. They were cold, alert, and predatory.

He placed the point of his knife in the hollow of Wyrdrune's throat, just over the trachea. "Believe it or not, I've probably saved your life just now," he said. "There's a man waiting for you in your room, a rather unpleasant gentleman named Mustafa Sharif. Does the name mean anything to you? Shake your head yes or no."

Slowly, all too aware of the knife at his throat, Wyrdrune shook his head from side to side. It took him a moment to realize the full implication of what the man said. If there was someone in their room, then what about Kira?

"Sharif works for Sheik Al'Hassan," the blond man said. Seeing Wyrdrune's eyes widen, he nodded. "I see you know *that* name. Now listen carefully. If you want to come out of this alive, you'll do exactly as I say. Agreed?"

Wyrdrune nodded.

"Good," the man said. "We're going to walk together down the hallway to your room. You're going to knock on the door, say that you forgot your key, and ask to be let in. Then you will quickly stand aside, away from the door, and press yourself up against the wall without making another sound. And you will do absolutely *nothing* else, whatever happens. Understand?"

Wyrdrune swallowed hard and nodded.

"Good. Come on, then."

They went out of the stairwell and down the hall together, the man holding on to Wyrdrune's arm, keeping the knife pressed against his side. They stopped at the door to Wyrdrune's room. The blond man glanced at him and nodded. Wyrdrune stepped up to the door, knocked three times, and said loudly, "Kira? Kira, it's me. Let me in, I forgot my key."

In a moment there was the soft click of the dead bolt being drawn back, the knob started to turn, and Wyrdrune immediately stepped aside and flattened himself against the wall.

The corridor was empty. The blond man had disappeared.

As Wyrdrune glanced wildly around him, there were three soft coughing sounds, coming in rapid succession from inside the room, and splinters flew from the door as three holes appeared in the corridor wall opposite the doorway. There was the sound of something heavy hitting the door and falling. A moment later there was the sound of something being dragged across the floor, and then the door opened and the blond man said, "Inside, quickly!"

He pulled Wyrdrune into the room and closed the door. A man's body lay sprawled facedown on the floor, staining the carpet with blood. There were red streaks on the carpet where the blond man had dragged the body away from the door and red splashes and smears on the inside of the door where Sharif had been thrown against it by the impact of the bullets and then slid down to the floor. Wyrdrune stared at the corpse wide-eyed, his stomach heaving.

"My God, you killed him!"

"I should hope so," the blond man said. In his gloved right hand he held a small black semiautomatic pistol with a short silencer screwed into the barrel. Crazily it struck Wyrdrune that the gun seemed very small to have done such damage.

"But how—how did you—" And then he realized there was only one way the man could have disappeared from the corridor and reappeared inside the room behind Mustafa Sharif as he was opening the door. "You're an adept!"

"I have some skill," the blond man said.

"Kira . . . where's Kira?"

"I imagine she's with Al'Hassan," the blond man said. "She may be dead by now, but I think he'll keep her alive as long as he does not have these." He reached into his breast pocket and took out the pouch containing the runestones. He tossed the pouch to Wyrdrune. "Open it," he said, gesturing at Wyrdrune with the pistol.

Wyrdrune loosened the drawstring on the pouch and shook the runestones out into his hand.

"Let me see them," the blond man said. He gestured with his pistol. "Carefully," he said. "No sudden moves."

Very conscious of the pistol aimed right between his eyes, Wyrdrune slowly held his hand out, the runestones resting in his open palm.

The blond man glanced down at them very briefly, not taking his gaze off Wyrdrune for more than a second.

"A number of people have gone to great lengths to obtain those gems," he said. "I'd guess they're worth a couple of hundred thousand, but that kind of money means nothing to a man like Al'Hassan. They must be worth a great deal more to an adept who knows their use." He gestured with the pistol. "Put them back in the pouch, please."

Wyrdrune complied.

"Now put the pouch down on the bed, clasp your hands on top of your head so I can see them, and step back." Wyrdrune did as he was told, and the blond man stepped up to the bed, picked up the pouch, and replaced it in his inside jacket pocket without taking his eyes off him for a moment.

"What *is* their use?" the blond man said.

"I don't know," said Wyrdrune.

"I don't believe you."

"Look, mister, I don't know who you are——"

"I'm the man who just saved your life," the blond man said, "which is ironic, considering that I was hired to kill you. However, my client recently suffered a fatal accident, for which you should probably thank the late Mr. Sharif. That was a fortunate turn of events for you, but I've incurred considerable losses as a result of this commission, and I intend to make good on them, one way or another. You're going to help me. Now, I'm going to ask you one more time, what is the thaumaturgic purpose of these gems?"

Wyrdrune hesitated, desperately trying to think of a way out of the situation. But there was no way out that he could see. Even if he could think clearly, there was no way to cast a spell faster than the blond man could squeeze the trigger. He was a professional, and he wouldn't be distracted.

"Even if I knew, you'd only kill me if I told you," Wyrdrune said.

"I suspect you'd tell me, anyway, if I shot out your kneecaps, but I don't think that will be necessary. We're in a position to help each other. You'd like to have your lady back and come out of this in one piece, perhaps even with some money in your pocket. And I would like to make good on my losses and pay off a personal debt to Al'Hassan. The runestones can help us both achieve our respective goals. Besides, you can't afford to do without my help. You're a hopeless amateur. Alone, you haven't got a chance against a man like Al'Hassan."

"You're asking me to trust you?"

"Have you any choice?"

Someone hammered on the door. *"Police!* Open up and stand back from the door!"

"Catch," the blond man said, tossing his gun to Wyrdrune. Instinctively Wyrdrune caught it.

The door was kicked in.'

"Freeze! Drop the gun!"

The cops crouched low, their arms extended, aiming their pistols at him.

"Drop the gun, I said! *Drop it right now!*"

Wyrdrune dropped the gun on the floor and quickly raised his hands. "Don't shoot! Don't shoot!"

The blond man had disappeared. Wyrdrune stared at the cops, then his gaze traveled down to the gun on the floor and over at the body of Mustafa Sharif. He felt sick.

"Wait," he said, "it's not how it looks. I can explain—"

They grabbed him and threw him facedown on the bed.

He felt his arms wrenched up behind him, and steel bracelets snapped over his wrists.

"No, wait! You don't understand—"

"Shut your mouth!"

He was yanked brutally to his feet and turned around.

And suddenly everything went absolutely still.

The policeman who had pulled him to his feet and spun him around stood holding him by the arm with his mouth open, staring at him, frozen like a statue. A uniformed policeman stood behind him, holding a gun pointed at him, utterly motionless. Another cop, his gun also out, was frozen in the act of looking at the dead body on the floor. Several people stood outside, looking in through the open doorway. They, too, were frozen into immobility.

"I knew I could trust you to get in trouble," Merlin said.

Wyrdrune spun around to see the old mage sitting casually in an armchair with his legs crossed, smoking his pipe. He took it out of his mouth and tamped the tobacco down with his forefinger. Then he snapped his fingers, and a tiny flame seemed to shoot out of his thumb. He used it to light the pipe, puffing out a cloud of smoke that smelled like pork roasting, then he blew his thumb out.

"Boy, am I glad you see you!" said Wyrdrune.

Merlin grunted. "I imagine so. You get in over your head more often than a drunken Irishman stumbling through a peat bog. I've never seen anything like it. Turn around."

Wyrdrune turned, and Merlin gestured absently, as if shooing away a fly, and the handcuffs sprang open and fell to the floor.

"First arson, then grand theft, and now murder," Merlin said. "You seem to be piling up quite a list of accomplishments."

"I didn't shoot that man, Professor, I swear it," Wyrdrune said.

"I didn't really think you did," Merlin said, getting up out of the chair. "You're the sort who couldn't hit the broad side

of a barn if you were standing in the hayloft." He glanced
down at the dead body. "What happened here?"

"I was jumped as I was getting off the elevator," Wyrdrune said. "I don't know who he was. I never saw him before. He said he was hired to kill me. He's an adept. He's
the one who shot that man—Sharif, that's what he said his
name was. He said he worked for Sheik Al'Hassan. He—"

"Wait a moment," Merlin said. "Slow down, you're not
making any sense. First of all, let's close the door before we
attract an audience." He waved his right hand, as if in a
gesture of dismissal, and the door slammed shut.

Wyrdrune sidled past one of the motionless policemen.
He glanced uneasily at the immobile figure, standing there
like a statue. He stepped up close to him and passed his hand
in front of his face.

"You sure they can't hear us?" he said. "This one's not
even breathing. They're not dead, are they?"

"Of course not," said Merlin. "Now calm down and tell
me how you managed to get yourself into this mess."

Wyrdrune took a deep breath and told Merlin what had
happened from the moment he stepped off the elevator. "I
never even had a chance to do anything," he said as he
finished. "Things were happening so fast, I couldn't think
straight, and the blond man didn't take his eyes off me for a
second. When the police came, he threw his gun to me, and
without thinking, I caught it. Then he teleported just as they
broke down the door—"

"Leaving the police to find you with a gun in your hand
and a dead body on the floor," said Merlin.

"And he also took the runestones," Wyrdrune said.

"Did he?" Merlin said. "Check your pockets."

Wyrdrune reached into his pocket and pulled out the
leather pouch. "I might have known," he said with a wry
grimace. "What happens now?"

"Well, obviously we're going to have to leave here before

anyone else arrives. However, first we should dispose of the body and the gun. It should help confuse the issue."

He gestured, mumbling under his breath, and the body disappeared. A moment later he had also disposed of the gun and all the bloodstains.

Wyrdrune glanced uneasily at the policemen. "Shouldn't you cloud their minds or something?" he said.

"Who do you think I am, The Shadow? There are limits to what even I can do, you know. I couldn't remove their memories of what happened here without risking damage to their mental faculties. It's a highly delicate process and I haven't got the time to attempt it. Besides, it's just as well. I'll remove your name from the hotel register, and that will complete the disposal of the evidence. They'll think you did it."

"Well, thanks a lot!"

"Don't be impertinent. You haven't got a position to think of. I do. I can't be seen to be involved in this. The press would have a field day, and there is far too much at stake for me to be concerned with the media and the police. I will require all my energies to deal with Al'Hassan."

"What do you mean?" said Wyrdrune. "You were his teacher. You're much more powerful than he is."

"Perhaps," said Merlin, "but Rashid has come a long way since he was my student, and there are powerful forces working through him. It will take all my strength to counteract their influence. I must have time to concentrate my powers."

"What about Kira?"

Merlin shook his head. "I can do nothing for her now. There is much more at stake than just her welfare. Besides, I don't think that Rashid will harm her. He'll probably try to use her as bait to bring you to him with the stones. Whatever you do, you mustn't let them fall into his hands. It will be up to you to help Kira. I can spare neither the energy nor the time."

"Up to *me*? But what can *I* do against a mage? I'm only a warlock, and if he's got *you* worried—"

"Even if you succeed in doing nothing but distracting him for just a while, it will help," said Merlin. "Besides, you're not as helpless as you think. Nor is Kira, for that matter. You have the runestones."

"But I don't know how to use them!"

"It makes no difference. They will use you," said Merlin. "You're growing stronger. You've noticed it yourself. That is the runestones' doing. They came back to you. For some reason that utterly escapes me, they've chosen you and your friend, Kira. There must yet be a third component to the triangle. Perhaps that's to be my role. I don't know. The runestones will make their choice in their own time. Either way, my task has already been decided for me. My responsibility is clear. You'll have to bear your share."

"Professor, I don't even understand what you're talking about!" said Wyrdrune.

"Come here," said Merlin. He took him by the arm, mumbled quickly under his breath, and teleported them back to his home on Beacon Hill. "Now we can talk without fear of interruption," he said. "Sit down and listen carefully. Events are moving more quickly than I expected. If that man, Sharif, was able to trail you to Boston, then Rashid already must have surmised that you would try to contact me. I don't think he will move against me yet, but it's only a matter of time. Under ordinary circumstances Rashid would know better than to try to pit his powers against mine, but Rashid is not himself. He has been taken over by the Dark Ones. I wanted you to bring Kira here before anything could happen, but Rashid has been too quick for us. It's what I was afraid of. Now both of you are vulnerable, the more so because she doesn't understand what's happening to her. To both of you."

"What *is* happening to us?"

"You're changing," Merlin said. "I can't say how, for certain, but I can guess why. We're dealing with a chain of events that began during the first thaumaturgic age. I was born during its last gasp. I thought it would end with me, with the collapse of Arthur's realm, but I know now that when Avalon disappeared into the mists, it was only marking a period of transition, a change in the natural balance of the world, the end of one cycle and the beginning of another.

"Long before the change began, there was a race of beings that has left behind only the barest traces of its presence—they can be found amid the ruins of old Egypt and Mesopotamia, in the crumbling temples of the Incas and the Mayans, the stone idols of the Pacific Islands, and the carvings in the shrines of the Thugees, the cult of Kali.

"They were once worshiped as gods," Merlin continued, "but they were physical beings, much like yourself, only a different race. Among the Celts, they were called the Old Ones. They were the deities of ancient Egypt, the gods of Greece and Rome. Among some of the Arabic tribes, they were known as the Djinn. The people of old Russia romanticized them in their legends as the Bogatyrs, and the Native American tribes of the Southwest knew them as Kachina.

"Study the mythology of almost any culture and you'll find signs of them in various incarnations: warriors who seemed to be immortal but who could be killed in battle; supernatural beings in human form who could become invisible, who could mate with mortals and transform themselves into various creatures, sometimes benevolent, sometimes terrible. Vampires, werewolves, witches, spirit beings, all these legends had their genesis with them. You know the legend that I'm the offspring of an incubus. And don't shake your head, Karpinsky, I know perfectly well how you students used to joke about it. It's not as much of a joke as you may think. I *am* a half-breed, the son of a human mother and a father who was of the old race. He was among the last of their kind. Or so I had believed."

"What happened to them?" Wyrdrune said.

"There was a war," said Merlin. "It happened long before I was born. The ancients called it the Ragnarök. The Götterdämmerung. The Twilight of the Gods."

"The struggle between good and evil," Wyrdrune said. "The creation myth. Then it really happened?"

"Oh, it was real, all right, although it had little to do with creation, mythical or otherwise. It was a mage war, a battle between white magic and black. To call it a struggle between good and evil would be overly simplistic. Nature's forces are neither good nor evil. They are merely existential. Good and evil are merely expressions of differing philosophies; they do not exist in and of themselves. You see, contrary to popular belief, there is no fundamental difference between white magic and black. Both make use of the same energies; the difference is one of application. I suppose you can say it's a difference of morality, which is entirely subjective. The question of morality was at the heart of what brought the war about. In all likelihood, the issues were probably more complex than that. There are no historical records of the conflict, after all. All I know of it is what I've dredged up from the recesses of my memory, from stories my mother told me in my childhood, and from legends passed on among the Druid priests, who embellished them no end until they were obfuscated into the myths. Myths which became, in their different ethnic interpretations, the basis for the folklore of so many nations.

"According to those stories," Merlin continued, "humans were the cause of it. Remember the legend of Prometheus, the god who was punished for bringing fire to mankind? It was a parable, but like many such stories, it may well have had some basis in fact. To the Old Ones, humans were an inferior race, little more than animals. They were useful for doing work, and if the stories I heard in my childhood are to be believed, they were occasionally used for food, as well. They were also used in rituals, for life energy is one method of utilizing thaumaturgic principles. When you cast a teleportation spell, for instance, it uses up more of your life energy than a less ambitious spell would, with the result that you feel tired. It takes some time for that energy to be replenished. The more powerful the spell, the more energy it requires, which is the price of magic. But whereas white magic utilizes energy in such a way that it might be replenished, black magic utilizes it in such a way that the energy source is often totally depleted. In other words, if your energy resource is another living being—a much more potent source than something which is either vegetable or mineral —that being is destroyed.

"The symbolism of the pentagram as protection against conjured demons originated with its use as part of a warding ritual designed to protect the thaumaturge from the energy-robbing consequences of his spells. Magic, like other natural forces such as electricity and water, follows the path of least resistance. Given a 'choice' between an energy resource that's thaumaturgically grounded by a warding spell and one that is outside the warded shielding, it will consume the unshielded resource. If it does not have that so-called 'choice,' it could dissipate, but there is every chance that it will consume whatever energy resource is most readily available, which is why careless practitioners of black magic were often destroyed by their own spells, or 'demons,' even within the boundaries of their warding pentagrams.

"The Old Ones were aware of this, of course," Merlin went on. "They were the masters of thaumaturgy, much as humans are the masters of technology, which in a sense follows the same principles as thaumaturgy, merely applying them in a different way. That's why the two can be compatible, within certain limitations. Wood used as a fuel or energy resource produces heat. A nuclear power plant follows the same principles; the difference is basically a matter of degree. Think of black magic as the nuclear energy of thaumaturgy. And its fuel, as it was practiced by the Old Ones, was human lives. An easily replenishable resource. The human sacrifices of the Druids and the Aztecs, the ritual killings of the Thugs, such practices were really vestigial remnants of these thaumaturgic rites.

"But as time passed, according to the story, there arose a feeling among many of the Old Ones that it was wasteful, senseless, even cruel to use humans in such a fashion. They came to believe that the same results could be achieved through other resources or even through less wasteful application of human energy, application that did not totally deplete its energy resources and result in human death. It was, perhaps, not as expedient, but it possessed the virtues of conservation. This was the beginning of white magic, differentiated from the black by virtue of its approach and application. Of course, this meant that white magic took a bit more trouble. It's always more difficult to utilize resources in a manner that conserves them rather than to expend them greedily without any concern for conservation. And the case for immediate reward weighs heavily in the balance. There were those among the Old Ones who were unwilling to give up the power they controlled, and they used up humans by the thousands. It led to competition for the human resource. What happened to the Old Ones was, in a way, not unlike the environmental crisis brought about by humans, which led to the Collapse. Only, in their case it resulted in a war far more devastating than anything humans ever faced."

Merlin was silent for a moment, staring thoughtfully at the floor. "Perhaps it was a function of natural balance," he said finally. "Neither the Old Ones, nor humans, apparently, could accept that there was such a thing as a limit to growth. Nature knows better. Nature has its own way of imposing limits. And it displays a tendency toward draconian solutions."

"They all died?" said Wyrdrune.

"No, there were survivors," Merlin said, "although not very many. My father was one. There were more human survivors, largely because there were more humans, and the Old Ones who survived were very much outnumbered. They soon learned to conceal what they were. They hid among the humans, interbred with them—to this day, humans with so-called paranormal gifts are born who, if they had the means, could probably trace their ancestry back to one of the old race. But if they could, I suspect they'd guard the secret carefully. Some feelings run deep, remaining embedded in human racial memory—the instinctive prejudice against anyone who seems the least bit "different." Once the Old Ones became scattered and lost their power over humans, they were mercilessly hunted down. The hunt continued even after the game had long since disappeared and the reason for the hunt was no longer remembered clearly. The persecution of the Druids, the extermination of the Aztecs, the Spanish Inquisition, the Salem witch-hunts, even in modern times, there still remain groups of Fundamentalist Christians who equate worship of nature and the quest for knowledge with Satanic evil. The old fears die hard."

"But if they're all gone," said Wyrdrune, "who are the Dark Ones?"

"I thought they were a legend," Merlin said. "A legend no one remembers anymore, unless one reads Dante or Milton or fabulists like Lovecraft and Hodgeson. The tradition they all drew on goes back to a very ancient story, one that hasn't been told in its original form since I was a small boy. The Dark Ones were among the most powerful survivors of the old race, the ones who would not give up the savage, old beliefs. In a sense they lost the war, but in another sense the victors did not win, because although they could subdue the Dark Ones, they did not have enough power to destroy them.

"According to legend, the surviving archmages of the white faction devised a spell to contain the Dark Ones for all time, a spell combining the most potent symbols of their art.

And to empower the incantation, they gave their lives, imbuing their own life energies into the symbols of the spell. I always thought it was a legend, nothing more, and yet you hold three of those symbols in that little leather pouch inside your pocket. So it seems that it was not a legend, after all. There *is* such a thing as hell. Rashid has found it."

CHAPTER
Nine

Riguzzo didn't much care for traveling by train, but he liked flying even less. He hated flying. It terrified him. He had heard too many stories about pilot adepts who had dropped their planes out of the sky. It took a lot out of a pilot to lift a heavy plane and hold it up all the way to its destination, which was why pilots were all fourth-level adepts who flew no more than once a week. Their flights were kept short—a transcontinental flight required several stops and several shifts of pilots—and their salaries were very high, but they aged quickly and spent much of their time recuperating from their flights. And even the best of them could drop a plane. Once he had almost been dropped himself. Cleary had given up trying to argue him into taking the shuttle flight to Boston and had resigned himself to making the trip by train. At least if something went wrong with the impulsion spells cast by the engineer adept, all the train would do was stop. Even so, Riguzzo had been a surly companion for the duration of the trip. Riguzzo didn't like to travel. What Riguzzo liked to do was walk. He did not trust magic users.

Even when they had to take a squad car to go out on a

call, Riguzzo felt uneasy. It didn't help that the department called the cops who drove the cars the "flying squad." They wore embroidered patches on their shoulders that matched the insignia painted on the squad-car doors—a rolling wheel with wings sprouting from it. The officers on the flying squad were low-level adepts as well as cops, but they were recruited from among the top ten percent of those passing their first-level adept exams. A good many of them were graduate students, going to school part-time in pursuit of more advanced certification, so they were very careful. They rarely got into any accidents. Most of them were not interested in the police force as a career; the salary was too low and there was no status associated with the job. Besides, the department insisted on such mundane things as haircuts and uniforms—or at least conservative civilian clothing for the detectives. It frowned on flowing robes and amulets and shoulder-length hair. Riguzzo had heard that there were cops who were magicians, but he had never met any.

Crimes involving magic use were generally handled by the ITC's investigative branch, a sort of international police force, but Riguzzo did not feel that was the way to go. The ITC was big, and getting bigger every day, keeping files on all certified adepts, but as magic use proliferated, the functions of the ITC became more and more diverse and the bureaucracy became more and more unwieldy. It was inevitable that sooner or later the ITC would have to restrict its investigation of crimes involving magic use to the more serious offenses, or to offenses that involved more than just one local jurisdiction, leaving the rest to the police. And the average cop was ill equipped to deal with an adept. Fortunately, so far there hadn't been any really serious crimes committed by adepts, at least no serious crimes in the way Riguzzo thought of them. There were the occasional thefts and larcenies, but the more ambitious crimes involving magic use occurred mainly on the corporate level. Thaumaturgic crime seemed to attract a better class of criminal. Riguzzo shuddered to think what would happen if they were ever faced with a serial killer who was an adept. He could not imagine a worse nightmare.

Sooner or later things would have to change. The police would have to modernize and start to recruit more adepts, attracting them with competitive salaries and benefits, and that would probably spell the end for ordinary street cops like himself. He was glad he'd be retired long before that happened. His retirement was not far off.

On the train trip up from New York City, after Cleary had grown tired of trying to make conversation with a partner who would only grunt in reply, Riguzzo had given a great deal of thought to how he could keep the ITC out of his case. He could not think of anything to stall them off with any longer. More than just one jurisdiction was involved now, and apparently what had happened in Boston left no doubt that the perpetrators were adepts. He had thought that there might be no real evidence that the Boston incident had been connected to his case, but as he sat with Cleary in the office of the captain of the Back Bay precinct, he watched his chances of retaining control over the case receding rapidly.

"These are the two officers who responded to the call," said Captain McGarry, indicating two uniformed policemen whom he had summoned to his office. "Sergeant Benson and Officer O'Dwyer. Lieutenant Riguzzo and Sergeant Cleary have just come up from New York."

They shook hands.

"Benson," said McGarry, "why don't you fill these gentlemen in on what went down at the Copley?"

"Sure thing," said Benson. "We responded to a report from hotel security at the Copley Plaza. Seems a maid was making up a room when she heard something funny and stuck her head out in the hall. She saw three holes in the wall that hadn't been there a couple of minutes earlier, and three holes in the door of the room immediately next door, directly opposite the three holes in the wall. She heard

voices next door and called security on the room phone.
Security at that hotel is sharp. They told her to stay put and
immediately called it in instead of barging in themselves and
taking a chance on bungling it. Not that we did much better," he added wryly.

"Hotel security did it right by the book," said Officer
O'Dwyer. "They made the call, sent a couple of people up to
cover the elevator entrance and the stairway exits on that
floor, and then they didn't make a move until we got there."

"We were cruising only about a block away when the call
came in," said Benson, "so we took it. We got there,
couldn't have been more than a few minutes after those shots
were fired. Whoever fired the shots was still inside. We went
in, with a couple of the hotel security people serving as
backup, and caught the suspect with the gun still in his hand
and a dead body on the floor. Blood all over the place. The
victim was an elderly male, shot three times in the back with
a 10-mm semiautomatic pistol. He was apparently on his
way to the door when he was shot from behind. There were
bloodstains on the inside of the door and on the carpet,
where the victim either crawled or was dragged away from
the door. We were unable to establish the identity of the
victim, because one moment I was slapping the cuffs on the
perpetrator, and the next I was staring at an empty room. No
perpetrator, no body, no blood. Even the gun was gone.
Everything had just vanished suddenly. There were hotel security people covering the stairway exits and the elevator to
make sure nobody came blundering into the scene while we
were making the arrest, and it wasn't until we checked with
them that we realized we had lost about three or four minutes. What's more, nobody came past them, either. The perpetrator must have hit us with a spell and teleported out. No
question about it, he was an adept."

"What makes you think he's the suspect we've been looking for?" Riguzzo said, glancing at McGarry. McGarry
passed it to Benson with a glance.

"We questioned the hotel employees," said Benson. "Nobody seemed to know anything about the victim. Nobody remembered even seeing him, but the perpetrator matched the description of the man the room was registered to. The man had checked in with a young woman. They registered as Mr. and Mrs. M. Karpinsky. We used an identigraph to create composite graphics of the suspects."

He opened a file folder he was holding and removed a printout, passing it to the two New York detectives. Riguzzo's heart sank. It was an almost perfect match of the composite drawing of the girl named Kira.

"Mrs. Karpinsky," Benson said unnecessarily. "Something about the face struck me as being familiar. I knew I'd seen it recently, so I checked it out against the recent bulletins back at the precinct, and sure enough, it matches with the sketch that we received over the zip-squeal from you people. The update correction that identified the suspect as a female, instead of a young male as originally reported, was what made it stick in my mind. Now here's what we came up with on the male suspect."

He removed another printout from the file folder. "Mr. Karpinsky," Benson said, "young male; late twenties to early thirties; long, curly blond hair; blue eyes; dimple in his chin. No match with your other suspect, but knowing that your suspect was an adept, as was the perpetrator, I had an idea, so I had another identigraph composite made. We took the same basic composite you have there and didn't change a thing about the facial features except to add some wrinkles here and there, a bigger nose, longer white hair . . ."

He handed the third printout to Riguzzo. ". . . and bingo," he said, "he was wearing a disguise when he pulled that job at Christie's. Seems like we've got your people here in Boston, Lieutenant."

With a feeling of resignation Riguzzo passed the printouts to Cleary. "Excellent work, Sergeant Benson," he said. He turned to McGarry. "Your people are very thorough."

McGarry smiled. "Wait. There's more." He glanced at Benson.

"Considering the perpetrator's age," said Benson, "the fact that he is an adept, and his presence in Boston, I thought it might be possible that Boston is his home base. After all, if he lifted the jewels in New York, it doesn't necessarily follow that he would come to Boston to dispose of them. With all due respect, your market for that sort of thing is a lot better than ours. His age suggested that it couldn't have been too long since he had been to school, and we have the finest thaumaturgic college in the country right here in Cambridge. So I tackled the student records at the local college while O'Dwyer ran a check for priors based on the composites. And we both came up with the same name."

He opened the file folder again and handed Riguzzo a photograph and an arrest report.

"Melvin A. Karpinsky, arrested four years ago on a charge of arson, reduced to reckless endangerment and subsequently dismissed. He actually used his real name to register at the hotel, believe it or not. He was arrested in connection with a fire at a concert. Apparently he was providing some magical special effects for the band, and one of his spells went out of control. The band was technically responsible, both since they had posted a bond against the eventuality of damage to the hall and because they had hired an uncertified adept to provide public entertainment, so rather than face a lengthy suit, the promoters settled with the concert-hall owners, and since an investigation determined that the fire was accidental, the charges against Karpinsky were dropped. He was, however, expelled from school as a result . . ."

He reached into the folder again and handed Riguzzo a copy of Wyrdrune's academic transcript.

". . . so technically he's not really an adept, since he never completed his coursework or stood for certification. His records indicate that he would be at the advanced graduate student level, which would make him—"

"A warlock," Cleary said, glancing at Riguzzo. "Pony said that the girl called him warlock."

Riguzzo rubbed his chin and nodded. "Looks like you guys have saved us a lot of legwork on this case," he said.

"I'm afraid it's not really your case anymore, Lieutenant," said McGarry. "I know how you feel. I imagine you'd like to hang on to this one. Frankly, so would I, but it's out of our hands. The ITC's got clear jurisdiction in this one. I had to call them in." Seeing the expression on Riguzzo's face, he added, "I'm sorry."

"No, you did what you had to do," said Riguzzo. He suddenly thought of his grandfather. Old Frank Riguzzo had also been on the police force, back during the Collapse. He had died at the age of ninety-seven, when Dominic was twelve years old. He was in a wheelchair, and his hands used to shake so badly, he sometimes needed help with eating, but he had been remarkably lucid right up to the end, when he had apparently fallen asleep in the middle of a Sunday spaghetti dinner. His head had fallen on his chest and he had started snoring, but the snoring had turned into a horrifying rattling sound, and before anyone could do anything, he'd died, right there at the dinner table. One moment he had been carrying on in his gruff manner about the old days, the next he was just dead.

He used to love to talk about the old days when he was on the force. It was all he ever talked about, an old man telling war stories, and nobody in the family ever used to listen to him except Dominic, who found the stories fascinating, even though he'd heard them all dozens of times. It got so he would ask for them by name.

"Poppi, tell about the subway fight," he'd say, and old Frank Riguzzo would launch into a gravel-voiced account of a firefight he'd been in with a gang of vicious derelicts down in the dark subway tunnels beneath the streets of the Lower East Side.

Cops weren't so much cops as they were soldiers then, the

last line of defense for the civilians trying to survive in a city gone berserk. They might as well have been in the army, only the army had far more important things to do, such as trying to put down small guerrilla wars in upstate New York or engaging mutinous National Guard battalions who had taken over towns out on Long Island. Dominic used to try to imagine what it must have been like during the Collapse, when everything just stopped and the world went crazy. Poppi had been a little crazy too.

Poppi had been there when it changed, when magic came back into the world. At first, said Poppi, they just heard the stories. It began in Europe first, then, very slowly, it had spread, but even so, it was a shock. The government was just trying to hold on—"like pissing in the wind," Poppi used to say—and then one day it suddenly had something to hold on with.

"He came to Washington with a delegation of apprentices," Poppi had said, recalling Merlin's arrival in America. "It seemed like he was everywhere, organizing and getting things under control, and Lord help anybody who gave him any grief. Anyone got in his way, why, he just killed 'em, magicked em' away, and never even broke a sweat."

Poppi always spoke about it with a kind of awe, as if he never really could believe it. He never learned to trust it, either, which was perhaps where Riguzzo got his bias. Magic scared his grandfather. He had seen what it could really do. But people had adapted. It seemed people could adapt to anything. In a remarkably short time, the world had changed, though in some ways it had not changed very much at all. Things didn't really look all that different from the way they looked in the old pre-Collapse tapes Riguzzo had seen in history class when he was still in school. The city still looked pretty much the same as it had in the old tapes; though it still showed signs of the violence during the Collapse, these were quickly disappearing. There wasn't nearly as much vehicular traffic and there were more bicycles than before, people dressed very differently and the city was much cleaner and greener; but at first glance there was not a great deal of difference. Thaumaturgy had simply become a part of everyday life. Looking back on the Collapse from an historical perspective, it simply seemed as if the world had gone into a brief spasm when everything went haywire, not unlike the energy blackouts that had taken place with greater and greater frequency in the years just prior to the Collapse, and then everything went back to normal. Only it wasn't the same. It would never be the same again.

They were sitting there talking about some kid who took a few college courses and learned how to cast some magic spells, Riguzzo thought, and now some bureaucrat from ITC was going to come in and take over the case, a bureaucrat who just happened to be a sorcerer, and they were going to go back to New York to resume investigating burglaries and muggings. Just routine. Cleary saw nothing unusual about it, McGarry didn't, Benson and O'Dwyer seemed to take it right in stride, and yet, even though he had grown up in a world where magic was alive, Riguzzo still somehow saw it partly through the eyes of his old grandfather, dead these many years. He tried to picture Poppi as young Frank Riguzzo, a tough, street-combat-hardened cop, sitting in his flak vest in the old, bombed-out squad room down in Manhattan South, and wondered what Poppi would have said if the door had opened and a long-haired man wearing robes and amulets had suddenly walked in, looking like some prophet from the Bible, and announced that he was taking over.

Why does it get to me like this? Riguzzo thought. *Why can't I just accept it?* It was as if, somehow, as a result of all those endless hours spent listening to his grandfather, Poppi had forged an imperishable link between the very different worlds in which they had grown up. In his own way, Poppi must have been a wizard too. He had made his experiences so vivid and alive that they had become Riguzzo's own experiences, as if he himself had lived them. And Poppi's world seemed somehow more real to Riguzzo than his own, as if that world were the real world and his was just a dream.

"Lieutenant?" said McGarry, and Riguzzo realized he had been off somewhere. "Anything wrong?" McGarry said.

Riguzzo shook his head. "Sorry," he said. He grimaced. "Must be getting old. I drifted off there for a minute."

"What were you thinking about?" McGarry said. "For a minute there, you looked as if somebody'd just died."

Riguzzo snorted and compressed his lips into a tight grimace. "Yeah. We did."

"How's that?" said McGarry, frowning.

"I was just thinking," he said. "We're on the way out, you know. Cops like us. It's changing. I sometimes get the feeling like I'm an old cowboy on a trail drive, watching the railroad coming in."

McGarry's frown grew even deeper. "I don't understand."

"Never mind," Riguzzo said. "It was just a figure of speech. It's not important. Anyway, it seems we could've saved ourselves a trip if the ITC's going to take over the case."

"Only the ITC insisted that we get you up here," said McGarry. "Special Agent Morgan wanted to coordinate with you personally."

"Figures," Cleary said. "They couldn't be bothered to have someone in their New York office take a file dump and forward it. No, we've got to haul our asses all the way up here just to give some jerk a briefing, as if we didn't have anything else to do."

Someone cleared her throat. They looked up to see an attractive, young, dark-haired woman dressed in a well-tailored business suit and open-necked white shirt standing in the open doorway. McGarry raised his eyebrows.

"Excuse me," he said, annoyed that someone should simply open the door of his office and walk in unannounced. "Can I help you?"

"Yes, I'm the jerk," she said, holding up an open leather wallet containing her badge and her ID. "Special Agent Faye Morgan."

Cleary flushed. "Ooops," he said uncomfortably. "Nothing personal. It's been a long day."

"It's getting longer," she said, with a sidelong glance at him as she put away her badge. "Is it possible to get a cup of coffee around here?"

"I'll get it," O'Dwyer volunteered. "Anybody else?"

"I could do with some," Riguzzo said.

"Make it three," said Cleary.

"Captain?" said O'Dwyer.

"Sure, why not?" McGarry said. He quickly performed the introductions.

O'Dwyer left to get the coffees. Speical Agent Morgan looked around for a spare chair and didn't see one. Riguzzo started to get up to offer his, but she shook her head and made an impatient gesture with her hand, beckoning him back down. "No, no, sit," she said. "I'll just grab a corner of the desk here—that's if you don't mind, Captain McGarry?"

"Not at all," McGarry said, clearing away some papers to make room. She perched on the edge of his desk and crossed her legs. She had extremely nice legs, Riguzzo noticed. She did not look like a sorceress. He thought she looked more like a business executive, very crisp in her manner, cool, professional. A no-nonsense type. She noticed Riguzzo looking her over and raised her eyebrows.

"Did you expect me to come riding in on a broom, Lieutenant?"

"I guess I expected someone who looked more like a sorcerer," said Riguzzo. "And I figured an ITC investigator would be older."

"Does my being a woman pose a problem for you?"

"No."

"I find that I am much more effective if I do not advertise

the fact that I am an ITC investigator," she said. "Much like a plainclothes policeman. As for my age, I'm older than I look. And I'm good at my job."

"I'm sure you are," Riguzzo said, feeling slightly foolish.

"As for the reason why I had you 'haul your asses up here,' instead of merely having the New York office pick up your case file, I could easily have done that, but it would have been counterproductive. I did, in fact, have the New York branch forward your files while you were en route, but you've put in a considerable amount of time on this case, and I'm sure you could contribute a great deal more to it than just your notes. I'd like to work together with you on this, and unless you have any objections, I will arrange to have both of you placed on loan to the ITC for the duration. After all, it's your case, and I imagine you'd like to see it through."

Riguzzo was surprised by the unexpected and, as far as he knew, unprecedented request. "I'd like that very much," he said.

"Good, then it's settled. Now I'd appreciate it if you'd brief me on this case. I've had a chance to look over your reports, but I'd like to hear it from you."

O'Dwyer came back with a tray of coffee cups, a jar of creamer, and some packets of sugar. As they drank their coffee, Riguzzo brought her up to date. She sipped her coffee and listened without interrupting, taking no notes, but Riguzzo had the impression that she would not forget the smallest detail. When he was finished, she pursed her lips and sat silent for a moment, thinking.

"You think the deaths of the fences named Fats and Porfirio Rozetti are related, of course?"

Riguzzo nodded. "Yes, I do, but I don't have anything to back it up."

"And the fire at the penthouse on Fifth Avenue as well?"

"I don't know about that one, but I have a feeling."

She nodded. "I'm inclined to trust your intuition. You say

you weren't able to come up with anything at all on the tenant, John Roderick?"

"Only enough to tell me that John Roderick was an alias," said Riguzzo. "Beyond that, a couple of petty-cash accounts, some tax records, a post office box, that's really about it. He's simply disappeared, and we haven't got the faintest notion who he really was. We're pretty sure that he was *not* an art appraiser, unless he was doing a land-office business in rare paintings or something on the side."

"What he does on the side is kill people, Lieutenant," she said.

Riguzzo and Cleary both stared at her.

"The ITC's been after him for several years," she said, "but we don't know much more about him than you do. He's the worst kind of rogue adept. An anonymous one. We don't know how he came by his knowledge. Unauthorized instruction in the thaumaturgic arts is a felony crime, and one of the reasons we'd like to catch him so badly is so we can find out who taught him what he knows. Another reason is that he's highly dangerous. He's killed at least fifteen people that we know of, and there's no way of telling how many other homicides he may have been responsible for. He's known only by the magename, Morpheus."

"Morpheus?" said Cleary.

"The God of Dreams," said Speical Agent Morgan, with a slight grimace. "He puts people to sleep. Our data banks are programmed to red-flag every unexplained occurrence that might be of thaumaturgic origin until they can be checked out. The moment the New York City Fire Department determined that your penthouse fire was thaumaturgic arson, it showed up in our files. I had our New York office look into it. They confirmed that the fire originated thaumaturgically, and they were also able to recover the remains of some highly sophisticated electronic equipment that had been severely damaged in the fire. The equipment was destroyed, of course, but they were able to pick up the trace emanations of what must have been a fortune in thaumaturgically etched and animated microprocessors. The trace emanations were very strong. They were able to reconstitute enough of the signature to determine that what they were looking at were the remains of Apollonius."

"Apollonius?" said Cleary.

"A sentient hyperdimensional matrix computer assembled by Yamako Industries and programmed by General Hyperdynamics in Colorado Springs. It was hijacked while en route to Langley. That was five years ago. Since then we've compiled a record of over two hundred break-ins at various top-security data bases possessing state-of-the-art safeguard systems. The break-ins were detected, but the safeguard systems were unable to lock on to the intruder and trace the signal. In other words, they were aware that their data was being picked clean, but there was nothing they could do about it. All of which suggests that there must have been hundreds, perhaps thousands, more break-ins among various data bases possessing less sophisticated safeguard systems that went undetected. In all the known cases, the same signature trace emanations kept appearing each time, almost as if Apollonius were showing off, arrogantly leaving a sort of calling card. It wasn't until we were two years into the investigation that we were able to establish a connection between Apollonius and Morpheus. It became obvious that Morpheus was getting access to certain information that only could have come from data raided by Apollonius. It took a while for us to establish that pattern, but it was unquestionably there. So either Morpheus was buying pirated data from whoever had stolen Apollonius, or he had Apollonius itself. It now appears that the latter was the case."

"How do you know that the man calling himself John Roderick was Morpheus?" Riguzzo said.

"I don't know for certain," she said, "but like you, I'm making some educated guesses. For one thing, the description you have of the man who called himself John Roderick doesn't give either of us a great deal to go on, but it does match the descriptions that we have of Morpheus from several sources."

"That's not much," said Cleary. "The same description could fit hundreds of different people."

"True," she said, "but hundreds of different people don't own million-dollar penthouses with top-secret hyperdimensional matrix computers in them. And the fact that Morpheus has been able to avoid capture for so long suggests that he was doing much more than simply buying information from someone who was using Apollonius. It suggests that he was using Apollonius himself to stay ahead of us. He even tried to break into our own data base."

"This all sounds like pretty high-level stuff," said Cleary, frowning. "How does a character like this Morpheus fit into our snatch-and-grab case?"

Riguzzo almost smiled. That innocent face and manner of Cleary's. That slightly stupid look of puzzlement was the most powerful weapon in the young detective's arsenal. It threw people off-guard, and they said things they never would have said to someone who seemed sharp and on top of things. He saw at once what his partner was trying to do. He was trying to get the ITC investigator to admit the possibility that it was much more than just another snatch-and-grab case, something they all knew already, but something that no one had yet come out and actually *said*, and he was trying to see if she would go so far as to admit the possibility that someone with great resources could be involved, someone wealthy enough to hire someone like this Morpheus. Someone like Sheik Al'Hassan.

But Special Agent Morgan wasn't going to play. She looked Cleary right in the eye and said, "We all know what's happening here, don't we? This may have started out as a simple snatch-and-grab case, but it's long since gone beyond that. You know who clearly has an interest in this. I know who clearly has an interest in this. But you're not so much

concerned about that right now as you are concerned about
whether or not there is a conflict of interest in *my* case. Isn't
that right?"

"I'm not sure what you mean," said Cleary, still looking
faintly stupid.

She smiled. "Then I'll spell it out for you, Sergeant, for
the record and in front of witnesses, right, Captain
McGarry?"

McGarry grunted, not quite sure what the conversation
was about all of a sudden.

"For the record," Morgan said, "I want two things out of
this case: I want to be able to close the books on it, and I
want Morpheus. When and if the runestones are recovered,
you can have them as evidence in your case. I have no
vested interest there. When the two perpetrators are apprehended, you can have them too."

"Wait a minute," said McGarry, "what about our murder?"

"You have a body?" she said, looking at him with an
arched eyebrow. "You have a murder weapon?"

"Well, no, but—"

"Then it seems to me that you don't have a case," she
said.

"Wait a minute," Benson said. "We *saw* the body! I saw
Karpinsky with the murder weapon in his hand! He hit us
with a spell and made them disappear! I could testify to that,
and hotel security could testify that we had lost—"

"And all this theoretical testimony would accomplish in a
grand jury would be the removal of the case from your jurisdiction," Morgan said. "Gentlemen, it's an ITC case, no
matter how you look at it, and I know that none of you are
very happy about that, but that's the way it is. Unless Karpinsky were to confess, you'd probably never get him on a
murder charge. We can get him on the snatch-and-grab, we
can probably get him on conspiracy, we can get him on several counts of violation of the International Thaumaturgical
Convention Covenants, but unless you had more concrete

evidence, he'd wind up walking on that murder charge. Assuming that he *was* the killer."

"What do you mean, *assuming*?" said McGarry. "Benson saw him standing over the body with the murder weapon in his hand!"

"Yes, but did Benson actually see him fire the murder weapon at the victim?" she said. "Doesn't it strike you that there's something incongruous about all this? If Karpinsky was able to dispose of the murder victim's body thaumaturgically, why did he even need to bother with a gun? If he could do that, why not just murder the victim through the use of magic? For that matter, if he could do that, why not dispose of you as well?" she said, looking directly at Benson and O'Dwyer, who stood like specters at a wedding, like little boys standing in the mist of a discussion among adults and not quite sure whether they should participate or not or whether they even belonged there.

"You say he hit you with a spell. Well, if he was able to do that, why didn't he finish the job? Why didn't he simply get rid of the only witnesses who could testify against him? If he was able to think it all out so completely as to remember to magically erase his name from the hotel register —and if the desk clerk hadn't remembered the name as a result of an unfavorable impression he'd had of the girl, we might not even have that—then why didn't he get rid of everyone who saw him?"

"Well," said McGarry hesitantly, feeling a need to come to the defense of his men, yet realizing with a certain degree of discomfort that the ITC agent was making some damn good points, "as I understand it, magic exacts a certain price in energy, isn't that right? Maybe that's why. Maybe he just didn't have the energy to do it. I mean, couldn't that be the explanation? Maybe that's why he used a gun instead of committing the murder magically, to save his energy?"

"Maybe," Morgan said. "It's certainly a possibility, but does it seem very likely to you that someone who's just committed murder and been caught standing over the body with the murder weapon in his hand would worry very much about being tired from expending too much energy? Seems to me he'd worry a lot more about leaving any witnesses around. He'd get rid of them, and then he'd have all the time in the world to quit the scene and go somewhere to recuperate."

McGarry grunted and nodded, grudgingly conceding the point.

"Besides," Morgan continued, "hasn't it occurred to anyone that what we're talking about here involves some rather advanced thaumaturgical skill? We're not talking about something as simple as levitation and impulsion spells to drive a cab—we're talking about spells that would require the abilities of a fourth-level adept at the very least, and even that would be stretching it considerably. This kid's only a warlock. He's not even a first-level adept! You don't get that kind of advanced knowledge from any home-study course, gentlemen. If Karpinsky's only a warlock, then how is it that he's managing to cast spells as if he were a full-fledged wizard?"

No one had a ready answer to that.

"What do you propose?" Riguzzo said after a brief silence.

"First of all, I propose to find out why they came to Boston," she said. "I don't think they're local. They stole the runestones in New York, they tried to fence them in New York. Now all of a sudden they show up here. Why? What connection do they have to Boston?"

"Karpinsky went to school here," Cleary said. "Maybe he's got contacts. Somebody he could hide out with until the heat's gone down."

"Then why check into a hotel?"

Cleary shrugged. "Maybe he wasn't sure of the contact? Maybe he needed to make a few calls?"

"Congratulations," she said wryly. "At least somebody's

thinking around here. Did anybody think to check on any calls that might have been made from that hotel room?"

McGarry looked sheepish. She picked up the phone and handed it to him. Feeling profoundly embarrassed, McGarry started to dial.

CHAPTER
Ten

Rashid knew the exact moment that Mustafa ceased to live. Kira lay helpless on the bed beneath him, thrashing and straining against the invisible force which held her, her arms spread out, immobile, as if nailed down, her legs spread as if bound by unseen ropes. Rashid bent over her on the bed, smiling as he watched her struggle. The expression on his face was almost tender.

The opulently furnished bedroom was a shambles. She had been dragged there, kicking and screaming, by two huge shaven-headed men as large as bulls, who had held her as easily as if she were a child. They had shoved her into the room and locked the door behind her. She had fallen face-down on the carpet, weeping with rage and frustration, and in a fury she had destroyed the room, tearing down the tapestries, smashing the mirrors with a chair, demolishing everything in sight and then hurling the chair through the bedroom window. It had fallen with a shower of glass to a courtyard four stories below, frightening a group of women who were sunbathing around a swimming pool that had a fountain in it. They looked up at the broken window where she stood, shouting down at them, screaming at them to help her, but none of them made a move. And then she heard the door opening behind her and she spun around as Rashid entered, dressed in a black satin gown, soft embroidered slippers on his feet.

She wrenched a piece of broken glass out of the window frame and brandished it before her, snarling at him. "You try to lay one hand on me, you son of a bitch, and I'll shove this right down your throat!"

Rashid seemed unconcerned about the damage to the room. He merely glanced around and said, "If I had known that you were going to be so abusive of my hospitality, I would have had the breakables removed."

She lunged at him, hoping to catch him off-guard, but he merely swept his arm out, and before she got to within five feet of him, she went flying back to land upon the bed. He made a gesture at her, palm down, as if pressing her down upon the bed, and she discovered that she couldn't move. She raised her head up off the bed, but she could go no farther; something was pinning her arms and legs down, holding her fast in an unbreakable grip.

"Let me go, damn you!"

He came up to the bed and stood at the foot of it, looking down at her as she struggled against the unseen force that held her. "You have an extraordinary tendency toward violence," he said in a mocking tone. "It seems to be your first response to any threatening situation. Has it ever occurred to you that such energies could easily be turned against you?"

"You go to hell," she said, staring up at him with defiance in her eyes. "I grew up on the streets. If you think rape is going to intimidate me—"

"Rape?" Rashid said, as if the idea amused him. He came around the side of the bed and sat down beside her. "Do you really think that I would need to resort to something as mundane as rape? There is much about you that I find attractive, but rape is not a function of sexual desire. It is a function of control, an assault upon a woman's most intimate self, born of inadequacy and a need to dominate. And I neither suffer from inadequacy, nor do I have to resort to rape to dominate you."

He bent over her, placing one arm on either side of her, bringing his face close to hers.

"I could stop your heart from beating with a gesture," he said softly. "Or I could speak a word and it would leap out of your chest, still beating, while I held it in my hand and watched you die."

And in that moment, as he bent over her, three bullets slammed into Mustafa Sharif, tearing their way through his body, shredding organs, and pulverizing bone.

Rashid jerked as if struck and clutched at his heart, gasping. The force that held Kira to the bed suddenly disappeared, and she sat up quickly, lashing out at him, clawing at his face. He saw the move, but he wasn't quick enough to avoid her, and only by twisting his face aside at the last second did he avoid losing his eyes. Her fingernails left bloody tracks on his right cheek, just below his eye, and he struck out at her, catching her backhanded across the face and knocking her down onto the bed again.

He caught her wrists and held her down while she struggled against him, both of them breathing hard as they wrestled on the bed. The jewel set in Rashid's forehead began to glow.

"No!" Kira shouted.

The beam lanced out from the jewel and struck her in the forehead. She screamed, arching on the bed, thrashing like a fish out of water as he held her down.

The blood trickled down his face as Rashid stared down at her, teeth bared. "So," he said, breathing hard, "it seems that your young warlock has prevailed over Mustafa, damn him for a bungling fool. Well, it is only the first move in the game."

His eyes burned into hers as she writhed on the bed,

bathed in the burning aura of the beam, her mouth open in a soundless scream. The pain was worse than anything that she had ever known.

"You feared something so trivial as rape," Rashid said. "As if I needed merely to possess your body when I could have your soul!"

His features swam before her, seeming to become transparent. His face appeared to shimmer like a ghostly mirage as it came closer, floating down toward her. The burning pain was suddenly replaced by a mind-numbing cold; freezing tendrils seemed to entwine themselves around her body, penetrating her.

"The violence in your nature is what will bind you to me," said Rashid, his voice echoing inside her mind. "Your baser instincts will form a bridge between your soul and mine. The harder you struggle, the more completely I will possess you."

She felt his presence in her mind like crystals of ice, chilling her and slowly melting, seeping through every fiber of her being and washing out her will, suffusing her with a pleasant warmth that slowly grew into the heat of passion.

It was as if she were floating somewhere between consciousness of her body and awareness of her astral state, and as she felt him pressing down against her, her arms involuntarily went around him and brought him closer. She felt his lips on hers, and she opened her mouth, receiving his tongue, feeling it touch hers. She wrapped her legs around him, unable to control herself, overcome by a fierce, animal desire to feel his flesh against hers, to have him deep inside her. She felt tears flowing down her cheeks. Rashid kissed them away and she lost herself.

"Concentrate," said Merlin, his finger placed over a line in a large, leather-bound book lying open before him on a lectern. Wyrdrune stood in the center of a pentagram drawn on the floor of Merlin's basement. The basement was dark and damp, unfinished, with heating and plumbing pipes exposed to view, running just beneath the ceiling. He could hear the gentle hum of the water heater. All around him were old chests and wooden crates covered with cobwebs, stacked high, pushed to the side and cleared out of the way. The small basement windows had been painted over, so that no light penetrated. The only light came from candles, two of them placed on the lectern by the book Merlin studied, five others in brass candle holders placed around the pentagram, one at each point. Wyrdrune licked his lips nervously. He was sweating. He shifted his weight from one foot to the other.

"What if something goes wrong?" he said.

Merlin's face looked gaunt and drawn in the candlelight. "Don't think of something going wrong," he said, knitting his heavy eyebrows. "You insisted on this. I'll do my part, though it's against my better judgment. You must do yours. Remember, we only have one chance. Rashid will not be taken by surprise a second time."

"How can you be sure you'll find her?" Wyrdrune said.

"I can't be sure," said Merlin. "I'm counting on the spiritual link that the runestones have forged between you. It is they who will guide you through the ether, not me. I can only send you on the journey. It will be up to you to return safely. You must act quickly. If Rashid is present, he will not hesitate for long. We can count on at most a second or two of surprise to give you time to act. If you fail, I won't be able to help you. We will have lost the element of surprise, and Rashid will know I was behind this. I only hope that I've made the right decision. You remember the words that will complete the transference spell?"

Wyrdrune nodded.

"Place the stones down at your feet," said Merlin.

Wyrdrune reached into his pocket and took out the small leather pouch containing the runestones. He placed them at his feet inside the pentagram.

"Are you ready?" Merlin said.

Wyrdrune swallowed hard and nodded.

"Remember, you will only have a moment. Do not hesitate for even one instant."

"Believe me, I won't," said Wyrdrune. He took a deep breath. "All right. Ready when you are, Professor."

Merlin looked down at the book open before him, one finger tracing out the words of the ancient spell as he began to speak it in a long-dead guttural tongue. His left hand was raised at his side, elbow bent at a right angle, forefinger and little finger extended, the other fingers bent, touching the palm, thumb placed across them. His voice sounded hollow in the dark basement. As he spoke, the candles began to gutter. Wyrdrune felt the beginnings of a cold breeze. His knees felt weak.

The breeze grew stronger as Merlin spoke the ancient spell, growing into a wind that circled around and around inside the pentagram, plucking at his clothes, taking on form and color, a whirlwind of bright cobalt blue that seemed to flame as it spun around him, increasing in force and substance. The candles placed at the five points of the pentagram were snuffed, their flames seeming to be drawn into the funnel, igniting it as it coalesced around him, moving closer to him, enclosing him in a cocoon of swirling blue flame.

Merlin's voice rose in pitch as he concluded the spell, and as he read the last word, he shouted it in a hoarse scream, extending his left hand fully, forefinger and little finger pointing, and a bright red spark seemed to leap up off the page. It traveled up his right hand, coursing through his body and wreathing it in a red aura, making his beard bristle and his white hair stand on end. It traveled along his outstretched left arm, bridged the gap between his extended fingers, and flashed from his hand, leaping across the distance between them, a bright red bolt of pure thaumaturgic energy lancing out across the darkened basement toward the

weirdly glowing funnel of blue flame that enclosed Wyrdrune, almost hiding him from sight. It struck the funnel and
was caught in its circular momentum, drawn into the maelstrom. It veined the swirling blue funnel with streaks of
crimson fire, and the sound of it was deafening as it spun
around faster and faster, its hue changing to a vivid purple as
it started to rise up off the floor like a tornado taking off. It
seemed to collapse in upon itself, and there was a bright
flash of orange lightning, accompanied by a clap of thunder
that blew out the black-painted glass of the basement windows. Wyrdrune was gone.

The borders of the pentagram had been blackened by the
heat, and lying within them, naked and huddled on the floor,
was Kira, her face buried in her arms. It was quiet in the
basement, save for the sounds of Kira weeping.

She raised her head suddenly with a jerk, gasped, and
looked around, not knowing where she was. Merlin hurried
toward her.

"Where am I?" she said in a frightened voice. *"Who are
you?"*

"You're safe," said Merlin, breathing hard and holding his
hand out to her. "Get up quickly. Get up and get beyond the
borders of the pentagram now, *at once!"*

Still dazed, she pushed herself up to her knees, looking all
around her. "What happened? Where am I?"

Merlin grabbed her by the arm and yanked her to her feet.
"Hurry," he said, pulling her along.

She stumbled, still disoriented, as he dragged her out
beyond the borders of the pentagram.

Wyrdrune's vision cleared, and he found himself lying on
a torn-up bed in a room that looked as if a war had been
fought in it. A man wearing a black satin dressing gown
stood with his back to him, pouring wine out of a decanter
into a crystal goblet. At the moment of Wyrdrune's appearance he spun around, and at the sight of him, he dropped the

goblet. It fell to the floor and shattered, staining the carpet with wine.

Wyrdrune closed his eyes and quickly spoke the words that would complete the transference spell. There was the sucking sound of air being drawn into a vacuum, and he disappeared, leaving a singed outline of himself imprinted on the bed sheets. An instant later he reappeared in Merlin's basement, within the borders of the pentagram. He collapsed to his knees, holding himself and hacking with dry heaves.

"*Get out!*" shouted Merlin. "Get out of there!"

Wyrdrune started to stagger out of the pentagram, but Merlin shouted once again, "*The runestones!* Take them, *quickly!*"

Wyrdrune turned, bent down and picked up the pouch, then lurched toward the borders of the pentagram. The moment he crossed over the line, he was struck by the concussion of displaced air as molecules whirling through the ether materialized within the borders of the pentagram, colliding with the molecules of air that had occupied that space and time. It struck him as a wall of force, knocking him off his feet and sending him flying to fall in a heap at Merlin's feet as shimmering points of light danced within the borders of the pentagram and a roaring like the death agonies of some giant beast filled the basement.

Merlin had taken off his jacket and wrapped it around Kira, and now she huddled against him, clutching him fearfully as she stared at the thing that had appeared inside the pentagram.

Wyrdrune looked back over his shoulder, and his bowels almost let go at the sight of the apparition that crouched on the space where he had been a moment earlier. It seemed transparent, with ionic fire coursing through it like an electrical storm as it rocked back on its haunches, threw back its mammoth head, and howled with rage. Its transparent claws raked the floor beneath it, striking sparks, and chunks of concrete flew up into the air as it tried vainly to break the boundaries of the pentagram.

"*Ambrosius*!" it screamed, its voice shaking the walls. "Damn you, Ambrosius! Where are you? *Where are you?*"

His right hand flat on the open book before him, Merlin extended his left arm toward the creature, fingers spread, energy crackling around them.

"Back, hell spawn!" he cried. "Back to your upstart of a master!"

Orange fire leapt from his outstretched fingers, slamming in a bolt of energy into the ravening creature trapped within the pentagram. It threw back its head and howled with pain as it became wreathed in orange fire, and then it seemed to fragment, a myriad of cracks forming in its transparent structure like fissures spreading through a block of ice. It shattered, falling apart into a thousand shards of spark-filled glass, showering to the floor and melting away into nothingness. The echoes of its howl reverberated through the room and died away into a silence permeated by the stench of ozone. Merlin sagged down against the lectern.

"My God," said Wyrdrune. "What *was* that thing?"

"Never mind," said Merlin weakly. "Help me upstairs."

Wyrdrune seemed to notice Kira for the first time. "Kira! Are you all right?"

She nodded mutely, taking Merlin by the arm. "Give me a hand with him," she said, her voice flat.

Together they helped the archmage up the stairs. The kitchen phone was ringing.

"I'll get it," Wyrdrune said.

"No, no, I'll answer it," said Merlin. "I think I know who it is." He reached out for the receiver, and Wyrdrune passed it to him. With a sigh Merlin took it and and held it to his ear.

"Yes, Mrs. Hofstedder," he said wearily, then flinched and held the receiver away from his ear. He rolled his eyes and put his ear back to the receiver. "No, Mrs. Hofstedder, I

don't have a dog. . . . Yes, I'm sure, Mrs. Hofstedder. . . .
Yes, I know about the howling, I. . . . I know. . . . Yes, I
know. . . . No, really, Mrs. Hofstedder, I promise you, I'm
not. . . . I'm sorry it upset your cats, Mrs. Hofstedder, but
. . . that's terrible, all over your new quilt?. . . . Yes, I understand, I . . . Mrs. Hofstedder . . . Mrs. Hofstedder?. . . . Now
there's no need for that sort of language, Mrs. Hofstedder,
I—" He flinched and held the receiver away from his ear,
then sighed and replaced the phone on its cradle. He shook
his head. "There's just no talking to some people," he said.
He glanced at Kira. "Are you all right, my dear?"

She gathered his tweed jacket around her and nodded.
"Thank you," she said.

"We'll have to see about getting you some clothes," said
Merlin. "If I could have my jacket back, please? Turn
around, Karpinsky."

Wyrdrune obediently turned around, though he had already seen her naked, and Merlin made a pass with his
hands. Kira suddenly felt herself dressed in a plaid skirt, a
frilly white blouse, saddle shoes, and knee socks.

"There, that's better," Merlin said.

She glanced down at her new outfit and made a face. "It
is?"

"What happens now?" said Wyrdrune

"Now the battle begins," said Merlin. "It will no longer be
safe for you two to remain here. Rashid knows where you
are now, and he will not hesitate to strike again the moment
he recovers. And he'll recover soon. His power has grown
greatly, and it will grow greater still. I must do what I can to
counteract it. I only wish there was more time."

"What do you want us to do?" said Wyrdrune.

"I only wish I could tell you," Merlin said. "Your fate is
not in my hands. The runestones will determine it. They
have bonded themselves to you, for reasons I can only guess
at. Rashid will have to destroy them to release the Dark

Ones, which means that he will have to destroy you. And me."

"Then we'll just have to kill him," Kira said.

Merlin raised his eyebrows. "Indeed," he said, "but that is far easier said than done. You have no conception of the powers that protect him. And you're not yet ready. If you attempt to move against him now, you'll surely fail. You are only two parts of the triangle. You must find the third before you can take on Rashid."

"I thought *you* were the third part," Wyrdrune said.

Merlin shook his head. "I think I would have felt it by now if I were," he said, "but the runestones have no link to me. I've been chosen for another purpose. It falls to me to be the stabilizing influence, to buy you time."

"Time to do *what?*" said Wyrdrune.

"When the time comes, you will know," said Merlin. "Listen to me. For centuries the Dark Ones have slept, but the power of magic in the world has grown, and now they have awakened. They have found their avatar: Rashid. With the runestones removed from the location of their tomb, the Dark Ones can reach out, through Rashid, and make their power felt. Rashid will have to make the climate favorable for them to escape. That is what I must work against. I must stop the encroaching force of their black magic, keep their strength from growing if I can, for if I can't, they may soon become strong enough to break free of their confinement. But as long as the runestones exist, there is a check to their power. The Old Ones have passed their mantle on to you, to the both of you, and to a third whom you have yet to find. When the three elements of the triangle are all brought together, then you can stand against Rashid. Until then he'll stop at nothing to destroy the runestones and you along with them."

"I don't understand," said Kira. "If that's how it is, why didn't he kill me when he had the chance?"

"Perhaps because he hoped to get at Wyrdrune through

you," said Merlin. "Perhaps because he couldn't. I don't know. Rashid is no longer the same man I once knew. He's been taken over, possessed by the power of the Dark Ones. He is lost. He will only find freedom in death now. But even if Rashid is killed, that in itself would not defeat the powers behind him. However, with Rashid dead, you would be able to replace the runestones to where they belong, thus sealing up the Dark Ones once again."

"Can't they be destroyed?" said Kira.

Merlin sighed. "I don't know," he said. "Once they were a race of mages, long before my time, but who knows what they've become now? They have survived for centuries. Even the Old Ones, who entombed them, weren't able to destroy them utterly. And I am only one. I don't know how many of them there are."

"What would happen if they got out?" said Kira.

"I shudder to think of it," said Merlin. "They were never bound by the moral considerations of the white magicians. Black sorcery is not inherently more powerful than white, but it can easily become so because the accumulation of power, gathered through the rituals of black magic, is accomplished far more rapidly than power gained through the white way."

"You mean, like a shortcut?" Kira said.

"In a word, yes," said Merlin. "A shortcut. Taking life energy from another is far easier than using up your own. Just as it's easier to mine the resources of the earth with no regard to the damage done to the environment, so it's easier to mine the resources of power with no regard to human life. I ought to know. I've killed many times, taking the life energy of those I destroyed, telling myself that it was unavoidable, done for the greater good, but that's the most seductive danger of black magic. Learn it now, for you will surely experience it yourself. It's almost impossible to know where to draw the line. How far does one dare to go for the so-called 'greater good,' and how does one justify the arrogance of appointing oneself the arbiter of what is good and what is not?"

"You do what you have to to survive," said Kira.

Merlin smiled wryly. "Is that all there is to it, then?" he said ironically. "Beware the simplicity of such philosophy, my dear. That is the very thing the ones whom Rashid serves are doing. They, too, are doing what they feel they must do to survive. How far would *you* go to insure your own survival?"

"As far as I had to, I guess," she said. "I've had to learn how to survive the hard way. No one was looking out for me."

"I understand," said Merlin, "but if I were to tell you that in order to survive, you had to kill Karpinsky, here, and perhaps old Mrs. Hofstedder next door, as well, and maybe the family across the street, a man and wife and their three infant children, what then?"

"Seems to me in that case it wouldn't be a question of their lives or mine," she said. "It would be me or *you*."

"Ah," said Merlin, "but what if I had you entirely at my mercy? What if there was no way you could prevail against me, if it was only a question of their lives or yours?"

"I guess I'd die trying to kill you," she said.

Merlin smiled. "An easy thing to say." He held up his hand to forestall her comment. "And I do not impute your motives in saying it. I only wish to point out that confronting such a question theoretically and dealing with the reality of such a situation are two very different things. During my long sleep I witnessed . . . well, let's say I dreamed . . . innumerable cases of people who were very virtuous sending others to their deaths merely to preserve themselves. And in every case they either told themselves they had no choice, or they convinced themselves that they were acting for the greater good. Not an easy thing to do, perhaps, when you are sending children to the ovens or shooting the helpless inhabitants of some small Asian village, but it is an easier thing to do than die. And it's easier to convince yourself you had no choice or that you have acted for the greater good than it is to live with the knowledge of your weakness and the glimpse of the darkness in your soul. Mine is as black as yours, believe me. It's the balance between light and dark that keeps us sane. Too much of one and you're a martyr. Too much of the other and you become a beast." He sighed. "I pity poor Rashid. That was him we saw down there, you know. That was what he has become."

He came up to Wyrdrune and placed his hands on his shoulders. "Perhaps that is where the Old Ones made their mistake," he said. "Perhaps they didn't destroy the darker ones among them because they were unable to. Instead they gave their own lives to protect those who would follow. Perhaps their blood flows in your veins," he said, then glanced at Kira. "And in yours as well. Maybe that's why they chose you. Or maybe it's because you're both still very young and you have not yet learned how complicated life can be. I don't envy you your coming education." He stepped back from them. "Go now. Find the one who will complete you. And seek strength in one another. Let the runestones guide you. I'll try to buy you time."

He gestured at them and spoke an ancient spell. They disappeared.

The unmarked car pulled up across the street from the large Victorian house on Beacon Hill and gently settled to the ground. Special Agent Morgan sat behind the wheel. She lit up a cigarette.

"I'll wait out here," she said.

Riguzzo raised his eyebrows. "You're not coming in?" he said.

"No," she said. "I think he would respond better to a couple of policemen than to an ITC investigator."

"Why?" said Cleary.

"Well, let's just say I don't think he'd be very glad to see me," she said. She seemed nervous.

"Something personal?" Riguzzo said.

"We've had our differences," she said. "It's been a while, but I don't want to antagonize him. He's an important man. Besides, he'd talk differently to you than he would to another adept."

"Any suggestions as to how to handle him?" said Cleary. "I mean, if you know the man . . ."

"Just be polite, low profile," she said. "It's a routine investigation, you're just following up leads, you know the drill. Just treat him as you would some corporate VIP back in New York."

"What if he should ask how come the ITC isn't investigating this, if it's a thaumaturgic case?" Riguzzo said.

"Good question," she said. "Tell him the ITC is looking into it, but they haven't officially stepped in yet. Karpinsky is not a certified adept, and there seems to be some question about jurisdiction as a result of that, purely a technicality. It's still your case and you're just following up a lead from the Boston PD. One of the things you're trying to determine is whether or not he's technically qualified as an adept. You'd just as soon turn the case over to the ITC, because you've got more than enough on your hands right now and you'd rather not deal with this one. See if that will prompt him. And pay attention to what he *doesn't* say and how he doesn't say it. Merlin has his own priorities, and he's never been a great respecter of authority. In other words, be deferential. Don't go leaning on your badge. He can be temperamental."

"Swell," said Cleary wryly. "We get on his nerves and he turns us into toadstools. I've heard some stories about this guy. You can *bet* I'll be polite."

"Maybe we should've called ahead," Riguzzo said.

"Do you normally call ahead and make appointments in such situations?" she said tensely.

"No, not usually."

"Then play it as you usually do," she said. "I'll wait for you out here."

They got out of the car and crossed the street, heading toward the big old house.

"What do you make of her?" said Cleary.

"I don't really know," Riguzzo said as they walked through the gate. "She doesn't throw her weight around like a lot of ITC types do, but she sure takes charge, all right. She seems competent enough."

"Seems kind of young," said Cleary.

"I thought of that," Riguzzo said. "It's hard to tell with an advanced adept, though. On the other hand, maybe that's the reason she kept us on the case. We don't know how experienced she is."

Something ran across their path and darted into the bushes. Instinctively Cleary's hand went into his jacket for his gun. "What was that?"

They heard a high-pitched giggle coming from the rustling bushes, and then all was still.

"Just take it easy," said Riguzzo, putting his hand on his partner's arm.

"This place gives me the creeps," said Cleary, looking around at all the ceramic gnomes placed on the overgrown lawn. "What are these things, a joke or what? Is that one there giving us the finger?"

"It's a lawn ornament, Al," Riguzzo said. "Will you relax, for chrissake?"

Cleary cast a jaundiced eye at the demonic face of the door knocker. "I don't think Christ has a lot to do with this," he said nervously.

Riguzzo raised his eyebrows. "You religious, Al?"

"Yeah, I'm a Catholic," he said. "Aren't you?"

"I don't know what the hell I am, tell you the truth," Riguzzo said.

Cleary grimaced. "Try being a Catholic," he said. "Especially these days. Feels like the whole world's a tuxedo and you're a pair of work shoes."

"I thought the church had modernized," Riguzzo said.

"Yeah, it's modernized," said Cleary. "Thaumaturgy's just an outgrowth of the power of God, and black magic is the work of the devil. The pope made that very clear. Only guys like Merlin will tell you that it's all the same thing, it's just what you do with it that counts. I tell you, I don't understand it. My father didn't understand it, my mother said novenas every day, and my sister got disgusted and turned Jewish. I'm just waiting for the adepts to start their own religion. That'll really tear it. Instead of going to church on Sunday, you'll take a hike out to the woods, strip off your clothes, and dance around a tree."

"That's nothing new," Riguzzo said. He raised his hand to the door knocker. Cleary grabbed his arm.

"Wait a minute." He licked his lips.

"What's bothering you, Al?"

"Don't laugh, Dominic, okay?"

"I won't."

"I'm scared."

"Of Merlin?"

Cleary sighed. "I've been hearing stories about this guy since I was a kid," he said. "He's killed people, Dom. Made 'em disappear. Just like that. And nobody ever said anything. It's not as if anyone could *do* anything about it, know what I mean? This man is above the law. Word is he's not even exactly *human*."

"No one is above the law, Al," said Riguzzo gently. "And about those stories, those were the old days. There were a lot of stories, and most of them were probably exaggerated. This is now. This isn't some evil wizard's castle, Al. This man is a university professor."

He grabbed the knocker and swung it hard three times against the plate.

The eyes on the door knocker's face opened wide. "What do you want?" it said.

"That's it, I'm leaving," Cleary said, turning around.

Riguzzo grabbed his arm. "Settle down, Al. It's okay. No big deal." Feeling a little uneasy, he turned to the door knocker and said, "Lieutenant Dominic Riguzzo and Sergeant Al Cleary, New York Police Department, to see Professor Ambrosius. We'd just like to ask a few questions, please."

The door swung open by itself. Riguzzo half expected it to creak, but it didn't. They entered and the door slammed shut behind them. Cleary jumped about a foot.

"I'm in the kitchen," a voice called out to them. "Straight down the hall and to the left."

As they approached the kitchen they smelled pork chops frying. Merlin was sitting at the kitchen table, a newspaper open before him. He got up as they came in and offered his hand.

"Good evening," he said pleasantly. "I'm Merlin Ambrosius. Please sit down. How may I help you, gentlemen?"

"We're sorry to interrupt your dinner, Professor," said Riguzzo, before he realized that the smell of frying pork chops seemed to be coming from Merlin's pipe. It caught him off-guard and he stood there, feeling confused.

"Everyone reacts that way," said Merlin, smiling at him. He took the pipe out of his mouth and stared at it. "I keep experimenting with the blend, but I can never get it quite right. I came close once, but though the taste was just about spot on, it would up smelling like a jockstrap and everyone complained about it. Can I offer you gentlemen some tea or coffee? Perhaps a glass of wine?"

"Please don't go to any trouble," said Riguzzo.

"No trouble at all," said Merlin. "I keep a pot on all the time." He snapped his fingers, and a steaming coffeepot appeared in the center of the table, along with two white ceramic coffee mugs. The mugs had names painted on them in large black letters. One was labeled AL, the other DOMINIC.

Merlin pulled out chairs for them and sat down. "One lump or two?" he said. A cup appeared before him, and the coffeepot sprouted legs and walked across the table, tilting itself and pouring the steaming brew.

They sat down at the table and glanced at one another. "Uh, I'll take mine black," said Riguzzo.

"Me too," said Cleary.

"I like mine sweet," said Merlin. He waggled his index finger and two lumps of sugar rose up out of the bowl and floated gently into his coffee cup. He pointed his finger down at the cup and made circular, stirring motions. The coffee started to swirl around inside the cup.

"Now, then," Merlin said, "what does the New York Police Department want with me?"

"We'd like to ask you some questions about a young man who may have been a student of yours some years ago," Riguzzo said. Cleary sat bolt upright, hands flat on the table, staring into his coffee cup as if afraid that it would jump up and bite him. Riguzzo consulted his notepad, although he didn't need to. "His name is Melvin Karpinsky, also known as Wyrdrune?"

Merlin puffed on his pipe. It now smelled like fried bananas. "Yes, I remember him. He was in several of my classes. He was expelled, as I recall. Unpleasant business."

"What kind of a young man was he?" said Riguzzo. "Was he a good student? Before he got expelled, I mean."

Cleary hadn't moved.

"He was impatient," Merlin said. "Somewhat headstrong, impulsive. He had promise, but he was in too much of a hurry. He might have made something of himself if he had been a bit more studious and methodical, but you know how some of these young people are. He thought he already knew all the answers. Frankly I'm not surprised to hear that he's in trouble."

"How do you know that he's in trouble, Professor?" said Riguzzo.

Merlin's eyes crinkled. "Because you're here, asking questions about him, Lieutenant. Also because he called me."

"When was this?" Riguzzo said, although he already knew from the record of calls made from the hotel.

"Only the other day," said Merlin. "He called me at my office, at the school. He wanted to know if he could come and see me."

"In reference to what, did he say?"

"In reference to some jewels he said he had," said Merlin, surprising them. "Enchanted runestones of some sort. He wanted my help in trying to determine what their use was."

"And did you tell him?" said Riguzzo casually.

"I read the newspaper," Merlin said, "and I even watch television on occasion. It struck me as significant that he was seeking to consult me about some enchanted runestones of unknown properties so soon after some enchanted runestones of unknown properties were stolen in New York. It might have been only a coincidence, of course, but it didn't seem very likely to me that someone like Karpinsky would be in a position to purchase such stones. Also, I am not in the consulting business. I thought his call rather presumptuous, under the circumstances. I do not react very favorably to people who want something for nothing, especially when it's a former student who was expelled as a result of some trouble with the law. Please don't misunderstand, but I have no wish to be involved with the police and I have a position to consider, as I told him."

"I see," Riguzzo said.

"Your coffee is growing cold, Sergeant," Merlin said to Cleary. Cleary gave a start and nodded, picked up his cup, and then set it back down again a second later without drinking from it.

"Tell me, Professor," said Riguzzo, "how would you assess Karpinsky's abilities as an adept?"

"Well, he was gifted," Merlin said, "but somewhat erratic. No discipline. No patience, as I've already said. He was on a scholarship, you know." He shook his head, breathing out a cloud of violet-scented smoke. "It didn't reflect well on me or on the school when he was expelled. It's the sort of thing a teacher really hates to see. Wasted potential."

"How much potential, would you say?" Riguzzo said.

"A great deal," said Merlin. "He was one of my best students. One remembers students like that. One has high hopes for them. That makes it all the worse when they let you down."

"I realize I'm asking for some speculation here," Riguzzo said, "but would you say he could have passed his certification exams—if he had taken them, that is?"

"His first levels? Certainly. He would have breezed right through them. As I said, a shameful waste."

"If he *was* certified," Riguzzo said, "based on what you know of his abilities, at what level would you place him now?"

Merlin raised his eyebrows. "You mean beyond the first level? I really couldn't say. That does call for speculation. Potential is hardly the same thing as certified ability. He might have done well on the more advanced-level exams if he had prepared himself adequately, but it would be difficult to say. It's been a number of years since he left school. He might have continued to pursue his studies on his own, though that would be difficult to do, and especially in the case of practicing the more advanced spells, it would entail a considerable degree of risk without proper supervision."

"Would you say it might be possible for him to attain the skill level of a wizard?" said Riguzzo.

"On his own?" said Merlin. "I shouldn't think so." He shrugged. "But I suppose anything is possible."

"Would you say he was capable of violence?"

"Everyone is capable of violence."

"But some people are more inclined to it than others," said Riguzzo.

"Indeed," said Merlin. "However, my impression is that he would not be one of those. Dishonest, yes, but violent? I suppose it's possible, but it would surprise me."

"The local police are anxious to question him concerning a recent homicide here in Boston," said Riguzzo, watching the mage for a reaction. "We have reason to believe that it's connected with the robbery of the Christie Gallery and that there's a possible connection with a couple of homicides back in New York as well, one of which was the result of arson. I believe the reason that Karpinsky was expelled had to do with a fire at a concert?"

"Yes," said Merlin, pursing his lips. "As I recall, he over-reached himself a bit and a fire spell went out of control. Fortunately, no one was seriously injured. You're telling me he's wanted for murder, as well as robbery?"

"At the moment he's only a suspect," said Riguzzo, "but we would very much like to speak with him. Our information indicates that he is keeping company with a young woman named Kira. Slim, pretty, dark hair, about five foot six or seven, around eighteen years old. Ring any bells?"

"I don't recall anyone like that among my students," Merlin said. "Still, I can't remember all of them, you know. Some stand out for one reason or another; others are just part of the crowd. I'm sorry I can't be of more help to you."

"I respect your desire not to want to be involved with the police, Professor," Riguzzo said, "but if Karpinsky should contact you again, I would very much appreciate it if you would let us know. You could call the Boston Police Department, ask for Captain McGarry."

"Not the local office of the ITC?" said Merlin.

"There seems to be some problem about jurisdiction," said Riguzzo. "The ITC is looking into it, but for the moment we're carrying the ball. I suppose they want us to do all the legwork for them before they walk in and wrap it up. Frankly, that's why Captain McGarry called us in. Ordinarily we wouldn't be pursuing an investigation in his jurisdiction, but there isn't much point to tying up a lot of man-hours on a case that's only going to get taken away from you sooner or later. This is a headache that no one seems to want, so I guess we're stuck with it, at least for the time being. Anyway, that's not your problem, Professor." He stood, and Cleary followed suit. "I'd like to thank you for your time."

"I'm sorry I couldn't have been more helpful," Merlin said. "I'll see you to the door."

"Please don't trouble yourself, Professor, we can show ourselves out."

Outside, Cleary shook himself. He seemed dazed.

"What was wrong with you in there?" Riguzzo said.

"I don't know," said Cleary. He glanced uneasily at the ceramic gnomes on the front lawn. "I felt ... strange. Numb, sort of."

"Are you all right?"

"Yeah, I ... guess so. It's like I sort of drifted off somewhere."

They walked down to the car where Agent Morgan waited.

"You don't think he did anything to me, do you?" Cleary said.

"Like what?" Riguzzo said.

"Like ... I don't know. Hypnotized me or something."

"You're being paranoid. You sure you feel okay?"

"Yeah, now I do. But I had the strangest feeling back there ..."

They got into the car.

"Well, we didn't learn much," Riguzzo began.

"I know," said Morgan.

"You know?"

"I listened in," she said. "I wanted to hear exactly what he said and how he said it." She glanced at Cleary.

"*It was you!*" said Cleary with a start. He became angry. "What the hell! Where do you get off pulling something like that? You've got no right!"

"Calm down, Sergeant," she said. "I was well within my authority to—"

"Wait a minute," said Riguzzo. "Do I understand this correctly? *You commandeered my partner's body* to listen in on that interrogation?"

"As I was saying," she said, "I was well within my authority as the agent in charge of this investigation to pursue whatever means are necessary to—"

"Dom—" said Cleary, suddenly grabbing Riguzzo's shoulder. He was looking out the window, his eyes wide.

One of the ceramic gnomes was walking toward their car. It came up the door on the passenger side and knocked on the window. Staring, Riguzzo rolled it down.

"Oh, by the way, Morgana," said the gnome, speaking with Merlin's voice, "don't be so shy next time. Did you think that I would be so petty as to bear a grudge for some two thousand years?"

CHAPTER
Eleven

They materialized inside the crammed apartment on East 4th Street, and Kira immediately sank down into the big chair, draping one knee-socked leg over the arm and dangling her saddle shoe.

"This popping in and out like this is getting real old," she said wearily. "I'm so blitzed, I can't even think straight." She glanced up at Wyrdrune. "What are *you* grinning at?"

"The new you," he said, referring to her outfit. "You look like you're about twelve years old."

"Yeah, well, if I am, you're in a pile of trouble. That's going to be the first order of business, warlock," she said. "I got to get me some decent clothes. I have to admit this beats wearing nothing, but not by very much."

"It's sort of a cute outfit, actually. I guess Merlin's not up with current fashions," Wyrdrune said. He stopped smiling abruptly. "You gave me a hell of a scare, you know."

"I was a little scared myself." She smiled wryly. "Thanks for rescuing me. What you did took guts."

"Did he . . . hurt you?" He kept thinking about her nakedness and how vulnerable she had looked.

"I don't really want to talk about it."

"It was my fault," said Wyrdrune. He felt as if he should comfort her somehow, take her in his arms, but her manner was the same as always, despite the schoolgirl costume. Street-tough and defiant. Her body language and her tense mood held him at a distance. *You're not so tough, you know,* he thought, and he said, "I should never have left you alone."

"Don't be stupid," she said. "If you'd been there, you'd probably be dead by now. Which reminds me, just how safe *are* we here?"

"As safe as anywhere else, I guess," he said. "Nobody really knows I'm here—except Merlin, that is. I keep pretty much to myself. I've been subletting this place from some actors who moved to the West Coast. They only keep it to have someplace to stay when they come into town every few months, and they never show up without letting me know in advance. They give me a break on the rent, so it works out. There's no record anywhere of me staying here, at least not that I know of. I don't get much mail, and the little I do get I pick up at my post office box. And the phone's not in my name because I never saw any point to going through the hassle. I'm glad of that now. Merlin and I discussed it, and he figured this would be the best place for us to be for now."

"I suppose so," she said. "It's a cinch we can't go back to my place."

"So *there* you are!" the broom said, swaying into the room. "Where *have* you been? And don't tell me you've been 'out.' What is it, too much trouble to let me know what's going on around here? You think maybe this is a hotel where you can just come and go anytime you please? Does anybody think to check with me? No, of course not, I'm just part of the furniture! A note is too much trouble, I suppose, a phone call, even? Should I hold dinner? Should I wait up? Should I start calling up the hospitals to see if maybe you were run over by a car? Does it occur to anybody that I might be frantic with worry here? Is it too much to expect some consideration?"

They glanced at each other and burst out laughing. And a moment later they were in each other's arms, kissing and clinging desperately as the tension broke and washed out of them in a flood of emotion.

"The schmoozing can wait till after dinner," said the broom. "When did you eat last? You must be starving. I'll go warm up some meat loaf."

"What did he mean about not bearing a grudge for two thousand years?" said Cleary. "What was that, some sort of joke?"

"I don't think he was joking," said Riguzzo, looking at Morgan strangely. "Special Agent Faye Morgan, ITC," he said. "You didn't even change it much."

"I've changed it quite a number of times over the years," she said, staring straight ahead.

"What are you talking about?" said Cleary.

"She and Merlin go way back," Riguzzo said. "*Way,* way back. Sit up straight, Al, you're in the presence of royalty. She's King Arthur's sister, Princess Morgan Le Fay."

"Half sister," she said. "And I'm not a princess. I never was, not really."

"But you almost had a kingdom once," Riguzzo said.

"Yes, once. But that was a long, long time ago," she said, staring straight ahead.

Riguzzo shook his head slowly. "No wonder you didn't want to go in and see Merlin. You're the one who put him to sleep for all those years. But he recognized your presence, anyway. That's what you felt, Al. You felt *her* fear. But Merlin seems inclined to let bygones be bygones. I wonder why. I don't know that I'd forgive you so easily if it had been me."

"I told you, Merlin has his own priorities," she said. "Maybe he's forgiven me. Maybe he just wants to see me squirm. I never could figure him out. And he's always scared me. But he's involved in this up to his neck. I just wish I knew why." She glanced at him. "Your knowledge of history is unusual for a cop."

"I read a lot," he said. "Chronic insomnia."

"Really?" she said, not taking her eyes off the road. "I can fix that for you."

"Thanks, but please don't bother. My insomnia is one of the few things I can count on these days. It's getting so that hardly anything surprises me anymore. But it explains how a woman who looks so young could rise so far in the ITC. Not so young at all, as it turns out. What's it like to live so long? To literally watch history taking place over generations?"

"Nowhere near as interesting as you might think," she said. She sighed. "It can get very boring, actually."

"How many others are there like you?" said Riguzzo. "Besides Merlin, I mean."

"Like me?" she said.

Riguzzo hesitated a beat and licked his lips nervously. "Immortals," he said.

She chuckled. "I'm not immortal, Lieutenant. I can be killed just as easily as you. And I do age, although at a rate far slower than yours. I can slow down my aging even more through sorcery, but I can't stop it completely. Eventually I'll die. I just don't know when."

"I've always wondered about Merlin," said Riguzzo. "It's true, then. There really was a different race before us, and some of them are still around. Merlin's one of them. And so are you."

She shook her head. "Not really. Merlin and I are half-breeds. I suspect that both of us would have died a long time ago if it hadn't been for our sorcery. My mother was a human, as was Arthur's father, Uther. Arthur didn't have the gene. He never suspected what I was. I didn't know myself, until I met Merlin. He was my teacher, you know." She glanced at him. "As to how many more of us there are, your guess is as good as mine. I've met a few over the years, an old man named Cagliostro, a seer called Nostradamus, an industrialist named Long, a few others here and there. Never any full-bloods—one of the Old Ones, as we call them. Many of them died in the Great Mage War. The others scattered. They interbred with humans, grew old, died out. Some were discovered for what they were and were killed. Their blood became diluted over the years. Every now and then someone turns up with unusually developed paranormal abilities, but they never really know where they got them from. It's the sort of thing you won't find in any of the history books."

"Does the ITC know who you really are?"

"Only a few of my most trusted colleagues know," she said. She smiled. "The rest just make jokes about my name. If they only knew."

"Why the ITC?" said Cleary. "Someone like you could live any way you wanted to. You could be rich."

"I am rich," she said. She smirked. "You'd be amazed what even the most conservative of investment plans can accomplish over several thousand years. But I keep it quiet. It would take a team of the best accountants in the world a generation to unravel my various assets and trace them back to me. I prefer keeping a low profile. A habit born of centuries of paranoia. If I decide you can't be trusted, I can easily make you forget you ever even met me. Perhaps I will, when this is over." She shrugged. "Or perhaps I won't. It doesn't really matter anymore. We sorcerers have come out of the closet, don't you know."

"You still haven't said why you're working as an ITC investigator," said Riguzzo. "Not that it's not a prestigious job, but I should think you could easily do better."

"True," she said, "but I'm not really interested. This job suits my purposes."

"And gives you easy access to a constant stream of information from all over the world," Riguzzo said, watching her for a reaction. "It's Morpheus, isn't it? You're doing this because you're after him. He's like you, isn't he? A descendant of the Old Ones. One who's gone bad."

"I gather you're quite good at your job, Lieutenant," she said.

"I don't miss much," he admitted. "Force of habit, I suppose. You work as a cop as long as I have, you learn how to read people, how to watch them closely without even thinking about it. You get a very intense look in your eyes when you're talking about him. Your body talks a lot too. This is something very personal for you, isn't it?"

She remained silent for a long moment, staring out at the road.

"I didn't mean to pry," Riguzzo said.

She glanced at him. "Yes, you did. But it's all right. I understand. You have to be able to trust the people you work with. And I want you to trust me, because I need your help." She turned to look back at the road. Her whole body was tense. "Morpheus is my son."

He stood at the window of his hotel room on the twenty-seventh floor, staring out at the city. He had only one suitcase, which lay open on the bed. He had started to unpack but hadn't finished. Several folded shirts lay piled on the bed, along with a leather case holding his toilet articles, some underwear, socks, a pair of expensive black slacks, and a black tunic that buttoned up the side. He had purchased a new 10-mm automatic pistol with a silencer and spell-warded it against metal detection. It rested in its black shoulder holster, visible now that he had removed his suit jacket, which was tailored so as to conceal the slight bulge. He would need to buy some new clothes. He had complete wardrobes in a dozen apartments in a dozen different cities, homes in several countries, some of which he hadn't seen in years. He could start over—although replacing Apollonius would not be easy and valued possessions had been de-

stroyed that never could be replaced—but he still had unfinished business to take care of.

The kid was a better adept than he had thought. He had
somehow managed to snatch the runestones back. No matter. He'd get them back again. He was dealing with amateurs. Gifted amateurs, perhaps, but amateurs nonetheless.
He'd had years to perfect his craft. Years and years and
years.

He had called room service and ordered a bottle of expensive, unblended Scotch. He held the glass in his right hand,
drinking it straight and neat as he stared out the window at
the lights of the city. His left hand held a cigarette, and the
smoke from it trailed up past his face. For the first time in
generations he felt as if things were slipping away from him,
out of his control.

He was an adept, although not an expert one. Not as
highly skilled as a sorcerer or a mage. Had he ever taken
certification tests, he would probably have certified as a
mid-level wizard. His education had been informal; he had
been taught by his mother in his youth, and what proficiency
he had was attributable to her demands on him, but though
he had practiced as she wanted, he had always disliked
magic. He found it useful on numerous occasions, but he
preferred not using it. It was part of *her* world, part of her
design for him, a design he had never really wanted any part
of.

The intervening years had erased his hatred of his father.
It had been dead for years, as Arthur himself was. When he
thought of Arthur now—and he could never quite bring
himself to think of him as "Father"—it was with a somewhat
poignant wistfulness. It had been a terrible waste. Perhaps
they might have had the normal relationship of a father and
his son, even of a king and his acknowledged bastard, despite the sinful circumstances of his birth, but Arthur had
never been able to face up to it beyond acknowledging his
son's existence as an unpleasant fact. And Morgan had been

poisoned by her hate and lust for vengeance. Or maybe it was lust for power. Or both. In any case, it no longer mattered, had not mattered for generations. What mattered was that she couldn't let him go.

For a while he thought he had escaped her suffocating influence. Everyone had thought him dead after the final battle, after the fall of Camelot and the vaunted age it represented, a time he had always perceived as being dedicated to vainglorious pride, ambition, and self-righteousness. How it had rocked them when Lancelot, the purest of them all, Arthur's own idealistic icon on a pedestal, had proved only human, after all. But even after it was over, there was no relief.

He knew his name would be forever linked with Arthur's fall, as if it were his fault that Guinevere and Lance fell to it like a pair of randy goats. It was all right, as long no one openly admitted it; they could sleep with one another beneath Arthur's own roof and pretend it was their guilty secret when Arthur knew about it, Merlin knew about it, Morgan knew about it, and half the palace guard and servants knew of the affair as well. That was the extent of Camelot's idealistic purity. Sweep the dirt beneath the rug and look the other way. But once the affair had been officially exposed, it was a different matter. *Then* Arthur had to stand upon his principles and watch his queen condemned to burn while he withheld his royal pardon, counting on his friend—the friend who had made him a cuckold—to rescue the woman they both loved and, in the act of doing so, condemn them both. The hypocrisy was nauseating. Arthur could condone the sin committed by his wife and his best friend, and even love them still, but he could not acknowledge the sin that he himself committed, nor bring himself to love his son, for that would reveal his own frail humanity, his own inability to live up to the lofty principles he had laid down for the entire kingdom. It was that which had infuriated the young Modred. His outrage over the injustice of it all and his de-

spair at being denied his birthright only served to fuel an
adolescent temper, so easily given to extremes, making him
an easy pawn for a manipulative mother who had her own
emotion-charged agenda.

Afterward, he had disappeared. For a time, he wandered
the countryside as an itinerant bard, and then a thief—a
prince reduced to petty theivery!—and finally a mercenary,
a vocation that eminently suited him. It called for nothing
but the most elemental human traits. In battle after battle he
forged himself anew, losing his old self in the white heat of
combat and creating, like a phoenix rising from the ashes of
the fallen Camelot, a new and very different man, a soldier,
given to simplicity of dialogue and action, a man who made
his way in life by way of physical accomplishment rather
than by way of thaumaturgic skill. The youthful emotions
that had consumed him and made him vulnerable were re-
strained, then numbed, and finally transformed into a cold
and ruthless pragmatism. He had no ideals beyond the preci-
sion of his craft, no morals beyond those defined by the
logic of the situation. He had seen enough of morals and
ideals in his youth, and he knew how easily they were equi-
vocated by expediency. He had sworn that he would never
stoop to the hypocrisy of self-righteous virtue, and he had
reconciled himself to what he had become. He did not pretend to be anything else but what he was.

He traveled the world and watched it change over the centuries. He lived many lives as many different people, but
always, essentially, he had remained unchanged—a black
knight errant who deceived neither himself nor others with
chivalric pretensions.

The only purity he recognized was that of craftsmanship,
and the purity of art. Especially art. The true artist, at least
in the practice of his craft, was incapable of deceit. His each
and every effort was a striving for an elemental truth. The
artist could no more hide the object of his quest than he
could alter the result. It was there in every piece of sculp-

ture, in each painting—Michelangelo's search for the god-like quality in man, Raphael's quest for his spiritual beauty, Bosch's visions of the dark side of the psyche, Gauguin's restless yearning for a primitive simplicity. Van Gogh could no more hide his own hysteria than he could resist the driving urge to capture the hysteria of nature. His paintings shouted with a divine madness, revealed the frenzied momentum of nature as plainly as they revealed the manic restlessness of his own soul. The artist ceaselessly revealed himself in his own work, and it was this breast-baring honesty that Modred cherished, the openness, the brutal frankness of bringing truth into the light of day. He found it on the canvases of the masters, but only rarely did he find it in people. And the irony of the fates so many of these artists came to did not escape him. Truth was not well tolerated in the world.

He had learned a lot over the years, and he understood enough psychology to comprehend himself. Sometimes too well. The well-examined life allows for little self-justification, and he knew that at the core of his persona he had not changed very much at all. No one ever does. He had restructured his worldview and his outward self, his priorities, and, to a large degree, even his personality, but deep down inside he was still the same young Modred, the outraged and angry boy who had dragged the ugly truth into the light of day and torn the veil from it so all could see. And then, as now, he could gain little satisfaction from it. The truth revealed did not necessarily set things right. It was merely the truth revealed. Sometimes, as with the paintings of Van Gogh, it could be beautiful. More often it was ugly. But whether it was beautiful or ugly, he had learned to accept it with equanimity and to settle for nothing less.

Morgan had never learned.

He thought of her as Morgan now, sometimes more impersonally as Le Fay, rarely as "Mother." He did not love her, and it had taken him years to learn that he had *never* loved her, nor had she loved him. What they had for each other in the place of love had been dependency, obsessive need. Their feelings toward each other had always existed in the context of their relationship with Arthur, and that relationship was poisoned. There was never any honesty, nor was there acceptance. On his part, all that was in the past. What he felt toward her now was, in a way, much worse than resentment, even worse than hate.

He felt pity.

And there was no room in his life for pity. He wanted nothing more to do with her. He wanted only to be left alone, but her pursuit of him had been relentless, spanning centuries. Over the years they had encountered each other several times, and he had always fled from her—not so much from *her* as from his feelings toward her. He did not like unfinished business, but that was the one piece of business in his life that would remain unfinished. The ony way to settle that relationship once and for all was to confront her with the truth, as he had confronted Arthur with it, but unlike Arthur, she would not accept it. The victory she had won over Arthur, through her son, had been a hollow one. Her so-called "triumph" over Merlin made a mockery by his return. Both men had refused to be cast into the simple roles she had devised for them. Both were too complex for such facile characterization. Her fulfillment had eluded her because she looked for it in things outside herself, and now the only thing that she had left to pin her reason for existence on was a son whom she had never learned to love, a son whose only identity to her was tied up with her ambition, her feelings of rejection, and her desire for revenge. And, like Arthur and Merlin, Modred refused the role she had assigned to him.

He closed his eyes as he stood at the window, thinking, "Morgan, Morgan, why can't you let it be? Find a life of your own to lead. Why must you insist on living it through me? How long must this go on? How many years? Must one of us die for the other to be free?"

She was somewhere close now. He could feel it. But he could feel something else as well, something much stronger than her presence. It was this disquieting feeling that occupied his thoughts now. He did not know what it was. It had something to do with the warlock and the girl and, indirectly, with Al'Hassan as well. He had always steered clear of Al'Hassan before, as he had scrupulously avoided Merlin since his reawakening. Both men were too powerful; both possessed enough thaumaturgic talent to discover him for who and what he was, given the opportunity. Modred had avoided them as he had avoided all the real power brokers, people who might have many convenient uses for a man such as himself, but who just as easily could have become an inconvenience themselves. He had plied his trade conservatively, picking his clients with care, charging them according to their ability to pay, and keeping most of them at a distance. He had always made it a rule to serve the petty warlords, never the princes and the kings, because with increased power came increased visibility. And for a man in his profession, the greatest power lay in being invisible.

Yet now he had set out to pay back Al'Hassan for the destruction of his penthouse, of his hyperdimensional matrix computer, and of his cherished paintings. It was unlike him. He had never before allowed personal emotions to interfere with his profession. A part of him realized that the intelligent thing to do would be to cut his losses and start fresh. He had brushed up against one of the heavyweights, someone well out of his league, and the prudent thing to do would be to chalk it up to experience and carefully avoid any further contact in the future. But some insults were too outrageous to be borne.

And there was something else.

He had found the warlock and the girl and picked up their trail easily. Perhaps too easily. He had lost the warlock back in Boston, and the runestones along with him, yet some powerful instinct urged him to return to New York City because he knew the warlock would return here also. *How* did he know? At first, he told himself that it was just a feeling, a hunch, the result of generations of experience as a stalker of men, and yet it was something more than that.

He hadn't liked the job from the very beginning. He had used Fats as an intermediary before in several of his jobs; men like Fats were useful, and he had not objected to undertaking a commission for him. But once he had found out the particulars, he hesitated. It was not his sort of job. He was a predator who preyed on other predators. Not for any moral reason; he did not delude himself that he only killed men who deserved to die, although that was usually the case. He killed those who had placed themselves into death's arena. They had bought into a game played by rules outside society, and consequently had incurred the risks that went along with it. But this was different. This was a case of a lowly, although extremely well connected, fence wanting him to take out two even more lowly snatch-and-grabbers, amateurs, little more than kids. It was distasteful. It was beneath him. And yet he had accepted the commission without really understanding why.

It should have been a very simple job. The work of a few days. But complications had quickly introduced themselves. The police were involved. Well, that was to be expected, but Porfirio Rozetti had been a wild card. And then Rozetti had been murdered. And then Fats was hit. And Al'Hassan's long arm had reached out and almost struck him down as well. And now Merlin was involved. *Why?* Why so much interest in a couple of kids who got in over their heads? What *were* those runestones that they were worth so much? And why did he feel this peculiar connection with the warlock and the girl? It was even stronger than the ancient link he shared with Morgan. They were like magnets exerting their force upon each other, aware of each other's proximity

long before they came together. It was like a sixth sense,
like an animal sniffing the wind and sensing the approach of
an intruder.

The kid's an amateur, he told himself. A bloody, small-
time amateur. So how had he managed to escape from the
police? And how had he managed to regain possession of the
runestones? And Merlin, damn him, he had gone to Merlin.
Where did *he* fit in? Surely Merlin would not involve himself in such a case merely because the warlock had once
been his student. There had to be much more to it than that.
What powerful spell did those runestones represent? And if
it was some ancient, terribly significant, potent spell, why
didn't Merlin retain them for himself? How had Al'Hassan
allowed them to slip out of his grasp?

Something was coming. But what?

He drew on his cigarette and sipped his Scotch as he
stared out the window at the night-shrouded city. His gaze
fell on the Tricorp Building, headquarters of the U.S. branch
of the ITC. Its tall, wide, pyramid shape towered over the
much older buildings all around it. Its unique architecture
was an indication of the future, the first sign of an old city
beginning a transition to a newer, brighter age. He stared at
its triangular shape, illuminated against the sky, and for
some reason he couldn't take his gaze away from it. It was
like some gargantuan symbol, pregnant with significance,
confronting him, waiting for him to decipher its meaning.

What was it?

CHAPTER
Twelve

He stood in dazzling sunlight, before an altar high atop a stone pyramid in a sweltering jungle. He was dressed in white ceremonial robes embroidered with gold and a tall, heavy, ornate headdress, like a war helmet with cheek-pieces and a crown of long, brightly colored feathers. Below him was a throng of copper-skinned worshipers, their arms upraised, their voices clamoring. He turned to them and raised a stone knife before him in both hands, clasping it point downward, raising it high over his head. They became utterly still. He turned, facing the altar, on which reclined the body of a naked virgin, just past puberty. She looked up at him, eyes wide, her body shivering, her lips slightly parted. A single tear rolled down her cheek and fell upon the blood-encrusted stone. He raised his eyes up to the heavens, staring into the blinding sunlight, and gave the invocation in an ancient language that he could speak only in his dreams. Then he brought the knife down hard, plunging it deep into the young girl's bosom as she screamed, rending the flesh, sending arterial blood spurting out in fountains. It spattered his white robe and shot up into his face. He plunged his

*hands into the bloody cavity and closed his fingers around
the still pulsing young heart. He ripped it from the chest and
held it high, displaying it to the cheering multitude as warm
blood streamed down his arms into his sleeves. . . .*

*His sandaled feet made not the slightest sound as they
walked slowly across the cold stone floor in the vaulted
chamber. Flames burned in tall and heavy braziers made of
bronze, throwing dancing shadows on the walls. His long
Pharaonic gown brushed the floor as he stepped within the
borders of the pentagram. A tall, cylindrical crown of gold
was on his head, a golden beard-piece fixed to his chin, his
eyes outlined in black and heavily shadowed in pigments of
blue and green. His cheeks were rouged, his lips reddened,
his face painted a glistening gold. He raised his head, and
his gaze fell on the naked sacrificial victim chained to the
wall before him, beyond the borders of the pentagram. Unable to meet the stare of a living god, the trembling young
boy looked down at the floor. His body was covered with
cabalistic symbols painted in black and gold upon his alabaster skin. His head was shaved. His finger and toenails
had been painted red, his cheeks and lips rouged, his frightened eyes delicately outlined in black and gold. There was
not a sound within the chamber except for the boy's labored
breathing and the clinking of his chains. Inside the borders
of the pentagram, the living god took a deep breath and
closed his eyes, bringing his hands up before his chest and
turning his palms outward. His head thrown back, his eyes
closed, he began to recite the incantation. A cold wind blew
through the chamber. The flames sputtered in the braziers
and then burned down very low. The chamber was in almost
total darkness now. And in that darkness, outside the
borders of the pentagram, a darker darkness gathered. It
seemed to flow and writhe across the floor, moving toward
the boy, resolving itself into a large black shape that rose up
like a wave. It crested and then crashed down upon the*

*naked boy. His high-pitched, throat-rending screams echoed
off the cold stone walls. . . .*

*They moved in single file, chanting, torches held high
against the night, entering the circle of the standing stones.
Four of them carried a litter strewn with fresh-cut boughs,
green and fresh-smelling, on which the offering reclined, a
young girl with hair the shade of fire and eyes as bright
green as the grass upon the gently rolling hills. He stood
within the center of the circle, the High Priest, as his
hooded, white-robed acolytes placed the litter down before
him, the young virgin sitting erect upon it now, eyes glazed,
face empty of expression. They formed a circle around him
inside the larger circle of the standing stones. He led her to
the altar, a large, flat stone placed across two shorter stones
set deep into the ground. He lifted her up onto the flat stone
and gently laid her down. The torches lit the night, throwing
shadows on the standing stones. His fingers closed around
the knife as he looked down at her. Her eyes cleared, and
she seemed to see him for the first time. She gave a gasp and
opened her mouth to scream as the blade came down. . . .*

Rashid's eyes flew open as he awoke with a start. He
swallowed hard and closed his eyes again, taking a deep
breath. His body was damp with sweat, and the silk sheets
were soaked and tangled by his thrashing. He moistened his
lips and sat up slowly, rubbing his forehead. His pulse rate
was high, his breath was short, and he had a throbbing headache.

Every morning was the same now. Insomnia plagued him
when he went to bed at night, vainly hoping for a sound and
dreamless sleep but knowing that when sleep finally came, it
would be fraught with nightmarish visions. He knew only
too well where those visions came from. There was nothing
he could do to banish them.

He pulled the tangled covers back and got out of bed,
feeling utterly exhausted. He walked unsteadily over to the

sideboard and poured himself a glass of whiskey from the bottle that he kept there. He was drinking steadily now, spreading it out throughout the day, but mostly at night, especially at night, and he needed a few shots in the morning to steady his ragged nerves. As he leaned against the sideboard, holding the glass in a trembling hand, he looked up into the mirror mounted on the wall and saw the face of an old man. The hair was long and lank, heavily streaked with gray, like the hair of an old woman. There were deep, dark pouches beneath his eyes, his skin was pale and wrinkled, his lips trembled slightly. The back of his hand was wrinkled and liver-spotted. It wasn't a hand so much as a claw.

Once, not very long ago, there had been servants to attend him in the morning, to bring him his breakfast, to assist with his ablutions, and to help him dress. Not anymore. Breakfast was a thing of the past now, and he had given strict orders that on no account was he to be disturbed until he came out of his bedroom. He did not want anyone to see him like this. He tossed back the drink, and then another, and stared into the mirror at the tired old man reflected there. As he stared at his reflection, waiting for the change to come, the jewel set in his forehead began to glow. The gray in his hair slowly became a lustrous black. The skin darkened and the wrinkles disappeared. The bags under his eyes faded away, as did the liver spots on his hands. He held up his hand, closing it into a fist and opening it again, feeling the strength returning to him.

Each morning he awoke looking much older, feeling more tired, more afraid. Each morning he was again restored. He could feel his strength increasing every time. It was as if he were actually living out the full span of the lives he relived in his dreams. They were making him over. It was as if he were dying in pieces and being resurrected in stages as a new and different being. Now he looked even younger than before, and he was terrified that it would stop, that one

morning he would awake as an old man and remain that
way.

At night they spoke to him. He felt their presence like
tendrils of ice being wrapped around his mind. They were
restless, impatient now that their long wait was almost at an
end. And in their weakened condition, they were hungry.
Rashid shivered at the thought of what he would have to do
to feed them. He had been working on the spells for weeks.
They terrified him.

He poured himself another drink, his hand steady now,
and he sipped this one slowly, savoring its taste. His plan to
use the girl to bring the warlock to him with the runestones
had failed, thanks to Merlin's interference. He could afford
to wait no longer. Ambrosius was the immediate danger
now. He knew. He had to know. And that knowledge meant
he had to die.

Merlin's fate was a foregone conclusion, but Rashid had
hoped that he wouldn't have to be the instrument of his old
teacher's death. It wasn't that he had any warm feelings for
the old mage; he did not regard Merlin with affection, nor
did Merlin think of him that way. They had not been in
contact for years now, except for that brief visitation he had
sent to Merlin's home following Kira's rescue. He should
have known better than to hope to catch Ambrosius off-
guard. The old archmage was as strong as ever. And just as
shrewd. That blast he had sent back through the conjured
entity had hurt. It had weakened him severely. Under ordinary circumstances it would have killed him, but these were
not ordinary circumstances. Things would never be ordinary
for him again.

He was neglecting business. It didn't matter anymore.
Today the board would meet, and it was almost certain that
they would vote him out of office. The official censure had
been the first step; now they would finish the job and have
him removed. There had been dozens upon dozens of calls,
none of which he had bothered answering, all from fright-

ened people whose power depended on his patronage, all greedy, grasping little double-dealers who had hitched their stars to his, and now they were in a panic, afraid that they would go down with him. His own staff was acting as if some sort of funeral were imminent. It had not escaped their notice that he was letting business slide, that he was keeping increasingly to himself, that he had started drinking heavily. All signs of a man on his way to ruin, they thought. An empire was about to fall. Little did they suspect what sort of empire would replace it.

They would give him power. More power than he had ever dreamed of. But at what price? And no matter how much power he held, it would always be subservient to theirs, in the manner they were showing him in dreams. It wasn't what he wanted. He had never wanted *this*. But he had no choice now.

Merlin's words came back to him, the words Merlin had spoken to him in his office years ago, when he had been in his last year of studies at the university.

"You've done well, Rashid," Merlin had said. "You've done very well, indeed. Much better than I had expected. I wanted to tell you that because I know that none of this has come easily to you and I can appreciate how hard you must have worked."

"I've had to work hard, Professor," he had replied. "My country has invested in my education and I had an obligation to my people. They were depending on me."

"Yes, I also appreciate how seriously you've approached your studies," said Merlin. "You will leave behind an admirable record at the university, one that will be difficult to surpass. However, there's much more to being an adept than mastering the skills, which you have done. There is also the philosophical approach, developing the proper attitude, learning to appreciate the spiritual nature of the craft. And that, I fear, you have not done."

He had reacted as if stung, because he had worked hard,

brutally hard, devoting every spare waking hour to his studies, cursing himself because it came less easily to him than to some of the others, and he had taken a fierce pride in his own progress. No one, he thought, could have been more severely critical of him than he was of himself. He drove himself unmercifully, and it was shocking to think that Merlin could have found him wanting in any aspect of his performance.

"But . . . I don't understand, Professor," he had said, wounded to the quick. "I am at the top of my class. You, yourself, have said that my record is beyond reproach. Where have I failed? What is it I have overlooked? Show me and I will make immediate amends!"

"I don't know if you *can* make amends, Rashid," said Merlin sadly. "Some things are too deeply ingrained to be changed. I'm referring to your ambition."

Rashid had frowned. "But how can you fault me in that?" he protested. "It is my ambition that has seen me through my time here, that has resulted in my progress! Where is the sin in wanting to excel?"

"There's no sin in wanting to excel, Rashid," said Merlin. "However, it is in your *reasons* for wanting to excel that the sin, as you put it, lies. You reveal yourself with your own words. 'Your people' are depending on you, you said. *Your* people?" He held up a hand to forestall Rashid's rejoinder. "Oh, I understand that the phrase is used colloquially to refer to one's fellow countrymen, but that isn't really how you used it, is it? You really do think of them as *your* people, as your possessions, as your birthright. No, wait, let me finish. I've been watching you carefully ever since you came here, and I'll be honest with you: I didn't think you would last out the first year.

"You're not a very popular young man, you know," Merlin continued. "You do know that, of course. It's revealed in your demeanor among your fellow students. You haven't got a single friend here, have you? From the very first you've held yourself above them, refusing to blend in, acting as if somehow you were being forced to perform some sort of necessary service as a condition of assuming the office to which your birth entitles you."

"I am a prince," Rashid said defensively. "I must bear myself accordingly."

"Oh, nonsense!" Merlin said. "You think I don't know the status of royalty in your country? Most of them are paupers, and a few cling to a pretense of nobility at the price of living constantly in debt, on the edge of financial ruin. I don't say this to belittle you, but to remind you of precisely where your responsibility to your people, as you put it, lies. Your country is nearly bankrupt. You were sent here to study the thaumaturgic arts in the hopes that you would succeed in bringing the benefits of thaumaturgy to your nation, which is sorely in need of the skills we teach here. You're a symbol to your people; you represent the hope for progress and education. But I don't believe you see yourself that way. You see yourself as a symbol, of that I have no doubt, but as a symbol of the return of power to a privileged few. Your ambition is not for the advancement of your country, but for the advancement of yourself and others like you. And I'm not even sure that you're terribly concerned about others of your so-called class. I think you're concerned primarily, exclusively, with yourself. You didn't come here to study the thaumaturgic arts as a means of gaining knowledge, you came in order to acquire power. Such an attitude in an adept, one who'll undoubtedly become a mage eventually, is reprehensible. And more than a little frightening."

"I see," Rashid said stiffly. "It is not my performance you find fault with, but my motivation. I submit to you, Professor, that it is not your province to judge me in that manner. You least of all, perhaps. Can you honestly say that in the old days, in your 'previous life,' as you refer to it, your own motives were entirely egalitarian? When you returned from your long sleep, was it the unselfish love of your fellow man that led you to destroy, yes, to *destroy* all those who stood in your way? Oh, yes, of course, you are hailed now as the great educator, as the founding father of the new thaumaturgic age, a veritable candidate for sainthood, to be sure, but what was it that brought you to this pinnacle you now occupy if it wasn't power? Throughout history there have always been those who lead and those who follow, and the difference between them could always be measured in one thing—*power*. The power of their own belief in themselves, the power to assume the role of leader, and the power to make others follow. Where would Arthur have been if it were not for your power behind him? Where would this country be today, where would most of the governments in the international community be today, if it were not for your power of leadership in helping to resolve the conflicts between them? And where do you think my country will be if someone—yes, perhaps someone like myself—does not take power and give it direction? Is that, then, where my fault lies, that I do not meekly assume the humble posture of the sorcerer's apprentice as the others do, but that I see a greater destiny beyond that?"

Merlin had let him talk until he'd run out of steam, watching him with a frown, smoking his pipe in silence. "Are you finished?" he said.

Rashid had taken a deep breath to steady his nerves. He knew that he had said too much, far too much, and he was amazed that he had the nerve to speak to Merlin in such a manner, but it had all come bursting forth, all his frustration and resentment, and now that it was out, he felt afraid.

"Yes, I am finished," he had said stiffly. "I suppose I am finished in more ways than one."

Merlin shook his head. "No, I won't hold it against you, if that's what you think," he said. "If I did, I'd be guilty of everything that you accuse me of. The fault is mine. I didn't teach you well. I've failed you. You've studied hard and you've learned much, but you haven't understood a thing.

You're like a musician who has practiced diligently until he has mastered his instrument, but you've never truly felt the music, and your playing will always be merely technically proficient, perhaps wonderfully so, but it will have no soul. I feel sorry for you, Rashid. You'll graduate with honors, but not with my respect. I take no pride in having had you for my student. I can only hope that when you realize your dreams of power, as I'm sure you will, you won't suffer from the nightmares that come with it. I know only too well what that means. You have yet to learn. Good day."

He had left the office in a daze of fury mixed with shame, feeling like a small boy who had been unjustly disciplined by an elder, one whom he had respected and admired, but who had disavowed him. It was unfair. His face had burned with shame and anger, and he was close to tears. He had resolved, in that moment, to prove Merlin wrong, to do much more than prove him wrong, to become as great a mage as Merlin was himself and to rub his face in it. He would show Ambrosius that his view of things was the correct one for his country. He would bring the knowledge he had learned back home and spread it, yes; but he would do much more than that. He would assume responsibility for lifting his poor nation out of its deprivation and restoring it to its rightful place as a world power. He would start an empire, give jobs to his people, raise their standard of living, create wealth, reconcile the feuding nations with each other, and unite them into a confederacy of republics that was a *nation* instead of just a name.

But it was not so simple.

He had succeeded in his goals, he had become a powerful man, world-famous, head of a vast financial empire, but every success had left him wanting more, feeling strangely empty, somehow denied. His hard work entitled him to enjoy well-deserved rewards, but satisfaction and contentment continued to elude him. The very dogs that he had raised soon started yapping at his heels, biting the hand that had first fed them now that they had the means to feed themselves. He was still respected, still feared—perhaps not so greatly anymore, now that they believed they had found a way to circumvent him—but he was now regarded as some sort of dinosaur, or to use the colorful metaphor an American publication had belabored, he was like the fast gun who had put on a badge and tamed a town, and now that the town was tame and prosperous, the aging gunfighter was considered an embarrassment. Although the marshal's gun hand was still as fast as lightning, the image of the gunslinger was not the one the town was anxious to promote. Now that the task had been accomplished, they argued with his methods, and while they were grateful for all that he had done, they wanted to be rid of him.

Merlin had been right. It galled him to admit it, but he had to give the old man credit. Power was an addiction. Once you're hooked, no matter how much you increase the dose, it's never enough. And while it may have started as the most direct means to a noble end, it had not taken long at all for it to become an end in itself. He had come to his present state seeking more power, when he had already gained more than enough to accomplish all that he had started out to do. And he *had* done it. He had met every goal that he had set himself, except perhaps to become as great a mage as Merlin, and now perhaps he had done even that—but there was only one way to find out for sure. He didn't want to do it.

What is it you're afraid of, Rashid?

He stared at his youthful reflection in the mirror, at the face of a man who appeared decades younger than he really was, a handsome, powerful man, envied by his peers, desired by women, feared and respected by those he had subdued, loved by his people—*his* people—who gave him the obeisance due a monarch, though his title was only nominal.

Are you afraid of Merlin?

And what would his people think of him if they knew

what he had become, what he was about to unleash upon them?

You were born to rule. The blood of Pharaohs runs in your veins.

A living god? He was not so much of a fool as to believe that. A high priest, perhaps—yes, that was fitting, the highest office he could aspire to in the coming kingdom.

Merlin would take even that away from you.

He shut his eyes, then opened them again and poured himself another drink. He knew whose voices spoke to him through his own mind. He feared them. He was in awe of them. He worshiped them. They were Power Incarnate. Everything that he had done had groomed him to be their acolyte.

He thought of a story he once heard, part of the mythos surrounding Merlin, the legend that Merlin lived backward through time. According to the legend, the past was Merlin's future, the future Merlin's past. Nonsense, of course. But then, before the dawning of the second thaumaturgic age, magic was also regarded as nonsense. *I wonder if you know,* he thought. Do you already know the outcome of all this? No, of course he doesn't know. If the old legend were true, then Merlin never would have come back, because in his past, the very near future, he would have met his death.

It has to be today.

If he could have reclaimed the runestones before Merlin was alerted, then the Dark Ones would have been freed and they would have seen to Merlin. He would have stood no chance against their combined power. But now that Merlin was alerted to the threat, it was too dangerous to leave him alive. Even now, he would be preparing spells to counteract the power of the Dark Ones, the power that flowed through him. One of them would be destroyed.

Rashid did not know if he had the power to prevail over Merlin, even with the aid of the Dark Ones, but he had an advantage that Merlin did not have. He did not have to pit his strength directly against Merlin's. The runestones were the key to the Dark Ones' containment. Now that they had been removed, the Dark Ones could reach out with their power. The runestones and the length of time that they had been contained had weakened them, but even so, their power was like nothing he had ever encountered. If they could be strengthened, they could break free. And they had shown him what to do in dreams.

They needed life energy to regain their strength, and he was the only one capable of giving it to them. But they were hungry. Very hungry. There was only so much he could give them before it was beyond even their power to replenish it. That was the reason for the dreams.

He would not strike at Merlin himself. Instead, he would cast his spells against others, releasing life energy the Dark Ones could consume. Merlin would be bound to try to stop him. And while Merlin was thus occupied, he would be vulnerable.

It has to be today.

"I'm going to go crazy if I have to stay cooped up in here much longer," Kira said.

She was once more in boots and trousers. The schoolgirl outfit Merlin had given her had been tossed in the trash as soon as she had bought new clothes. They had stocked up the refrigerator and the pantry, and a new, larger television set had been purchased to replace the one Wyrdrune had dropped. He sat before it now, watching the all-news channel, staring moodily at the screen. Kira was irritated at his lack of reaction. Since their shopping trip, they had been staying inside the apartment, and she was getting cabin fever.

"Between you staying glued to that television set and the damn broom trying to stuff me full of food, I'm starting to lose it," she said.

Wyrdrune turned toward her. "I'm sorry, Kira," he said.

"I don't like this waiting any more than you do, but I can't think of anything else to do right now."

He reached into his pocket and took out the pouch. He kept it on his person constantly, placing it under the pillow when they slept. He held it in his hand, staring at it, as if expecting it to say something to him. He shook his head.

"Merlin said we'd be guided by the runestones. I don't know how they're supposed to tell us anything, but I don't have any sense of what to do. I've got to keep track of what's going on out there," he said, jerking a thumb toward the television screen. "Something's bound to break soon. I just know it. I need to know what's going on before I can figure out what we should do."

"All right, so you can tune in the evening news," she said, "but do you have to stay planted in front of that damn thing all day? I'm starting to go stir-crazy in here."

"So read a book or something," he said. "There's several hundred here to choose from."

"Oh, great," she said sarcastically. "The police are looking for us, you've got a hit man out there trying to find you, Al'Hassan wants us both dead, and you say 'Read a book'! Shouldn't we be *doing* something?"

"Like what?" he said.

"How should *I* know?" she said, her temper flaring. "You're the adept around here, not me! Hell, all I wanted out of this deal to begin with was a simple score, and now all of a sudden I'm caught up in some kind of bizarre magical plot!"

"Fine," said Wyrdrune, his own temper getting short. "If that's the case, then you can take your cut of what's left of the money and just go."

"Don't think I wouldn't if I could!" she said. "I never wanted any part of this! I've been teleported from one place to another till I'm dizzy, attacked by goons and almost killed, raped—"

Wyrdrune jerked around to stare at her. "He *raped* you?"

"So what? What do *you* care? While you and Merlin are busy planning how to save the world, it all comes down on me! And I'm just supposed to sit here and take it and wait till you decide to tell me what to do? What are we *doing* here? Why aren't we going to the police and telling them what happened? Why aren't we taking the money we've got left and hiring a lawyer? Why the hell aren't we *doing* something?"

He got up and came toward her, holding his arms out. "Kira, I'm sorry, I didn't know. I thought that . . . well, I was afraid that—"

"Just keep away from me!" she said. "It'll take more than a hug and a pat on the back to make things right!"

"Kira—" He tried to take her in his arms, but she shoved him away so hard that he went staggering back and fell over the coffee table. He rubbed his elbow where it had struck the coffee table and got up to a sitting position on the floor, staring at her in bewilderment as she glared down at him.

"I'm sorry," he said in a hurt tone. "I just wanted to—"

"Just leave me alone!" she said, turning away from him and going into the kitchen. The broom was bustling around in there, sweeping the floor with itself. She kicked out at it viciously, sending it flying across the room to strike the wall and fall back to the floor with a clatter.

"What? What?" the broom said. "What did I do already? Such a temper—"

Kira glared at it with such fury that it quickly scuttled back into the broom closet and shut the door behind itself. A second later it stuck the top portion of its handle out cautiously, but a thrown cup caused it to quickly dart back inside the closet as the cup shattered on the door.

She turned toward the kitchen cabinets and pulled open one of the drawers. She reached inside, and her fingers closed around the handle of a ten-inch butcher's knife. She pulled it out, staring at the keenly honed blade. She glanced back at the living room where Wyrdrune had resumed his position in front of the TV set, his back turned toward her. He was hunched forward in an attitude of dejection.

Kill him.

She stared at the knife, holding it before her, her eyes glazed and unfocused.

Kill him now!

Slowly she started to move toward the living room, her eyes on Wyrdrune's back. In a daze, she approached him, turning the knife over in her hand, grasping it firmly by the hilt so that the blade was pointed down. Only a few feet separated them now. She raised the knife high over her head—

"Look out! Look out! *Behind you!*" the broom cried from the kitchen.

Wyrdrune turned quickly, glancing over his shoulder, and his eyes widened with shock at the sight of Kira with the knife raised high over her head—

There was the sound of breaking glass and a sharp, abrupt cough, a *chuffing* sound, and the bullet struck the knife blade, knocking it from Kira's grasp as she cried out.

She clutched her hand and blinked several times, shaking her head, and then her eyes cleared and she suddenly realized what she had been about to do.

"Oh, my God," she said.

The man on the fire escape reached through the broken glass and released the catch, then raised the window and stepped through into the apartment, holding a silenced automatic pistol in his right hand.

"*You!*" said Wyrdrune, staring at him with disbelief.

"That's twice I've saved your life now, warlock," Modred said. "Sorry about the glass, but I didn't want to risk deflection. There was only time for just one shot."

Kira stood there looking stunned, still holding her hand, which stung from the impact of the bullet wrenching the knife out of her grasp. "I almost killed you," she said in a small voice, barely louder than a whisper. "Oh, God, that's what he meant. . . ."

Wyrdrune looked from her to Modred, feeling shocked and confused.

Modred gestured toward Kira with his pistol. "Go on," he said. "It seems you have something to settle here. I'll wait." He leaned against a bookcase, watching them, holding the gun loosely at his side.

"Kira," Wyrdrune said, staring at her uncomprehendingly. *"Why?"*

"It's *him*," she said, unable to look at him. "Oh, God, he's in my head! I didn't understand. He said that he could have my soul—"

"Rashid?"

She nodded jerkily. "He said the violence in my nature would bind me to him. I didn't understand. I thought he only wanted . . . I thought . . . ." She burst into tears. "I'm sorry! Oh, God, Melvin, I'm so sorry!"

He held her while she cried. He could feel her struggling for control, her body going tense, terrified now that *any* emotional display would allow Rashid a foothold. She got herself under control after about a minute and looked up at him, wiping away her tears.

"Forgive me," she said.

Wyrdrune smiled. "Melvin?" he said.

She attempted a weak grin. "I guess not, huh? Think I'll just go back to warlock." Then she stopped smiling, and her eyes filled with fear. "What am I going to do? I *can't* leave you, but if I stay, he might take control of me again and I might . . ." Her voice trailed off.

"I think we've got a more immediate problem on our hands right now," said Wyrdrune, turning back to Modred. "For someone who was hired to kill me, you've got the strangest way of going about it. How did you find us?"

"I honestly don't know," said Modred. He reached into

his pocket. "Perhaps these have something to do with it." He held the pouch containing the runestones in his hand.

Wyrdrune's right hand immediately slapped his own pocket, but of course, the pouch was no longer there.

"I suddenly felt their weight in my coat pocket while I was on the fire escape," said Modred. "And I don't know how I know, but I'm convinced they led me here. I find it all rather confusing. I was hoping you could explain it to me."

"It's him," said Kira, staring at Modred. "He's the one!" She glanced at Wyrdrune. "Don't you see? He's the one that we've been waiting for! He's the third part of the triangle!"

Modred frowned. "What's this about a triangle? What does a *triangle* mean to you?"

Wyrdrune watched him cautiously. "Does it mean anything to you?" he said.

"I'm not sure what it means," said Modred, "but it means something. Lately, every time I've seen something triangular in shape, I've had the most peculiar feeling, as if it were something very significant."

"It is," said Kira.

"I've told you once before, warlock," said Modred, "I'm not without some skill when it comes to thaumaturgy. I know when I'm under the influence of an enchantment. And I also know that a mere warlock does not possess sufficient skill to overcome me with a spell." He raised his weapon casually and pointed it at Wyrdrune. "I'll ask you the same question I asked you once before, and this time I want an answer. What is the purpose of these runestones?"

In the brief moment of silence that followed, the voice of the newscaster on the television set suddenly sounded very loud.

"This just in . . . it appears that a massive explosion at a home in the exclusive Boston residential area of Beacon Hill has claimed the life of the eminent thaumaturge, Merlin Ambrosius. For a special on-the-scene report, we now go live to correspondent Bruce Miller."

The screen showed an image of a large Victorian mansion wreathed in flames as a reporter with a microphone stood across the street from it in the foreground, framed on the right side of the screen. There was a cacophony of sirens as firemen struggled to put out the blaze and police arrived to hold back the crowd of onlookers.

"I'm standing just across the street from the residence of Merlin Ambrosius, internationally known archmage and educator," said the reporter. "As you can see, the fire here is raging out of control, and the concern now is to prevent it from spreading to the neighboring houses. A short while ago, this block rocked with the concussion of several massive explosions. Reports as to their number vary from between three to six. As we were setting up here, yet another explosion shook the house and blew out part of the left wall. According to our information, Professor Ambrosius was inside the house at the time of the first series of explosions, and it seems virtually impossible that he could have survived. Irma Hofstedder has resided next door to Merlin Ambrosius for the past thirty-five years, and she was home when the explosions occurred."

The shot widened to show a squat, gray-haired, little battle-ax of a woman wearing a print dress and holding two squirming cats in her arms.

"Mrs. Hofstedder, could you tell—"

She did not give him the chance to finish. "It was his *magic* what done it," she said, drawing herself up fiercely and staring belligerently at the camera. "I *told* him and I *told* him, no good would come of it, no good at all, all the time sitting down there like a spider with his conjuring and spells and all, 'tain't Christian, 'tain't Christian at all, and *now* look what he's gone and done! All the times I've called up and complained, but they wouldn't listen to me! Well, *now* you see what comes of it! It's the devil's work, that's what it is! And my poor house next door to his, look at it, look what they're doing!"

There were fierce thunderheads gathered directly over the neighboring houses, pouring forth a deluge of water as the fire department's sorcerer adepts fought to keep the flames from spreading while the lay firemen trained hoses on the blaze.

"Even if the fire doesn't spread to my house, there will be all that water damage," she said. "I never had a chance to close the windows! And my vegetable garden and my precious roses! All ruined, I tell you! I'm going to sue the fire department! I'll sue the police for not putting a stop to all his conjuring all those times I've called them! I'll sue City Hall! I'll sue the university! I'll sue—"

"Thank you, Mrs. Hofstedder," said the reporter, moving away from her with the mike. "As you can see, the neighbors are understandably distraught. However, it should be pointed out that at this time there is no evidence to indicate the explosions that resulted in the fire were the result of thaumaturgy. And there may be evidence of foul play. Shortly after the first of the explosions occurred, one of the neighbors witnessed two vehicles speeding away from the scene."

He moved over to his right, and a young man who was standing by, just out of camera range, appeared in the shot with him.

"Steven Rasnic resides in the house directly across the street from the home of Professor Ambrosius," said Miller. "Mr. Rasnic, could you tell us what you saw immediately following the first explosion?"

"Well," said Rasnic, speaking slowly and deliberately, "we were just getting ready to sit down to dinner when we heard the first explosion. It blew all the front windows right into the house. I thought maybe a gas main had burst, and I ran to the front door. As I opened it, the next several explosions occurred—at least three of them, one right after another. Debris was falling down into the street and our front yard, and I saw several men running across the street. There were four of them, and they jumped into these two cars that were pulled up in the street right in front of our yard. They took off at top speed in that direction, down the street. I didn't get a very good look at them, but it looked as if they were running from the direction of the professor's house. And the gate to the professor's yard was open. Of course, it could have been blown open by the force of the explosion, but he never leaves it that way." And, as if rebutting the old woman's testimony, he added, "We've never had any problems with the professor before. He's always been a good neighbor. He kept mostly to himself. I can't believe he would have been doing anything in there that would endanger the community. I think those men I saw had something to do with this."

"You're suggesting that this could have been murder?" the reporter said.

"I don't really know. But I never saw those men in this neighborhood before," said Rasnic, "or those cars, either. I'm not saying I could recognize them if I saw them again— I'm sure I couldn't—but they were in one hell of a hurry to get away."

"Thank you, Mr. Rasnic," Miller said, moving away from him and turning to the camera. "So there you have it, at least one witness reports seeing a number of men apparently fleeing from the scene. It is not clear at this time if they had anything to do with the explosions, but as police and fire marshals pursue their investigations, we will be reporting on their progress. As of right now, one thing seems certain, and that is that Merlin Ambrosius has perished in the explosions that ripped apart his home. Reporting from Boston, Bruce Miller, TVN News."

"We take you now to Cambridge, Massachusetts," said the anchorman, "where reporter Kathleen Williams is standing by at the university—"

"I can't believe it," Wyrdrune said, staring at the television. "He *can't* be dead! Not Merlin!"

"Merlin was not invulnerable," said Modred. "If he was in that house when those explosions occurred, it's doubtful he could have survived. But knowing Merlin as I do, I wouldn't write him off until they discover his remains."

"What do you mean? Who *are* you?" Wyrdrune said.

"I've been known by a lot of names. More than I care to remember, really. Michael Cornwall will do as well as any other."

"Modred," said Kira, staring at him intensely.

He started; his gun hand jerked toward her. "*What* did you say?"

"Your name is Modred," she said, her gaze locked with his, speaking as if she were surprised at the sound of her own voice.

He went pale. "*How do you know that name?*"

"I know it too," said Wyrdrune slowly. "My God, you're Arthur's son."

"Your god had little to do with it, Karpinsky," said Modred. He glanced down at his gun and sighed, then returned it to its holster. "I believe I need a drink. You haven't any whiskey, I suppose?"

"Light beer," said Wyrdrune.

"Light beer," said Modred with a wry smile. "Well, I suppose light beer will do."

"Broom!" said Wyrdrune. "Bring us three beers!"

The broom cautiously ventured into the living room. "Is it safe in here, or am I liable to be blasted into splinters?"

Modred's eyes widened slightly and he smiled. "We're quite finished with the shooting," he said. "I'm sorry you were frightened."

"Frightened? What frightened? It's a wonder I have any bristles left living in his madhouse. You want I should just bring the cans, or do you drink out of a glass like a normal person?"

"A glass would be just fine," said Modred. "Thank you."

"You want I should bring a bowl of chips or pretzels, maybe?"

Modred's lips pursed in amusement. "No, just the beer, please. It's not necessary to go to any trouble."

"Trouble? What trouble?" said the broom, heading back into the kitchen. "Digging bullets out of the wall, *that's* trouble. Replacing broken windows, locking up the cutlery, trouble I've got plenty of—what's the bother with a bowl of corn chips . . ."

"You have an unusual familiar," Modred said, grinning.

"Too damn familiar if you ask me," said Wyrdrune.

"I believe I rather like it," said Modred.

"Good. You want it, it's yours."

The sound of tops popping came from the kitchen, and a moment later the broom brought in a small tray holding three cans of light beer and one glass. "We're out of corn chips," said the broom.

"Thank you, broom, it's all right," said Wyrdrune wearily. He sat down on the couch, and Modred and Kira each took a chair.

Modred took a healthy slug of beer and made a face. "Nectar of the gods," he said sarcastically. He looked curiously from Wyrdrune to Kira. "I haven't heard my truename spoken in a very long time. It brings back unpleasant memories. It should disturb me that you know it, yet somehow it doesn't. I'm not sure why. It seems we have a great deal to discuss."

"How can you be Arthur's son?" said Wyrdrune. "According to history, you died after the fall of Camelot."

"Reports of my death were greatly exaggerated, to quote Mark Twain," said Modred. "The line between history and legend blurs increasingly with time. They told many lies about us. Some versions of our story claim that Morgan was my mother, others that it was her sister, Morgause. All agree that I'm Arthur's bastard son, and that part of it is true. My mother was Morgan Le Fay, Arthur's half sister, but she was no more Queen of the Faeries than I am an elf, unless one wishes to stretch the definition of faerie to include the old race, who were the basis for most of the old legends. Morgan's father, Gorlois, the Duke of Cornwall, was one of the Old Ones, though he concealed it. You know about the Old Ones? Merlin told you?"

Wyrdrune nodded.

"Then you know about the Dark Ones too."

"Yes."

"This all has something to do with them, doesn't it?" said Modred. "And Al'Hassan. I know he's involved. He's the only one who'd dare to put a contract out on Merlin. That's what it was, you know. It has all the earmarks of a gangland hit. I've heard rumors that Al'Hassan was involved with organized crime. But he's involved with much more than that now, isn't he?"

"He's been taken over by the Dark Ones," Wyrdrune said.

"And while he had you, he cast a binding spell on you," said Modred, looking at Kira. She looked away from him. "Your emotions are the catalyst. Violent emotions. It's where his power base lies. *Their* power base."

He took the pouch containing the runestones and tossed it on the coffee table.

"And our power base lies here," he said. "Three runestones, three of us, three sides to a triangle. Tell me what it means."

"It's an ancient spell," said Wyrdrune. He started to recite it:

"Three stones, three keys to lock the spell.
Three jewels to guard the Gates of Hell.
Three to bind them, three in one,
Three to hide them from the sun.
Three to hold them, three to keep,
Three to watch the sleepless sleep."

The leather pouch on the coffee table suddenly seemed to collapse in upon itself. Simultaneously Modred gasped and doubled over, clutching at his heart. Wyrdrune cried out, and his hands went to his head, holding it with pain. Kira grabbed her right hand and screamed.

"God, what *now*?" the broom said, hurrying in from the kitchen. "Are you all right? What's happening? What *is* it?"

Tendrils of smoke curled up from Kira's right hand. Wyrdrune knelt on the floor, holding his head and moaning, wisps of smoke seeping out between his finges. Modred's breath came in short gasps as he clutched his chest. Frantically he tore open his shirt.

A bright red ruby gleamed against his skin, embedded in the singed flesh over his heart.

Kira opened her hand and stared at the shining sapphire embedded in her palm, and as Wyrdrune took his hands away from his head, they saw a softly glowing emerald embedded in his forehead.

CHAPTER
Thirteen

Riguzzo had felt sick throughout the flight back to New York, sitting rigid in his seat, much to Cleary's amusement. He had suggested taking the train back, but Morgan wouldn't hear of it. She countered with a proposal that she teleport them back, but that frightened Riguzzo even more than flying, so he had acquiesced, taken several drinks, and decided to suffer through the flight. He was profoundly relieved when they landed, thinking the worst was over, but as they were getting off the plane, Morgan doubled over with a gasp and clutched at her heart. Riguzzo immediately grabbed her and picked her up, rushing out into the deplaning area while Cleary ran ahead, shouting for medical help. One of the passengers waiting to get on another plane was a physician, and hearing the commotion, he hurried over.

"I'm a doctor," he said, pushing his way through to where Riguzzo knelt over Morgan, laid out full-length on the carpet. "Let me through, please, I'm a doctor!"

"Give us some room, dammit!" yelled Riguzzo.

The doctor knelt and took Morgan's wrist, measuring her pulse.

"I think she's having a heart attack," Riguzzo said.

"An ambulance is on the way," said one of the airport security officers.

"Pulse is strong," the doctor said, frowning. He checked her pupils. "Pupils dilated, though. Her skin's cold and clammy, breathing is shallow and rapid and she's sweating . . . I'd say she was in shock, but her pulse seems all right. I haven't got my bag, damn it. . . ." He bent over and listened to her heart. "Jesus, she's started fibrillating! We need a goddamn crash cart now!"

"Pound on her chest!" Riguzzo said.

"It won't do any good," the doctor said, his voice reflecting his concern. "When the heart is fibrillating like that, you've got to stop it first with shock and then try to start it up again and hope like hell it works!"

"Can't we do something?" Cleary said.

"*Where's that ambulance?*" the doctor shouted. He spotted the security officer with his radio. "Get on that thing and get the airport paramedics here with a crash cart *right now!*"

"They're on the way," the security man said. "The ambulance will be pulling up right outside the gate."

"Coming through, coming through!"

The airport paramedics pushed their way through the crowd, carrying a portable cor zero cart with them. The doctor was ripping open Morgan's blouse. "Get it in here!" he said.

One paramedic moved in with the electrode paddles while the other reached into a bag and handed the doctor a stethoscope.

"*Clear!*"

The paramedic hit the juice, and Morgan's body spasmed, jerking briefly. The doctor listened. "Again—now!"

"*Clear!*"

Her body jerked once more as power flowed through the paddles.

The doctor checked again. An expression of relief came over his face. "We've got it," he said, still listening to her heartbeat. He glanced up at Riguzzo. "We'll get her to a hospital right away, but I think she's going to be all right."

The onlookers started to applaud.

They took her down to the ambulance on a gurney, and Riguzzo showed his badge to one of the attendants. "I'm riding in with her," he said. "Al, report in and meet us at the hospital."

Her eyes fluttered open as they started administering the IV, and she turned her head toward Riguzzo. "Dominic . . ."

"It's all right, Faye, don't talk," he said. "You've had a heart attack. We're taking you to the hospital."

"No," she said, shaking her head and trying to sit up against the straps of the gurney. The attendant immediately urged her back down, gently but firmly.

"Please, ma'am, you'll have to relax. You're going to be all right now."

"My son," she said. "Something's happened to my son. . . ."

The attendant glanced up at Riguzzo. Riguzzo shook his head. "She's delirious," he said.

"Dammit, I'm all right!" she said, sitting up and snapping the restraining straps. She shoved the amazed attendant away hard, and he fell back. With one hand she ripped the IV out of her arm, and with the other she grabbed Riguzzo's wrist, squeezing it hard and saying something quickly under her breath.

The next thing the ambulance attendant knew, both she and Riguzzo had disappeared.

They materialized in a penthouse suite high over Fifth Avenue. The place was under construction, and there were spattered drop cloths, stepladders, and buckets of paint all around them. The rugs had been pulled up, and there was a tang of smoke in the room, mingled with the smell of paint. Riguzzo looked around, and it took him a moment to realize why the place seemed so familiar. It was the penthouse apartment of John Roderick, alias Morpheus. Her son, Modred. The renovators had been hard at work, but the place was still only partially rebuilt and still smelled of smoke.

"No, no, no," Morgan said, moaning, staring around dejectedly. "He isn't here. . . ."

"Of course he isn't here, Faye," said Riguzzo, releasing his wrist from her grasp. It felt sore. "Damn, I didn't realize you were so strong. I wish to hell you'd warn me before trying something like that again. I'm not as young as I used to be, you know. And for that matter, neither are you. Please, let me take you to a hospital."

She sat down on a small, folding stepladder, an expression of dazed confusion on her face. She looked as if she were about to cry.

"I really think you should be examined by a doctor, Faye," Riguzzo said gently. He took off his jacket. "Here, put this on."

She stared at the jacket uncomprehendingly for a moment, then looked down at herself and realized for the first time that her blouse had been torn open, exposing her bosom. With a self-conscious smile she took the jacket and put it on, buttoning it up.

"Thank you," she said. "I didn't realize. I hope I didn't embarrass you."

"I've been married a long time," Riguzzo said. "And after some of the things I've seen on this job, the sight of a little female flesh isn't going to raise my blood pressure. Besides, you're young enough to be my . . . well, that is . . ."

She smiled. "To be your great-great-grandmother fifty times over," she said. "You're a good man, Dominic. Thank you for your concern, but I'll be all right now."

"Faye, you've had a heart attack—"

"No," she said, shaking her head, "although that well-meaning doctor almost killed me. In a moment, I would have been all right if he'd left me alone. You mustn't make hasty assumptions about me, Dominic. I'm not like you."

"I'm sorry. I thought—"

"Never mind," she said. "It's over. Whatever happened's over now."

"What *did* happen? You said something about your son."

She sighed. "Modred," she said. "I told you about the affinity we have for each other. I can always sense it when he's near. He's near us now, somewhere in this city. Something happened to him. I thought at first that he was dying, but he's still alive. Alive yet . . . changed somehow. Something feels different." She looked puzzled, concerned. "I don't know what that means. We've got to find him."

"I can understand how you feel, Faye," Riguzzo said, "but you've just had a shock and—"

"It concerns him," she said. "Something terrible is happening. I know it. Don't ask me how."

"All right," Riguzzo said. "But you realize what has to happen if we find him, don't you? I'll have to place him under arrest."

She smiled wryly. "Modred? Good luck. No jail would ever hold him."

"If what you tell me is true, Faye, he's a killer. He has to be stopped."

"Better men than you have tried," she said. "No offense, Dominic, but you may as well not waste your time. You'd never take him."

"I'll have to try."

"Don't," she said. "Please." She came up off the folding stepladder and approached him. "I'm not asking for my sake, believe me. He'll kill you."

"It's my duty, Faye." He paused, looking into her eyes. "And yours."

"Duty," she said bitterly. "Don't tell me about duty. I've seen too many people die needlessly because of *duty*. Do you think he's just an ordinary man? He's managed to survive for several thousand years! He's seen more battles than you've seen meals!" She slapped at his potbelly contemptuously, and Riguzzo looked pained. "I'm sorry," she said, shaking her head. "I didn't mean to hurt your feelings."

She sighed and went over to stand by the window, staring out at the city spread out below them. "He's out there, Riguzzo, and I'm afraid for him."

"If and when we find him, one of us will have to take him in," Riguzzo said. "If not me, then you. Whatever else your son may be, he's a professional assassin. I know that has to be a very hard thing for a mother to live with, but the law is the law, and as an officer of the ITC, you're sworn to uphold it."

"The law is the law," she said sarcastically. "My son and I were both alive long before your precious law. And if you're going to dangle oaths before me, I've broken oaths far older and far more binding than any allegiance I owe to the ITC."

"I see," Riguzzo said. "Do I take that to mean that both of you consider yourselves above the law? Because it was written by mere humans? I just want to be clear as to where we stand here."

"Oh, don't be a fool, Riguzzo!" she said, spinning around to face him. "You should see yourself, standing there stiff with righteousness and virtue! Can't you understand that things are nowhere near as simple as you see them?"

"Maybe not," Riguzzo said. "Why don't you explain it to me? I've been known to be flexible."

"Have you got any real evidence with which to build a case against him?"

"Perhaps not, but I suspect you have."

"I wouldn't give it to you. It isn't your jurisdiction, anyway."

"Then you'll have to build the case against him."

"Dammit, Riguzzo, *he's my son!*"

"I guess it will be up to me, then. I'm sorry, Faye."

She snorted. "You're a fool. He'll kill you."

"Maybe," Riguzzo said. "The question is, will you try to stop him?"

"Are you seriously asking me to choose between you and my own son?"

"No, that would be a very simple choice. The choice you'll have to make is a lot more difficult. I suppose an argument could be made that it isn't any real choice at all. I don't have the right to judge you, Faye. I'm only a man, stiff as I may be, though I doubt it's with righteousness and virtue so much as with arthritis. But I know what I have to do. I've got to live with the choices I make. And so do you."

She stared at him, a sad, ironic smile on her face. "You remind me of his father." She looked away from him, back toward the window. "There isn't any real resemblance, but I look at you, a balding, fat little Italian cop in a cheap suit and shoes run down at the heels, and you make me think of him. It's the way your silly little badge is every bit as important to you as his crown was to him."

"I'll take that as a compliment, in spite of the unflattering description," said Riguzzo. "But you still haven't answered my question."

"You won't back off, will you?" she said.

"I don't see how I could."

"I could have you taken off this case," she said. "I have that authority, you know."

"I know, but you won't use it."

"What makes you think so?"

"Because you're scared."

"Of *you*? You must be crazy."

"Oh, not of me. Of yourself. It's like you said, you're not like me. I can't imagine what it's like to live for several thousand years, but I'd guess it would give you a very different feeling about time. I guess if I knew I had the kind of time you've got, I'd feel differently about a lot of things. Like if I was after something that I'd ordinarily consider a waste of time, something that seemed hopeless, I might take a lot longer to give up on it. I'm not sure what you planned on doing about your son, but from what you've told me, it seems pretty obvious that he doesn't care about you. He is what he is, and there's nothing you can do to change it. I think maybe that's finally starting to sink in."

Riguzzo shrugged. "Maybe I'm not capable of understanding what you've gone through all these years because I don't know what it means to be immortal, but you're still part human, and I can understand that part. It's the part of you that's scared to give up on something you've been after for so long because you're not sure what you'll have left if you let it go. You don't really need me on this case, Faye. You never did. There's no real reason why you should have kept me on. I think you did it because you're starting to get scared and lonely and you need to have a crowd around you. If not me and Al, then it would've been McGarry and his people or some of your fellow agents from the ITC, only I don't think you'd have wanted them along as much because they wouldn't have been as easy to control as a couple of street cops grateful for the chance to make points with an important case.

"Only you see, it isn't points with me. It never was. It's a job I happen to take very seriously, so I like to keep my priorities straight and do it right. And while I'm doing it, I like to watch out for my partners, which in this instance happens to include you—and you're in trouble, Faye. You've been in trouble for a long, long time. I'm not saying I'm the guy to get you out of it; you're a powerful adept, you know more than I could ever learn, and you could probably take me with one hand tied behind your back even if you didn't use magic. You're a superior being, and you know it and act like it. But you're also part human, and nobody human is all that tough. One moment you're coming across as a tough, professional investigator, a sorceress able to hold her own with anyone and anything, and the next you're acting vulnerable and asking Al and me to trust you because you need our help. You've got to face up to a few things, and the fact that you haven't done it for over two thousand years isn't gong to make it easy."

"So what's your prescription, doctor?" she said sarcastically.

"You're not listening, Faye. I told you, I'm not the guy to get you out of this. It's not my place and I'm not equipped to do it. You're going to have to do this for yourself. And I wish to hell you'd get around to it, because I haven't got the time to wait. I'm not immortal."

"All right," she said, suddenly looking tired. "What do you want me to do?"

"What do *you* want to do, Faye? What did you hope to accomplish when you found your son?"

"I . . . I just want him back, that's all." She sighed. "He's not being himself. He's rejected everything he is, everything he could be."

"Don't you think it's a little late for kings?" Riguzzo said.

"I don't mean that, of course," she said. "I'm not a fool. But he's been running from himself ever since he left me. He has it in him to be a mage as great as Merlin. Instead he's chosen to become . . ." She turned away. "It's such a waste, what he's done with his life!"

"What about what you've done with yours?" Riguzzo said. "With everything you've done and seen, with all you know, isn't it also a waste for Morgan Le Fay to be nothing more than a glorified cop? I don't know, maybe it isn't, if that's what you really want. But is it?"

She didn't answer.

"You know, it's arguable how responsible we are for what our kids turn out to be," Riguzzo said gently. "I mean, we can do our best, trying to raise them right, to give them opportunities, to instill our values, but they still turn out pretty much the way they're going to be, regardless of what we do. Parental influence has to count for something, but it isn't everything. Not by a long shot. As a cop, I've seen a lot of cases where parents who were fine, upstanding, caring citizens had kids who were habitual criminals. And I've also seen cases where parents who were scum somehow wound up with kids who managed to turn out just fine. It seems to me the choice is up to Modred. It's possible he could turn it around. We've been known to make some deals. He'd wind up serving time, but then what's a little time to an immortal? Even if they gave him life, which could be an interesting judicial test considering his life span, he'd be up for parole in twenty years. For him that would be a drop in the bucket. He could make a fresh start, if that's what he really wanted. If it isn't, I don't see what you could do about it. But you could give him that choice."

"I can't imagine Modred letting anyone put him away," she said. "I told you, no jail would ever hold him."

"Not if he didn't want to stay," Riguzzo said. "Jail's a hard place to be. But I can't imagine anyone giving Modred any trouble if he's all you say he is. They say jail never succeeds in rehabilitating anyone, but I know that isn't true. I've seen convicts come out of jail with a whole new outlook on life. Sometimes it's just a way of letting them work off their guilt so they can forgive themselves. Maybe all he needs is for someone to give him that opportunity."

"You think it's that simple?" she said.

Riguzzo shook his head. "No, nothing ever is. He's not my son. I don't know what drives him. I don't know if it's guilt or anger or just plain meanness, but two thousand years is a long time to keep the fires burning. Maybe he's tired. I know *you* are."

She started to cry. Riguzzo put his arms around her, and she held him tightly, sobbing against his chest. They remained that way for a long time in the burned-out apartment while the sun went down over the city.

And all the lights went out.

The workers at the plant heard the screams from inside the control room of the power station. They hurried up the stairs with battery-powered flashlights and broke down the door. No one knew why it was locked, but the locked door lost all significance when they saw what lay behind it. The control room personnel, including the chief engineer adept and his assistants, had all been slaughtered, their bodies torn apart, the pieces flung throughout the room. Blood was everywhere: on the control panels, on the indicator screens, on the floor, and on the ceiling. There was no sign of who—or what—had done it, and they couldn't call for help. The phones were dead. There was no power in the city.

In Washington, D.C., the lights went out during the bottom of the sixth inning at RFK Memorial Stadium—all except for a dark blue glow that seemed to writhe and shimmer, pulsing like a giant heart in the middle of the diamond, just behind the pitcher's mound. As the pitcher turned to stare at it, tipping his cap back on his head, something grabbed him and lifted him high into the air. He screamed briefly, and then half of him went flying toward first base; the other half went arcing out toward center field. Huge paw prints, thirty feet across, appeared in the ground as something *huge* bounded across the field and leapt into the stands. Bodies started flying everywhere as a screaming human wave surged toward the exits, people trampling each other in blind, unreasoning panic as they fled the unseen thing that roared like an express train and mowed through them like a scythe.

In China, about two miles from the center of Peking, disaster struck at Peking Station, trapping over two hundred thousand people when the four columns holding up the shell-shaped roof of the ten-story-high, beamless concourse suddenly collapsed, crushing everyone beneath it. It was a crude sacrifice, lacking any ritual, but it served its purpose. Thousands of souls gave up their life energy, and the tile-inlaid ring circling the pit in the Euphrates began to crack and buckle.

"It's a blackout," said Riguzzo, staring out the window at the lightless city.

"No," said Morgan, standing very still behind him in the darkened room. She suddenly felt very cold. "It's something worse. *Much* worse."

On the island of Hawaii, Mauna Loa and Kilauea both erupted simultaneously, sending a shower of rock and ash high into the sky. A mushroom cloud of fire-charged smoke appeared above each of the volcanos, and within each of them something cried out and stirred the smoke with the beating of large wings. The top parts of the clouds seemed to form themselves into giant shapes, like manta rays, and they started to move northwest, toward the islands of Maui, Molokai, and Oahu.

In South America, a series of huge waterspouts, several times the size of the tallest skycrapers in Rio de Janeiro, rose up out of the waves and rushed across the Baia de Gaunabara, toward the Ilha das Cobras and along the coast to the Santos Dumont airport, moving on toward the port of Rio de Janeiro, towering over the 1296-foot-high rock known as

Sugar Loaf and gathering momentum as they split and hurtled inland, toward Copacabana and the Morro do Corcovado. Buildings were leveled, and hundreds of thousands perished as the walls of water struck, churning across dry land like tornado funnels, destroying everything in their path. The altar atop the massive stalagmite began to tremble as tremors formed cracks throughout the rock, sending pieces of it crashing to the floor of the subterranean chamber.

In Moscow, it started to rain fire on Kalinin Avenue. People on the street turned into running torches, and the high-rise office and residential buildings burst into flame. The fire consumed the October Concert Hall and spread to Komsomol Square, igniting the Leningrad Hotel. East of the Kremlin, the Pakrovsky Cathedral and the cluster of onion-domed churches around it, which had stood since the sixteenth century, started to crumble as the flames licked through them, blackening the icons and the Byzantine murals painted on the ceilings. Many thought it was the Second Coming, and they dropped down on their knees, praying even as they burned. It was a second coming in a way, but one that had little to do with prayer. The borders of the ancient pentagram in the subterranean chamber burst into blue flame and became obliterated. A brilliant, hellish glow came from deep within the pit, rising up toward the ceiling of the chamber like the beam from a giant searchlight.

As he sat in the torchlit presence chamber of his palace, Rashid trembled violently, his hands white-knuckled as they gripped the arms of his throne, his face contorted in a grimace of agony. He was dressed in his ceremonial black sorcerer's robes, his black kaffiyeh held on by the gold, cobra-headed circlet on his head, the gem set in his forehead glowing white-hot and blackening the skin around it.

The throne was wreathed in an emerald-green aura, giving his skin a pale, deathly look. The veins stood out sharply in his forehead. His teeth were clenched and bared as the lips drew back from the gums. His muscles spasmed as fierce tremors racked his body. His back was arched so sharply, it felt as if his spine would snap.

Devastating force flowed through him as energy from deep beneath the earth was channeled through his body. He was aging rapidly, his years passing like seconds. His hair had turned pure white, his skin taking on the consistency of parchment veined with capillaries, the flesh sagging and folding into wrinkles, the hands gnarling into talons, green flames burning in the pupils of his eyes.

The metal of the throne started to melt beneath him, softening and flowing like wax on a burning candle as energy radiated from him, passing through the palace walls and making the entire building shake. People ran screaming through the halls. The water in the fountains of the palace courtyard frothed and boiled. Like a runaway chain reaction, waves of searing energy slammed through the building corridors, making tapestries and paintings burst into flame, consuming everything, turning fleeing figures into skeletons that staggered on for a few steps, then crumpled into heaps of charred bone on the floor. The ground around the palace cracked into steaming fissures that radiated outward through the city like jagged wheel spokes from the epicenter of an earthquake.

In the half-renovated shell of the dark penthouse apartment, a voice came out of the air, a voice strained with urgency and effort.

"Morgana, for God's sake, help me!"

"Merlin!"

"Come to me now or all is lost!"

She threw her arms out to her sides and tilted back her

head, chanting in an ancient Celtic dialect, and blue sparks, like hurtling fireflies, shimmered in the air as they spun around her, faster and faster, growing brighter as they started to form a funnel of crackling energy around her, almost obscuring her from view.

Riguzzo hesitated for a moment, staring in astonishment at the sight, then he lunged forward, through the swirling mass of sparks, feeling wind tearing at his clothing and static electricity making his hair stand on end as his arms closed around her waist. There was a roaring in his ears as the blue funnel lifted them up off the floor, spinning them around and around with dizzying speed. He clung to her with all his strength, unable to breathe as the thaumaturgic whirlwind sucked time and space away from them and sent them hurtling through the ether . . .

. . . and then they stood in darkness, in a cavernous stone chamber on a rock floor that heaved beneath them, while before them, illuminated in a massive shaft of brilliant light that rose up from deep beneath the earth, Merlin stood atop a towering stalagmite, on a ledge over a pit, his long blue robes billowing around him, his white hair streaming in a hurricane-force wind. His arms were raised high over his head, and bolts of lightning shot down into the pit as chunks of stone fell from the ceiling of the cavern, and cracks opened in the rock walls.

"Sweet Jesus . . ." said Riguzzo.

"You fool!" said Morgan, grabbing him by the shoulders. "What have you done? You're going to die!"

"I can't hold them, Morgana!" Merlin cried. *"They're channeling their strength through Al'Hassan! You've got to stop him!"*

"Come on!" said Morgan, grabbing the dumbfounded Riguzzo. "I can't leave you here!"

"What's happening?" Riguzzo shouted over the noise, but his words were lost on the wind that swept them away

as Morgan's fingers closed around his wrist and he was
yanked into a maelstrom of swirling particles of light that
left an afterimage on his retinas like tiny fireworks exploding, and then everything went black as he lost consciousness.

CHAPTER
Fourteen

They suddenly shared fragments of memories that had never been their own, memories belonging to a race that lived before the dawn of history. They remembered the great war of mages and the millions who had died. They remembered an upheaval the likes of which the world had never seen: cities bursting into flame, islands breaking apart and sinking beneath the waves, tempest winds of pure thaumaturgic energy sweeping across the land and leveling everything standing in their way.

They saw glimpses of a solemn ceremony, held deep beneath the earth, and they heard the screaming of the renegade mages called the Dark Ones as they were lowered into a black pit, imprisoned in a shimmering funnel of whirling, crystalline blue fire shaped by the combined powers of the most powerful of the surviving white magicians; robed, hooded figures marshaling the last ounces of their strength to hold the black magic of their antagonists at bay.

They saw two of their number carrying a heavy golden chest inscribed with mystic symbols and placing it upon the lip of the rock ledge over the pit, welding it in place forever with beams of thaumaturgic force. And there they gathered,

one last time, to shoulder the responsibility of the knowledge that they bore and shared with those they had imprisoned deep beneath the earth. They placed the runestones
inside a small jewel box made of bronze, where they lay
upon black velvet trimmed with gold, arranged in a triangular pattern. Then all save one of them gathered around and
joined to form the living triangle, flooding the cavern with
white light as they gave up their lives to the spell of self-
transmogrification, infusing the runestones with their own
life energy, giving vitality and sentience to the inert gems
that would become the three-in-one, bounding time, space,
and the ether into a dimensionless congruity contained
within the pentagram, inside the circle of the cavern that
would be their tomb.

Then only one stood, alone atop the towering stalagmite. He
bent down and picked up the small bronze jewel box and
placed it within the golden chest, sealing it inside for all
eternity, for that had been their plan. He then descended to the
floor of the cavern and walked out through the tunnel they had
blasted in the rock, sealing it behind him. He went out to join
the others of his kind, those few who had survived, scattered
throughout the world, the weaker, younger ones who had not
yet mastered the abilities they had been born with and now
never would, not fully, for the Age of Magic had ended in a
holocaust, and there would be only brief flickers in the coming
years of the flame that once burned brightly, before it finally
would be extinguished.

He took off his sorcerer's robe and left it on the ground
where it fell, never to put it on again. He banished his magename from his memory and went out into the world under his
truename, Gorlois, the youngest and the last of the ruling
council of white mages. He made his way to a windswept
island to the north and found a home among the tribes there.
For years he lived alone, a hermit treated as a sage by the
primitive nomadic tribes, but in time his solitude became too
much to bear, and he took a wife from the tribe known as the

De Dannan. She bore him a son named Merlin. Being human, time passed more quickly for her, and with the hard life that they lived, she seemed to age before his eyes. It became painful to watch, and one day he left her, telling himself he had no business taking human wives. He vowed never to take another. The years passed, the world changed, and Gorlois changed with it. He became a warlord, forgetting his past as he embraced his adopted human future, and soon his loneliness made him forget his vow and he took another wife, a beautiful young woman named Igraine. With her he had three daughters—Elaine, Morgana, and Morgause. And he continued to forget until one day a man named Uther, aided by the son he had abandoned, gave him what he really wanted all along, the only forgetfulness that's final.

"So now we come full circle," Modred said, touching the gem over his heart. He looked up at Wyrdrune and Kira. "My cousins," he said softly. "One descended from Morgause, one from Elaine. And now my brother and my sister. To think I might have killed you."

"I don't think you could have," Kira said, looking up from the softly glowing jewel set in her palm and meeting his gaze.

"Oh, yes, I could have," said Modred. "I killed my own father, whom I never understood—perhaps because I did not choose to—and I've been killing ever since. I've become quite good at it. Perhaps it was meant to be."

"It's started," Wyrdrune said, staring out the window at the lightless city. "God, I can *feel* it." He looked to Modred. "Damn it, why did they wait so long? Why bring us together only at the last minute? There isn't enough time! I don't know what to *do*!"

"Pull yourself together," Modred said. "It would have made no difference if we'd had more time. There was no way to prepare ourselves for what we're about to do."

"I've never killed anyone," said Wyrdrune. He swallowed hard. "I'm afraid."

"So was I, when I went into my first battle," Modred said. "And the second and the third. The fear lessens with time, but it never goes away completely. It's always worst just before a battle, but once the fighting starts, there's no time for it anymore. And there's no time now."

A bright red beam shot out from the glowing ruby in Modred's chest, striking the jewel in Wyrdrune's forehead. A thin shaft of emerald light came from Wyrdrune's gem and struck the stone in Kira's upraised hand. A brilliant sapphire light came from the gem set in her palm and struck the ruby in Modred's chest.

The triangle was formed.

The room seemed to become insubstantial all around them. It faded away, and they stood amid a field of stars, standing still yet moving, turning around a central axis, their former position marked in time and space by the blue, green, and red glowing borders of a triangle. They came full circle, forming a second triangle to intersect the first, and the pentagram became complete, its borders erupting into flame, burning with multicolored fire. As the flames subsided, the rock walls of a giant cavern faded into view around them, and as they stepped forward, inside the borders of the pentagram, the rock ledge above the pit collapsed and Merlin plummeted down. . . .

Riguzzo felt a cold stone floor beneath him as he gasped for breath and struggled to push himself up to his hands and knees. Through blurred vision he saw a garishly illuminated throne at the far end of a long room with a high ceiling. A light that seemed to pulse and throb came from the body of an emaciated figure writhing on the throne. He shook his head to clear his vision as he sobbed for breath like a half-drowned man.

Above him, Morgan stood with her arms raised, a blue aura crackling around her outspread fingers. She flung her arms out straight before her, and a bolt of blue fire leapt from her fingers and lanced out across the room, striking the figure in the throne. The old man seated there was bathed in violet light and he jerked hard, becoming rigid, and for a moment the pulsing waves of light that were shooting out from him wavered and dimmed.

"Merlin!" shouted Wyrdrune as the old mage fell. He stood motionless, unable to believe what he had just witnessed, and then the shaft of light coming from the pit began to flicker as Morgan struck out at Rashid, and Wyrdrune and Kira both felt, rather than heard, Modred's voice.

"Now! Now, while they weaken!"

Beams of thaumaturgic energy linked them together as they raised their arms and the borders of their glowing triangle extended outward, rising up to form a pyramid of light over the pit. They heard screams echoing up from its depths as their combined strength suffocated those within and in that moment—

—Rashid rose up from his throne, his gnarled hands clutching the arms for support as he fought against Morgan's power. The jewel set in his forehead blazed, sending a searing bolt of white-hot energy slamming into Morgan. It caught her squarely in the chest and flung her clear across the room. She struck the wall and fell—

—and Modred gasped with pain and collapsed, clutching his chest. The spell broke, and the Dark Ones came streaming from the pit.

"Faye . . ." said Riguzzo, pushing himself up off the floor.

"Modred!" Wyrdrune shouted.

"No!" Kira screamed with rage and frustration, and her instinctive fury opened up the way for Rashid to take control. Unable to resist him, her mouth twisted in a snarl and she spun toward Wyrdrune, the sapphire in her outstretched

palm blazing forth a beam of energy that struck Wyrdrune full in the back.

Riguzzo reached inside his jacket and drew his service revolver, emptying it into the figure on the throne. Rashid jerked as each bullet slammed into his chest—

—and Kira staggered as he lost his hold on her—

—while Riguzzo stared, still holding his empty gun aimed at the old man on the throne, who clutched spasmodically at his bleeding chest with one hand while he raised the other toward Riguzzo, fingers trembling and outstretched. . . .

And suddenly Rashid was bathed in a bright crimson aura. He screamed as his white hair burst into flame. His robes caught fire, and his deeply wrinkled skin blistered and burned, and the throne beneath him melted into slag as the heat consumed him until nothing but a charred skeleton remained, slumped in a steaming lump of molten metal.

Kira knelt down beside Wyrdrune, cradling his head in her lap as he grimaced in agony.

"Oh, God, what have I done? Are you all right? Please, *please* tell me you're all right!"

"I'll live," he said, wincing with pain. "I think. How's Modred?"

"I don't know, I—" She glanced around. There was no sign of him.

Modred stared for a moment at the blackened bones of Rashid Al'Hassan, then he turned and walked over to where Morgan lay motionless upon the marble floor. He crouched down beside her and turned her over. Her face was ashen. She had aged incredibly. Her eyes flickered open and she stared up at him, a dying old woman breathing her last.

"My son," she said.

"Mother."

"Forgive—"

And she was gone.

He closed her eyes and stood, looking down at her, wishing tears would come, but he had no tears left, not even for her. "There's nothing to forgive, Morgana," he said softly.

He turned and saw Riguzzo standing there, holding his revolver at his side.

"You're her son," Riguzzo said.

"Yes," said Modred, frowning. "Who are you?"

"Detective Lieutenant Dominic Riguzzo, NYPD. You're under arrest. You have the right to remain silent..."

Modred started walking toward him, the sound of his heels echoing in the torchlit chamber.

"You...you have the right to..." Riguzzo swallowed hard and raised his gun.

"It's empty," Modred said, gently taking the revolver out of the policeman's hand.

Riguzzo sighed. "Oh, hell...what am I doing?"

"Come on, Detective Lieutenant Dominic Riguzzo," Modred said. "I'll take you home."

EPILOGUE

The fires slowly died in Moscow and they began to count the dead. The tally would take a long time to complete, and explanations would be slow in coming, ranging from theories about some sort of freak volcanic eruption to a meteor shower to a spell by some government sorcerer gone out of control. One government would furiously accuse another, but as the news came in from all around the world, news of the tragedy in Peking, of the disaster that had occurred in South America, of the slaughter in Washington, D.C., and the cataclysm in the U.S.R., the accusations dwindled and became replaced with dread, and with relief, that somehow something far worse had been averted, though no one was quite certain what it was, what had begun it, or what had brought it to a halt. It had been magic. Of that much they were certain. And as the people on the Hawaiian islands watched two impossibly huge, wing-shaped clouds dissipate above them and rain ash down upon the sea, some thought they heard cries, like those of wounded beasts, and old fears started to return.

In a small apartment on East 4th Street, Wyrdrune lay

stretched out on his stomach on the bed, wincing as Kira applied bandages to cover the burn ointment on his back.

"I still say you should go to a hospital," she said. "You're hurt bad."

"I'll be all right," he said. "No hospital." He sat up slowly as she finished, and he winced with pain.

"That's got to hurt like hell," said Kira, looking at him with concern, feeling awful that she had been responsible.

"It stings a bit," he said, gingerly putting on a bathrobe, "but I'm not about to try explaining what happened to a doctor."

"Don't be ridiculous," she said. "We could make up a story that—"

"*No*. That's final. I'll be fine. Thanks."

"For what?" she said miserably. "I did it to you. I almost killed you twice."

"*Rashid* almost killed me twice," he said. "And Rashid is dead. You won't have to worry about him anymore." He sighed. "But it's not over. Between the four of us—Merlin, Modred, you, and I—we managed to kill some of them, but some escaped. That's why I'm not going to a hospital. We have to find them and finish what we started."

"Forget it," she said. "You're not going anywhere for a while. You're going to stay here and eat broom's chicken soup and let me change your bandages until your back is healed. I'm going to stay right here and take care of you and that's final."

Listen to her. Modred's voice came to them from some-where. *She's right. We've hurt them, and they've fled to hide and lick their wounds. As long as we remain alive, they'll never be as strong as they once were. They'll be vulnerable. We'll find them. And when they're ready, they'll try to find us.*

"Where are you?" Wyrdrune said aloud.

*I'll be there when you need me, wizard. But for now, eat
your chicken soup.*

Modred lit a cigarette and gazed out the window of his
hotel as the sun came up over the city. He was looking toward the Village, in the direction of East 4th Street. He
smiled. He was the last survivor of the Age of Camelot, but
he was no longer alone. He turned from the window, picked
up the phone, dialed room service, and ordered a big breakfast.

"Where the hell were *you*?" said Cleary as Riguzzo came
shambling into the squad room and slumped down into the
chair behind his desk.

"Morning, Al," he said distractedly.

"*Morning, Al*?" Cleary stared at him. "What do you
mean, *morning, Al*? Where the hell have you *been*? Where's
Faye? You never showed up at the hospital, and I didn't
know what the hell to think! I've been up all night trying to
figure out where in hell you disappeared to! Do you have
any idea what's been going *on*? Christ, *look* at you, you look
half dead! What the hell *happened*?"

"I don't know," Riguzzo said, shaking his head.

"What do you mean, *you don't know*?"

"I mean, I don't know. I can't remember a damn thing.
You got a cigarette?"

"A what?"

"A cigarette."

"You're going to smoke?"

"Yeah, I think so."

He took out his pack and tossed it on Riguzzo's desk.
"Dom, are you okay?"

"Yeah." He lit a cigarette, inhaled, coughed, then reached
inside his jacket and pulled out his gun. "I seem to have
fired my weapon," he said vaguely, "only I don't remember
doing it." He frowned. "I'm going to have to make out a

report, but I haven't got the faintest idea what I'm going to say in it."

"Faye, Dom. What happened to Faye?"

"Faye?"

"Jesus, Dom, don't tell me you forgot about her too?"

Riguzzo stared at him blankly.

Cleary came around the desk. "Dom," he said, "you don't remember *anything*?"

Riguzzo looked up at him with a dazed expression. "Not a goddamn thing," he said. "It worries me." He looked around the squad room. Everyone was staring at him. "It must've been some night," he said.